Scars of Obsession

by

Darryl Bowen

RoseDog❧Books

PITTSBURGH, PENNSYLVANIA 15222

ISBN 978-1-4349-9317-5
Printed in the United States of America

First Printing

For information or to order additional books, please write:
RoseDog Books
701 Smithfield Street
Pittsburgh, Pennsylvania 15222
U.S.A.
1-800-834-1803

Or visit our website and online catalogue at www.rosedogbookstore.com

ACKNOWLEDGMENT

To My daughter Melissa. You are the greatest source of Joy in my life. Thank you for your patience and understanding during the writing of this book. You have filled my heart to bursting with tremendous pride and I thank God for you daily. Also to my mother who has supported me, believed in me and propped me up with her unwavering strength and positivity.

CHAPTER ONE

Sleep evaded him with a growing certainty until finally he'd had enough of the waiting game. Sean flung the duvet aside and swung his legs out of the bed. Had time travelled as slowly as he imagined or had it sped by unchecked by his much troubled and searching mind? The springs of mattress pinged and twanged back into their daytime position as each in turn became free of his weight. Hate was a word that he'd almost eradicated from his vocabulary but it described his feelings for his cheap bed and its torturously lumpy, unsupportive mattress perfectly well. He stretched out his arms and arched his back forward then twisted his torso from left to right and back again to counteract the stiffness in his muscles. A fleeting moment of doubt for his next course of action left him as quickly as it arrived. Pulling on his jeans he quickly dressed so not to feel the effects of the chilled air on this late February, early morning. He clomped wearily down the stairs to the lounge and ruffled his short mid-brown hair. Keeping the silence he yawned with only the sound of the air rushing in and out his gaping mouth reaching his ears. Scratching the side of his hand against his two days old stubble he resigned himself to his plan of venturing out into the night and maybe, hopefully clearing his mind.

"Come on Moll!" he called to his border collie and glanced at the digital readout of the clock on the VCR, the only working timepiece in the house. He'd ritually packed away all the clocks in the house when he'd left his job as a production manager. He had kept one clock; it had never worked but it had been with him since he'd bought it at the age of nineteen in a Torquay flea market, some sixteen years ago. The time was close to what he'd expected, ten past four. Molly observed him with growing interest until he put on his hat and coat. With an un-energetic single swish of her tail she prised herself from the chair and stretched her front paws out in front of her. Stiffly she trudged her way towards him and the front door. Her tail swished more enthusiastically when he bent down to apply her collar and lead and in a moment they were stepping through the front door. Sean breathed in the crisp night air and exhaled it as a vapour that billowed around before quickly disappearing to rejoin the invisible cold air. They moved at a good pace, helped largely by Molly's eager pulling at the lead to bring to a swift end the boring part of their walk through the silent streets. Once over the main road with only the sight and sound of a milk float whirring its way towards them they reached the start of the canal. Sean bent down and freed her to do what she loved best in life, sniffing out and giving chase to foxes, rabbits and adventurous cats. She had no malice in mind for her quarry of foxes and cats; with them the fun was in the chase but for rabbits it was to be an entirely different story and a swift end. Once he had watched as she ran down a young inexperienced fox that made the mistake of breaking cover and running across open ground. She'd intercepted it before it got half way across the field and as it cowered terrified and waiting for its imminent and gory despatch from this world she had merely batted it playfully on the nose with her paw for it to run again.

They moved further from the red glow of the town and into the living dark of the country night. Molly ran on ahead, her nose an inch from the ground as she searched out the scent of her would-be quarry. Sean sauntered on alone again in the darkness. He sought to free his mind or come up with a combination of words that could do the work of magic and open the door to a new direction and much yearned for future. The sudden noise of an alarmed coot made him jump out of his skin and tense up inside a fraction of a second. He slowed his pace further in the hope of passing by any other potentially noisy birds un-noticed. The sky was dark with only the wispiest of clouds that couldn't diminish the light of even the faintest of stars. The three quarter moon hung low, almost touching the dark silhouetted trees on the ridge. The light seen through the leafless branches illuminated the cold, still waters of the canal and gave it a steely blue sheen. Walking on and under the eerie red brick railway bridge his pace quickened until the bridge was far behind him. Molly waited at the nearby intersection to see which path he would take. Sean chose to head up to the wider and lighter cycle track as Molly again sped off ahead and disappeared into the dark. The cycle path took the high ground for half a mile or so until it dropped down and branched out either into the pasture fields or back towards the town through the industrial estate. Its wide grass verges were perfect rabbit habitat. Molly shot out from the hedgerow on his left and crashed head long into the hedgerow on the right in hot pursuit of an unfortunate night revelling rodent. Sean slowed his pace to a dead slow and gazed up at the night sky. Picking out the brightest star in the sky he knew to be Venus he decided to offer up a prayer. Confident that he was alone on the ridge at this ungodly hour he spoke aloud his unprepared prayer as if he were talking one on one with the Goddess herself.

"Venus, I love someone . . . I mean really love someone I don't know why because I know nothing about her but her name. I only know that life has ground to a halt because I can think of no one and nothing but her! She's awesomely beautiful, long jet black hair, beautiful bronze skin that fades to coffee in the winter. Her eyes are big, brown and sloe. The contours of her face are perfect and precise. She has the most perfect lips that barley seem to move when she so seldom speaks and a jaw-line I could kiss forever. . . . Venus, she fixes me in her cold and calculating gaze and sees straight into my soul, daring me to speak my Love of her and at the same time forbidding it!" Sean paused for thought then continued to put voice to his feelings though now in a lower tone sensing that Venus had come down and was standing beside him. "She never smiles! She's not polite or welcoming but when I'm standing in front of her . . . my chemistry goes berserk and I am left wondering how she can remain so . . . patiently calm . . . Venus, surely there has to be a reason beyond her obvious beauty that I feel so completely captivated by her. There has to be a reason why she fills my every waking moment and keeps me from sleep!" Beginning to feel his prayer was futile and that no answers would be coming forth he raised his voice to shouting pitch and with his eyes firmly fixed on the brightness of her star he bellowed at the very top of his voice.

"I LOVE HER, I LOVE JESSICA KAHN WITH ALL MY BEING AND I WILL LOVE HER FOREVER!" Satisfied that he'd brought his prayer to an appropriate ending and keeping his unblinking eyes firmly fixed on Venus he listened into the silence for her telepathically transmitted reply. The silence stretched out from one second to the next then his attention was suddenly interrupted, something drew his eyes down to the hedgerow on his left. He stood motionless and scoured his surroundings for any further movement. Again something moved to his left and the ivy leaves seemed to glow for a second. His heart began to beat fast as his blood seemed to cool and meet with the cold night air at the surface of his skin. As well as his now pounding heart his mind also began to race. Had he attracted the attention of some local spirit, a ghost that roamed this track-way in search of an undefended, opened mind to wreak its havoc upon? The Light appeared again this time much brighter and all too real to explain away as the product of an over-tired mind. It was growing in strength and intensity feeding from his increasing state of panic. The want to flee the area overwhelmed him but his legs proved unresponsive and sent their own message to his brain that any thought of relying on them to propel him to safety would certainly end in failure. The Light danced around him more menacingly and lashed out at his body testing its newfound physical properties. It had the better of him and was searching out a vantage point from which to launch its attack and chase his very soul from its moorings within him. His legs re-confirmed their previous message. 'Turning to jelly, do not attempt flight!' If Sean thought that he couldn't be more terrified he was about to be proved very wrong. Next came the most terrifying, ear-splitting scream of some enraged demon the likes of which he'd never heard before. It would be on him in seconds and after ripping him apart would carry his torso back to hell as its sick trophy. People went missing all the time. This must be what befalls of those that are never found. No, there was no ghost and no demon. He was reaping the wrath of God for his pagan prayer. God himself had set upon him a terrifying, sword wielding avenging angel. Screeching from the heavens it was swooping down at blistering speed. Its white-feathered wings outstretched to slow its descent and synchronise its attack with the dancing light there to illuminate him in the darkness. In seconds it would slice his head cleanly from his body with one swipe of its flaming sword. The terrible sound increased in volume and still he remained power-less to take any kind of evasive action. The heart-stopping scream sounded again now even louder and definitely coming from behind him. His heart pounded vio-lently against his rib cage as if it was trying to escape from his doomed body and his bowels sent the message to prepare for a sudden and imminent evacuation. Sean closed his eyes and waited for the end in the hope that his acceptance of his fate would lessen the punishment that would follow his death. Cursing his feeble legs for their early capitulation and his own stupidity for angering the one true God he clenched his eyes shut and felt a sudden rush of air break over him. He opened his eyes as a helmeted cyclist shot past him. He saw the red glow of the bike's rear light, the yellow reflective strip of the rider and heard its tyres crushing the gravel into sand beneath them. Again the air filled with the horrifying cry of the assassin angel as the cyclist eagerly slowed his rate of knots to negotiate the next sweeping bend. A voice from his would-be executioner called out to him. "WELL GO HOME AND GIVE HER ONE THEN!" Sean watched the red light disappear around the bend and again heard the screeching brakes applied to slow the speed-ing contraption just enough to take the next bend. With his eyes opened wide and still fixed in the direction of the speeding cyclist he exhaled deeply and felt the ten-sion ebb away from his rigid body. Gradually he gathered his thoughts and regained his composure. His heart rate began to slow and a burst of laughter erupt-ed from his lips. Still not certain that his trembling legs were ready to carry him he forced himself forward to where he knew to be a stile. There he could sit and have a much needed cigarette whilst his legs recovered from the shock.

Molly came to see him at the stile and with a low, gruff bark made it known that he was blocking her way over. Sean stood and moved aside allowing Molly to leap from plank to plank and into the field beyond. Again he sat himself down and fumbled through his pocket to retrieve his cigarettes and lighter. As he lit the cig-arette the hand holding the lighter still trembled. His relief that he was still in the land of the living manifested itself into uncontrollable and self-mocking laughter that rose from deep inside him and travelled up through his ribcage to his heaving shoulders. He laughed so hard that he couldn't close his lips around the cigarette and had to wait for the involuntary laughter to subside before he could draw from it.

Finishing his cigarette he whistled his unique call to Molly who re-appeared at his side in seconds. Together they headed homeward along the track in the direc-tion from which they had come. The idea of waiting on the bridge to watch the sunrise left him due to the plain fact that he was more than ready for his bed and sunrise wouldn't happen for another ninety minutes or more by which time he would be back in his unfriendly but warm bed and sleeping for England.

On his return home he realised that the walk and its lesson in true terror had done something for him. It had taught him that what he feared didn't necessarily exist and a life that was static and immobile was no life at all. He should turn and face his fears head on and would probably find that they weren't so very terrible after all. He smiled and a new determination surged through him. He would in a few hours march down to the bank and declare his love for Jessica, to Jessica. He would calmly and casually ask her that she allow him to take her out one day or evening to a place of her choice. He would then stand erect and absorb her absolute refusal with strength, dignity and honour. That done he would get on with his life and throw himself back into his novel and save himself from the impending return to wage slavery. If it turned out that he was in fact deluding himself about his ability as a writer he would return to taking in lodgers and find a simple low pay job with the minimum of responsibility and live only for the weekends and long walks in the hills with Molly. Maybe he'd become a refuse collector or a council gardener and be quite content in his new life. It was a great revelation, instead of living in the hope that one day Jessica would bare her breasts to him and demand that he meet her after work for rampant, passionate and bitingly violent sex he would accept the inevitable now, have it confirmed in the morning and get on with his life.

He woke with the sunlight streaming into the bedroom. Shielding one eye with the back of his hand he looked to observe the angle at which the light entered his room. The light illuminated only part of the far wall mostly striking the ceiling; this indicated the time to be around nine to nine thirty. He'd only been asleep for around three hours so there was more sleep to be had and he turned his back to the window and waited to drift back to sleep. His first thought of the day was a question to himself. Did he still have the resolve that he had conjured up only hours earlier? Could he kill off the hope that one day he would be with her? Would he take the bull by the horns and with one spoken sentence of a few carefully chosen words, yet to be decided, put an end to his obsession with the girl at the bank?

His addiction to her compelled him to visit the bank almost on a daily basis. He'd juggle money from one bank to hers and back again in order to feed his addiction to her beauty. He soaked up her image and attempted to commit to memory every line and angle of her face. She exuded such a powerfully commanding charisma that he was all too often tongue tied when standing before her. Her expression never altered from the serious. She dealt quickly and efficiently with each and every customer. He had seen her smile but that was when she had shared a private joke with a colleague and that was months ago. Sean felt certain that her stony faced exterior was her defence mechanism perfected over the years to deter further advances from the smitten. An un-ending stream of proposals and invitations from the hopeful undoubtedly blighted her life. Sean had refrained from encroaching on her peace of mind and in doing so also kept his hope alive. No, sleep would not be forthcoming with such a life changing duty to perform just moments ahead. Thoughts queued up and came one after the other with no respite. Thoughts that had been with him and grown in intensity ten thousand fold since he first laid eyes on her.

From the first sight of her to making his feeling known to her had taken him almost a year. Maybe she would realise that he was the sender of the Valentine card, the only one to be displayed all that special day. It was then that he had been given the confirmation his troubled mind so badly needed to know that she was surely still single. Indeed the card had been a source of immense pride when he had observed it twice that day, once in the morning and again in the late afternoon standing alone on the filing cabinet below the calendar clock. A single, solitary, hand crafted Valentine card of red and gold. Never in his thirty-six on this earth had he been moved to handcraft such a thing. The poem within the card had taken him three days to construct and again it was a first. There had been many drafts of rhymes to accompany the card but finally in the early hours of February 11th he had achieved a poem that seemed to perfectly sum up and express his belief in her divinity.

Forgive my intrusion but this must be said,
You're in my heart, my soul and running through my head.

Never before have I seen anyone such as you,
So what my heart does tell me, I know it to be true.

Your Beauty goes beyond what this world has ever seen,
Outshining Cleopatra and Sheba's own Queen.

Not Helen of Troy nor Roxanne it's true,
Could ever come close or hold a candle to you.

So if I were a brave man this way I would pave,
To Love and be near you, each day as your slave.

So now you know you're worshipped, you're Loved and Adored,
Just think of my poem whenever you're bored.

Sean still procrastinated on whether or not he should have used the ending . . . if ever you're bored, but had finally decided that by using . . . whenever you're bored, implied some understanding that she was so much more than what her hum-drum job allowed her to be. Surely the occasional moment of boredom was a sad fact of her daily working life and so, whenever, was a more fitting word to use.

With no hope of a return to sleep Sean flung the covers from him and headed into the shower. He afforded himself an extra long, extra hot shower from his usual three-minute wonder showers designed to keep the gas bills down to a minimum. He had enough funds in his three bank accounts to pay the mortgage and keep him from a reluctant return to employment for another eight months or so. His hopes were pinned on his novel to boost his dwindling savings but with his head filled with only thoughts of Jessica he had ground to a complete halt. He had also surprised himself with how little he knew of the Roman period in which his book was set. The vast amount of research needed had already slowed his progress and he knew the timescale he had set himself of six or seven months was wholly unrealistic.

Out of the shower, shaved and dressed to impress he made his way to the kitchen for a bastard strength coffee, an intake of nicotine and a light breakfast. He listened to the radio as he drank his coffee and lit his second cigarette. All there remained to do was a quick brush of his teeth and an extra dosing of aftershave. Molly threw her weight at the back door to be let back in and fed. Sean opened the door just enough to allow her to pass through and closed it quickly behind her. Immediately she checked her bowl that wasn't empty long before he emptied a sachet of morsels into it. As she noisily chomped her way through her breakfast Sean went to the front room and checked his appearance in the mirror. He could've done with a bit of a trim but was pleased with the scruffy and wet look his short brown hair had taken with the aid of the cheapest hair gel. It darkened his hair colour and even hid the flecks of grey at the sides. He would show Jessica a Sean that she'd never before encountered and fix her in his grey, blue eyes as he spoke the words yet to be decided on. He paused facing the front door and re-confirmed his resolve to do what a man had to do. Opening the front door he called out to Molly, who was licking every trace of food from her bowl in the kitchen.

"Be a good girl, I won't be long!" and with that he was headed for the bank. Sean had a plan to keep his negative and cowardly thoughts at bay by means of a chant. Reciting over and over again, sometimes aloud he chanted. . . . 'Get it done and over with and get on with life!' Ten minutes later and still reciting his chant he stood at the door of the bank. Lifting his chin and straightening his posture he stepped into the bank and immediately viewed Jessica at her counter. There were no other tellers on duty and no customers waiting. His stomach muscles tightened and his blood stopped flowing to his extremities. He froze to the spot as she looked over to him, her face serious as ever. As he moved forward he drew his wallet from his trouser pocket and felt his thumb begin to tremble. In true form Jessica simply looked at him and waited for him to speak first. All the other tellers always smiled and asked how they could be of help but not Jessica, she dominated every customer with her steely gaze and contented silence. Sean took the appropriate bankcard from his wallet and saw that his hands were shaking very noticeably. When he looked across at her he saw that she too was watching his trembling hands. He passed the card under the glass into the metal tray. He had to speak.

"I'd like to withdraw £100 from this account please!" He felt his face burning hot and feared that he was blushing no ordinary blush but a beetroot red blush that would condemn him in her eyes as. . . . Weird. Jessica took the card and looked coldly at him then at the card then at him again. With her second glance into his face her eyes widened, she'd noticed the blushing and looked questioningly at him.

"Is the cash-point outside not working?" She enquired.

Sean's brain went into overdrive and compelled him to do and say exactly what it told him. "Oh yes, probably yes but. . . ." Sean couldn't hear his own thoughts because his heart was throwing itself against his ribs and pleading with him to walk away. He tried desperately to find words but knew that he was rapidly losing his composure. Jessica waited and waved his card slowly from side to side in front of her.

"I actually came to say. . . ." Sean's head and heart were giving him alternate messages. In the turmoil of his increasingly hopeless situation he managed to re-engage his brain.

"I have . . . for a long time now . . . I've. . . ." Think of the Valentine card and tell her what you feel, the voice in his head prompted him. Finally with his planned strength, dignity and honour absent he blurted out some basic, honest words.

"I think you are the most beautiful woman to ever walk the earth and I wondered if I might . . . be able to spend some time with you, somewhere . . . some time . . . maybe?" Sean breathed out deeply and slowly back in. He'd done it. Momentarily he dropped his gaze from her eyes then resumed his focus on her and waited to hear her refusal. Jessica's look of confusion melted away as she tilted her head marginally to one side and smiled widely at him.

"Tomorrow's Saturday and me and some of the girls go for a drink at the Red Lion after work. You could have a drink with us there if you like . . . around 12.30?" Jessica smiled again and Sean saw a kindness in her face that was totally new, truly genuine and utterly brilliant.

"Yes, okay. I'll pop along and see you there. Thank you!" Sean couldn't believe her positive response. He beamed the happiest, widest of smiles the likes of which his face had never before performed.

"Do you still want the £100?" Jessica again waved his cash-card in front of him.

"Err, no, no thank you." He spoke through his smile as his lungs sucked in air in short, sharp, excited jitters. His strength now returned to him with a vengeance. He gripped the edge of the counter with both hands so tightly that he thought a section of the three-inch thick plastic coated chipboard might break off in his hands.

Jessica slid the card back under the glass and smiled again. Sean returned it to his wallet and began to back his way out of the bank not wanting to take his eyes from her smiling face. Jessica's smile widened and gave way to a burst of shy, embarrassed laughter that she tried too late to hide behind her hand so she swivelled in her chair to face her colleagues in the background. Sean backed away until he neared the door and began his turn to negotiate his exit unaware that another customer was already entering the bank. He completed his turn and smacked his head into the edge of the approaching solid oak door. Reeling back in shock and embarrassment he immediately tried to numb the pain by pressing his hand tight to his forehead. The impact had been severe so he checked the palm of his hand for blood but there was none. Offering an apology to the little old lady who eyed him with concern and then contempt he took over the job of holding the heavy door to allow her to complete her entrance. He checked again to see if his forehead was bleeding then nervously checked over his shoulder to see if Jessica had observed his misfortune. Luck was with him. Jessica remained facing in the opposite direction and totally oblivious to his mishap. Wasting no more time and with the old lady beyond the arc of the door he was now free to make his speedy exit. In just two solitary steps his passage became suddenly problematic. The old lady was trailing a shopping trolley. His forward momentum kept his upper half travelling but the progress of his legs was ended and there was nowhere for him to go but over. Head first he toppled to the floor, his legs now detached from the ground followed the rest of him over the trolley and into a crumpled heap. Mercifully the bulging shopping trolley had remained upright so he took a moment of immobility to take stock of the new situation. As he glanced over to Jessica's counter his fear became reality. Sure enough she was surveying the scene and craned her slender neck to see more clearly what was happening. Rolling onto his knees he rose to his feet as the old lady pulled her trolley free of the door and watched voyeuristically as it closed on him. Surprised by the doors second assault he was momentarily pinned between it and the doorframe for a further embarrassing moment of haplessness. Pulling her trolley sharply towards her she glared at him through her large, thick spectacles. Sean pushed against the doorframe until he had room enough to lay a hand back onto the door and push it to the open. Free of the door he let it close behind him and faced the woman to take her scorn before offering his apology.

"Are you on drugs? What's the matter with you?" The old lady confronted him then in a moment of what she believed to be clarity her expression changed to one of realisation and fear. Her jaw dropped.

"Oh gosh, oh bloody hell! It's a robbery!" On uttering the word 'robbery' her false teeth ejected from her mouth that remained both gaping and silent. The sound of the false teeth clattering to the hard floor put her in mind of a firearm somewhere being cocked and primed for action. Abandoning her trolley she backed away from the desperate, identifiable man and let out a blood-curdling series of very loud screams. Sean halted his advance and waved his hands in front of her.

"No, no it's not a robbery. I just fell over your trolley that's all! Everything's O.K!" Jessica came from the side security door at a good pace and put her arm around the old lady to lead her to the waiting area. Her screaming stopped as she squeezed Jessica's arm and told her not to look at the robber or he might do for her too. Sean hovered in the background as two more of Jessica's colleagues came to attend the old lady. One of them held a glass of water and as she made her way to the panic stricken woman she slid on the upper set of false teeth and fell heavily to the ground with a thud accompanied by the shattering of the glass tumbler. The second of the bank clerks made it safely to the seating area and sat herself down beside the old lady who could now see Sean bending over the floored clerk.

"Oh won't somebody help that poor girl? Somebody should stop him!"

Jessica leaned over to block the old lady's view but had to double check for herself what was going on. Sean offered the fallen clerk his hand, which she took, and he pulled her to her feet. She dusted herself down as he picked up the pieces of broken glass and both sets of false teeth. Next out from the secure area was Karla. Giving Sean a wide birth she brought a replacement glass of water and handed it across to Jessica. The previously felled clerk returned hobbling and bent forward in obvious pain and discomfort from her lower back. In her hand she held reams of blue paper and she gingerly lowered herself to the floor and began to soak up the spilled water. Sean placed the shards of shattered glass and false teeth on the receptionists' desktop and offered to take over the mopping up operation from the discomforted clerk who politely declined his offer. There was nothing else for him to do so he caught Jessica's attention by waving his hands in the air and mouthed the words, aided by more hand movements and finger pointing, "I'll go now!" Jessica smiled and nodded and Sean exited the bank.

With the commotion over with he felt the pain of his own injuries return to him. He exercised the shoulder that had taken his full weight when he crashed to the ground then rubbed his hip. His forehead throbbed and he felt the sore area that appeared to be swelling up with the palm of his hand. All in all he had won a huge and wholly unexpected victory. He had left the bank with a different sort of pain than what he'd prepared himself for and felt fantastic. The months of worshipping her in secrecy, the untold hours of running scenario after scenario where he would sweep her off her feet and immediately engage her in an explosion of passion were ended. His most re-run fantasy of handing her a cheque from an adoring publisher of £310.000 and offering her £100.00 for a single date was no longer required or relevant. He was now in a parallel world where his dreams mingled with reality. He was actually to meet with Jessica in a social capacity the very next day. In fact he would be sitting with her and supping ale inside the next 26 hours. A rush of adrenalin coursed through his veins and quickened his step. He headed down the town with no thoughts of where he was going. He wandered the high street with a huge grin on his face that made his cheeks ache but every time he manually prised it away with his hand it returned inside a minute. It soon dawned on him that the importance of the following day called for a new shirt at the very least. He made his way to the Officers Club and perused the racks and rails soon picking out a thickly woven black shirt. Black was perfect because apart from her bank issue red jacket he had only ever seen her wearing black. Yes, she loved black so the shirt in hand was a definite buy. The idea to follow up his black shirt with a pair of black jeans was quickly dismissed as a step too far, too Gothic. With that thought something worrying struck him like a thunderbolt from the blue. Maybe Jess was a Goth. One of those who roamed the town centre draped in black and chained by some extremity to a fellow Goth of equal piercing and badly applied black make-up. No, this couldn't be true of Jess she was far too individual, far too composed, too elegant, mature and responsible to give herself such a label. She had the best reason to wear black and that was that it simply suited her. It suited her long, jet-black hair it complimented her bronze skin and implied depth beyond any other colour.

Sean paid for just the shirt and was eager to get home and share his groundbreaking news with someone. With springs for legs and frequent rushes of adrenalin he was home in record time. Through the front door Molly greeted him. He bent down and rapidly ruffled her fur the wrong way along the length of her body.

"It's done Moll, I am to meet with . . . The Her!" Sean kissed Molly on the head and stood to take his coat off. He paced up and down the living room with a huge smile, occasionally raising his head to God and with arms outstretched shouted his many thanks. Molly took her place back in her chair and watched his increasingly strange behaviour with interest and a hope that his excess of energy would result in a good long walkies.

Sean decided that the only person available who would appreciate his news would be his ex-workmate and long-time drinking partner John. Sean had called a halt to his twice-weekly nights out with John and Carl some three months previously. He'd seen that his savings were being depleted at an unsustainable rate due to his potentially premature departure from gainful employment. His funds could no longer take the strain of his social life so he'd had to change his lifestyle to suit. Of course with his abstention from the nights out he also had to forego the sporadic sex that came with them. He didn't miss the infrequent one-night stand, his heart had become the property of Jessica a long time since and his loyalty to her was an important part of keeping alive the hope of one day being with her. As he came to see it, if he continued in his drunkenness and pursuit of meaningless sex he wouldn't deserve her. He had to prove to the unseen but ever present ancestors and matchmakers that he was worthy of her. If he could prove that his heart was loyal to her without possessing her he might one day be rewarded with the gift of achieving his ultimate goal. His most private belief had paid off, he was on the verge of being with the Divine Jessica and there could be no greater reward on this Earth than to be the one to be with her.

A strange thought then occurred. An unknown memory from back at the bank now made itself known The sound of her stilettos on the bank's tiled floor as she came through the security door resounded in his memory. It was a unique sound he'd not noticed in the bank but here it was replaying in his head. It wasn't the rhythm of her heels on the hard surface it was the actual sound they made that captivated him. Again and again he summoned the sound of her shoes. He thought back to the incident and recalled an image of her black stilettos slightly scuffed around the toe and in need of some attention but the sound they made was the sweetest sound he'd ever heard. He sat himself down on the sofa and let the thoughts and images wash over him. For the first time he'd been standing on the same surface as her and even though she wore 4 or 5-inch stilettos she only came up to the level of his chin. She was daintier than he ever realised. The moment when she had led the little old lady to the seating area heralded another memory for him. She wore tight black trousers that rapidly flared out from the knee and he'd seen her knicker line. A mild dose of adrenalin surged again and he shook his lecherous thoughts loose choosing instead to return to the memories of her sound and her sublime smile.

The next thing to do was to phone John at work. He pulled his mobile from his trouser pocket and dialled. In two short rings he was through to Andrea the receptionist.

"Hello, Precision Mouldings."

"Hi, can you put me through to John Baker in the stores please?"

"Hi is that you Sean?" Andrea inquired.

"Yes, hi Andrea." Sean knew he was in for a gossip fest followed by an onslaught of prying questions.

"How are you? What are you doing these days?"

"Oh I'm doing fine, enjoying my freedom. Living life stress free!"

11

"Oh well done. Nothing's changed here. We all still miss you, there's been one giant cock-up after another downstairs."

"Yeah, I don't doubt it. Anyway Andrea I'm on a mobile and haven't much credit left. I'll pop in and see you all one day soon!" Sean had no intention of keeping to his word.

"All right, I'm putting you through now, byee."

"Hello stores John speaking."

"Hello John Speaking, how are things?"

"Fuck me its Sean of the Dead! If you're wanting your job back I'm afraid they've given it to an Aardvark"

"An Aardvark?"

"Yes that is correct an Aardvark has your old job and is doing it rather better at it than you did. Busy little thing, just gets on with things and keeps it's head down!"

"Yeah John I haven't much credit so are you going to be in the George tonight?" Sean considered it best not to go into detail over the phone as it'd take far too long with John obviously in a strange humour mood.

"Yes I'll be there with Carl at about eight-ish if I must. Are you thinking of coming out?" John asked sounding surprised.

"Yeah! I'll pop along and have a couple." Sean told him.

"To the pub?" John inquired. His voice sounding ever more surprised.

"Yes!" Sean snapped.

"With alcohol, fights and your mum?"

"Yep! I'll see you at eight!" Sean didn't wait to hear more of John's surreal banter and hung up.

Sean felt tired and deflated. His big news wasn't going to rock anybody's world but his own. It was at best a pre-date meeting and in truth John probably couldn't even recall his mentioning her on any occasion. Sean yawned and led himself down on the sofa. He tucked a cushion under his head and closed his eyes.

CHAPTER TWO

SEAN'S DREAM

Something black moved swiftly and silently through the open kitchen door followed by a second shadowy figure. Leaving the door wide open behind them they made their way through the kitchen and paused at the door to the lounge. Molly sniffed the air and then settled her head back down to sleep. Smoothly the two dark figures entered the lounge and took position standing over the sleeping Sean. One of the figures produced a length of rope from somewhere in its midriff and pulled it taut between his hands. He nodded to his accomplice and they simultaneously burst into action. Turned onto his stomach and pushed deep into the sofa he had his arms pulled from under him and pressed into the small of his back, his wrists forced together. He tried to roll over and off of the sofa to the floor but was prevented by the first figure who then applied even greater pressure on him and brought his knee to rest on his neck. Sean felt the rope being applied to his wrists, round and round in quick succession. It was now or never. He mustered all his strength to serve him in one desperate two-second burst. It worked he'd thrown off his assailants, the rope unwound from his wrists and he was on the floor. Before the figures could effectively respond he rolled over and over towards the front door, his legs flailing violently into the air to keep his attackers at bay. Finally he hit the door and began to rise from the floor. His arms were now free to take over the work of swinging through the air warding off his foes. SMACK! He'd caught one of them square on the side of the head. The Foe didn't fall. The impact made his hand numb up instantly and before he could fully withdraw his fist for a second strike he was pinned by the throat to the closed and locked door. A huge force pulled him forward and threw him again to the ground. As before he was pinned. The pain of a knee heavily coming to rest between his shoulder blades, the force of which he'd been thrown to the floor and his apparent exhaustion made him close his eyes and accept the inevitable. Again his assailants pulled his hands behind his back and applied the rope. He let his limbs relax and become compliant to the needs of his captors. Roughly grabbing hold of his shirt collar whilst the other figure caught hold of the rope around his feet he was hoisted into the air. They carried him face down as if to use him as a battering ram, back through the house and out into the garden. Waiting on the long garden path there stretched a Chinese dragon of brilliant yellow, red and gold. A third all black figure he now made out to be either a Ninja or Special Forces stood by the dragon with a hefty wooden pole. Sean dropped his head and stared down at his concrete path until he was hoisted into the upright position. He was pushed and pulled about until they had completed lashing him to the pole and again transported to the horizontal. He gathered his defeatist thoughts together and asked one of the ninja where they were taking him.

"We take you now to meet with your Master!" A voice answered but which one spoke he didn't know.

"But I'm free, I'm a free man, I have no master. I wont submit to this. I don't even like men!"

"You've submitted already!" A voice told him as he was raised up still higher for the pole to rest on the shoulders of two ninjas. With a sudden drop in altitude, a sideways move and the regaining of height he was secreted away in the belly of the dragon. Symbols crashed, horns blew and prayer bells rang out with an underlying bass of drums beating a slow march as they vibrated the air. They moved out of the garden and through the unusually busy nighttime streets. Firecrackers fizzed and exploded all around. In no time at all the tarmac roads became cobbled and the accompanying noise ceased. They travelled over a significant wooden echoic bridge, up a number of stone steps and through an enormously wide doorway. The dragon performed a 90-degree turn and fell still. A Ninja appeared inside the dragon with him and to Sean's deep concern began to cut his upper half free. Before he could get the words of warning out his upper half was freed and with his feet still secured to the pole he swung head long to the stone floor. Somehow he managed to break his fall with his chest and lifted his head up just in time to keep it from being his first point of contact with the stone floor. All air in his lungs was expelled in a second. He realised that he represented the dragon's penis and with no movement possible he remained gasping for air and straining to hear anything.

"Award his chain and bring him to me!" A distant female voice commanded.

At last his feet were cut free and they fell hard to the floor. A collar was brought up and snapped shut around his neck. The cold of the heavy iron only added to his discomfort. The Ninja pulled him from beneath the dragon and continued to drag him the length of the great hall. Sean was in too much pain from his winding and his bindings past and present to get to his feet. All he could do to ease his pain was to hold on to his collar with both hands and take the strain off his neck. Finally his journey came to an end at the base of more steps and the excess of chain clattered to the ground.

"You're mine now and I want you to be a good boy and behave accordingly!" The female voice addressed him. "Your heart has made a wise choice. An impeccable choice! Serve me well and you will find the love you seek to be blissfully sublime! Wear my chains with great pride! Its every link gives you the freedom and scope to serve me better! Remember these words and be good. Do right by me and we will be together and make each other whole! I will be as much yours as you are mine and our love will be among the rarest there has ever been!"

"Jess! Jessica, is that you? Sean waited to hear more but the voice fell silent. He lifted his head to see her but all he could see was an enormous, luxurious bed surrounded by beautiful silks that draped down from a ceiling too high to bring into view. A Cheetah chained at the foot of the bed caught his attention and cussed him as it swished its tail from side to side. All around were scattered and piled sumptuous pillows and cushions of rich, intense colours.

"Hello!" Sean called out to her.

"Hello!" He needed to see her and confirm that the voice was that of his Jess. He climbed the four steps trailing his chain behind him and surveyed the rich, oriental surroundings. The Cheetah walked to him and rubbed its head affectionately against his hip.

"HELLO!" He tried one last time but there was no reply. Instead he heard the faint footsteps of his abductor come closer and the clanking sound of his chain as it was pulled taut. Suddenly he was pulled backwards so hard that he left the ground and flew over the steps back toward the stone floor.

CHAPTER THREE

Sean woke with a jolt from a missed heartbeat, still expecting to impact on the stone floor. Collecting his thoughts he checked the time. 19.23 in electric blue told him he had little time to get ready and get to the pub. His stomach rumbled, demanding something to work on. He was in full agreement and had no intention of pouring ale into an empty, growling stomach. With time a deciding factor he put a burger into the microwave and lit a cigarette whilst he waited the ninety seconds for it to cook.

His slept in clothes would remain on, after all he wasn't on the pull and he swore to himself that he wouldn't be going on to a club. All the same he checked his wallet to make sure he had enough funds for just such an eventuality.

He stroked Molly under the chin, flung his coat on and buttoned it up to the neck. He didn't look at her as he left but called out his usual goodbye.

"Bye Moll. I won't be long. Be good!" He stepped along the front path and there was something in what he'd just said that made him recall his dream. 'Be good' he thought had triggered an immediate and total recall of his dream. He should've walked at a decent pace but his thoughts were on his strange and lucid dream. Despite his steady pace his walk up the hill to the old town laboured his breathing and his dream was soon out of mind. He undone the top button of his coat and synchronised his pace to his breathing. Vowing to stop smoking at the earliest opportunity he reached the apex of the hill. Turning into the high street the sights and sounds brought back memories of his in regular nights out that seemed now to be from a past life. He leapt the three steps of the entranceway to the George Inn and stepped inside. John and Carl weren't at their usual spot at the end of the bar so he made a quick sweep of the whole interior. The alcove was completely taken over with a large party of students who had requisitioned most of the chairs and stools from other tables. Two groups of middle-aged locals stood at the bar and around the podium was another grouping of office workers or possibly estate agents. Leaning over the bar he was greeted by Sue.

"Hello stranger! A pint of best?"

"Yes please Sue!" Sean began to realise that he had missed this part of his life. Sue put his drink in front of him and took his money. Whilst she sorted out his change she commented on John and Carl's unusual lateness that evening. Sean settled on the only available bar stool and took the first gulps of his ale. He soon worked out that the group of estate agents were in fact police. He noticed that they were the loudest group in the whole pub but it was what they said that gave them away as police officers. D.S this. D.C.I. that sounded with regularity. Turning on his stool he brought into view the group of four men and two women. The first sight of one of the women officers made his heart beat faster and his brain seize in shock. Dressed in a black trouser suit and with long black hair she put him in mind that it was his Jessica. She stood with her back to him. Soon enough he was able to dismiss the woman as his Jessie when he noticed her fuller build and increased height. His hot flush of concern melted away and he turned to face the bar. Stubbing out his cigarette he experienced a force slam into his shoulder that forced him forward across the bar. Then came another slap and another. Big John appeared beside him and continued pounding of his shoulder.

"Sean you old bugger you made it!" John finally ceased his backslapping and leant heavily over the bar.

"Good to see you Sean!" Carl clearly unsteady on his feet appeared the other side of him.

"You too, you two!" Sean replied and patted Carl's upper arm. "Did you start early tonight or something?" He questioned them on their obvious advancement in intoxication.

"We had a few tinnies and a little splifter at my place before we came out" Carl said and took the drink handed to him by John. Carl's legs found it difficult to remain standing and stationary at the same time so Sean stood and offered up his stool.

"The return of the three Amigos!" John raised his rather full glass and waited for Carl and Sean to chink their glasses with his. Sean followed by Carl trailing beer over his trousers and the floor chinked their glasses to John's and took long gulps of ale.

"To us!" Carl returned his glass to the center of their little circle. John and Sean followed Carl's lead and they toasted themselves again. To Sean's disappointment his comrades turned their heads towards him and waited for him to propose a toast. Sean thought for a moment.

"To the three Amigos!" To his relief and amusement his buddies accepted the toast. Sean emptied his glass and stretched to the bar for his second pint. John put his hand on Sean's shoulder.

"No, wait a minute, we've done the three Amigos. You gotta do another one!" He said swaying then raised his head letting out a loud and proud belch.

"Okay, here's to freedom from the clock!" Sean raised his glass.

"No, we're not having that old chestnut! Some of us are perfectly happy being miserable at work!" John looked at him with impatient eyes.

"Okay, okay, gentlemen I give you the Queen!" Sean raised his glass.

"Nope, can't stand her!" John cut his toast dead in its tracks.

"Kylie Minogue?" Sean offered a quick alternative.

"Too short!"

"Halle Berry?"

"Too tall!"

"Sharon Stone?"

"Too old!"

"Demi Moore?"

"Hair too short!"

"Umm. . . . How about Cameron Diaz then?"

"Too spunky!"

"Kate Moss?"

"Too skinny!"

"Holly Valance?"

"Too loud!"

"Audrey Hepburn . . . in her hey-day?"

"Too . . . monochrome!"

"Kierah Knightly?" Sean offered anticipating compliance.

Carl's eyes lit up as he smiled and looked to John for his acceptance.

"Hmmm . . . big eyebrows and no tits . . . to speak of!" John declined only after careful consideration.

"Right then, this one you shall not DARE to refuse me. . . . Twats please raise your glasses and drink to the health and the everlasting beauty of . . . Angelina Jolie!" Smiles all round they happily toasted the uber sexy Angelina.

The toasting proceedings came to an end and Sean sought to see if he could catch a glimpse of the Asian policewoman. She had changed her position in the group and Sean saw that she was indeed eye-catchingly pretty. As if she had felt his eyes on her she looked straight over at him. Sean withdrew his prying eyes and rejoined his pals. John and Carl gulped their beers in silence and Sean felt the urge to see if the woman was still looking over. Sending his pupils to the corners of his eyes he turned his head ever so slowly in her direction. She was talking on her mobile some distance from her group of friends with her free hand pressed against her ear. A mere two seconds must have passed before she turned about to look directly at him again. Sean quickly turned away vowing not to chance another glance.

John put a hand on his shoulder and pointed out a table that had just been vacated. The three of them made their way to it with Sean getting there first and choosing the chair that faced away from the police pack. Sean settled into his chair and John plonked himself heavily down on his. Carl completely misjudged his approach to the allotted chair and came down on it at too acute an angle. The aborted landing came too late to save him and he fell sideways to the floor. The chair came to rest sideways on the floor next to him as the liquid in his glass sloshed around but didn't spill.

"I just remembered, I don't like that chair!" He said with all the dignity he could muster as he sat up and crossed his legs faking contentment to be seated on the floor. John returned Carl's chair to the upright and seated himself on it. He offered Carl his stool and pulled it across nearer him. Carl gratefully accepted the offer and rose from the floor to be seated. John still held the leg of the stool and looked across at Sean giving him a wink and a shifty, sideways glance toward Carl. Carl began his second descent and John pulled the stool away at exactly the right moment. Carl's second descent passed the point where he expected it to end. His expression burst into total bewilderment followed by the resignation that again he was to be reunited with the floor. John and Sean were in a fit of hysterics as Carl lay on the floor with his arms and legs sticking up in the air. John replaced the stool and fought to quell his laughter. Sean seemed to have his under control but when Carl eventually rose from the floor it all began again. Now they took the mantle of being the noisiest group in the pub. Almost all the eyes in the pub were on Carl until Sean helped him to his feet and walked him forward to straddle his stool and successfully come to rest upon it.

John was still chuckling to himself when he stood to get the next round of drinks. Sean signalled and told him it was his round. He walked up to the heaving bar and found himself standing next to the Asian woman officer. He kept his eyes looking straight ahead but her presence and close proximity seemed to be compelling him to verbally acknowledge her. He fought off his compulsion and put her tremendous sense of presence down to her resemblances to Jess. He waited his turn as Sue moved about the bar in something that resembled a fast-forwarding action. The pub was filling up fast and he knew he was way down in line to be served. Sue returned to the Asian officer and as she handed her, her change the woman leaned over and spoke loudly in her ear.

"I'm going to get this man to help me carry the drinks but I don't want him to lose his place! Okay?"

"Yeah, fine love!" Sue reassured her then took a second to give Sean an obvious wink.

Sean realised that the Asian lady was talking about him. She had an array of drinks in front of her on two bar trays. She took hold of the tray with the six tumblers and two tall drinks, then, without taking her eyes from her own drinks tray she spoke to him.

"Will you be all right with that one?"

"Yeah, okay, fine! I'll be fine!" Sean lifted the second tray and followed her through the crowd to the podium. He slid the tray onto the podium pushing aside numerous empty tumblers and pint pots. With no word of thanks forthcoming he discharged himself from being of any further assistance. He turned to go back to the bar when he heard the woman call loudly across the podium to him.

"Just a minute!" The woman finished clearing her tray that he'd brought over and offered him the two trays.

"It'll save me another journey!" She held out the trays at arms length and stared into his eyes. Sean's indignation melted away in the instant she looked into him. She'd probably appreciated his help even if she didn't see the need to show it.

"Okay!" He took the trays from her and returned to the bar.

Sue was still working the bar alone and was clearly doing her best to get through everyone in turn. Sean felt sure that the Asian woman had made some kind of point but to whom she had made it and what the point was eluded him. He eventually made it back to his own table with three more pints. John and Carl were pretending to be dead with Carl slumped over the table with his arms hanging limply down to the ground and John draped backwards in his chair eyes shut tight and mouth a-gape. Sean put the drinks down and after taking a few gulps of his own, he busied himself collecting some glasses from surrounding tables. He took them up to the bar to a grateful Sue who shouted her thanks over the noise and gave him the thumbs up. He took one of the trays that remained on the bar and paused to think a moment then returned to the podium to collect their glasses too. He deliberately avoided eye contact with the Asian woman but felt her eyes on him all the while. He returned the glasses to the bar and the smiling appreciation of Sue. On his return to his table he found John and Carl in deep discussion about someone new at their work named Neville Vaark. Carl let him into the joke that his name was Mr Vaark and he was extremely hard. He's an . . . Aardvark!" Carl divulged and cracked up into fits of laughter. Sean smiled at the pun and bided his time, refusing to get involved in work place politics. He showed his total disinterest by sitting back in his chair and keeping out of earshot.

There was something strange about the young man who came next into the pub that made Sean track his movements with interest. He was wearing biker boots and jacket but had no helmet with him. His short, flattened, bleached blonde hair suggested he had been wearing a helmet recently and most strangely of all, he was still wearing his leather summer gloves. Sean watched as the man made his way, not to the bar but to the tables in the far corner. The wiry, young biker engaged one of two seated men in conversation. He leant heavily over the table and suddenly unleashed a series of lightning blows to the man's face and head. The man sought cover under the table but the biker tipped the table aside and began to kick and then stamp on the now screaming man. Sean stood to see more clearly what was going on, as did all the students at the tables opposite. The beaten mans friend now stood and tried to pacify the biker. One well-aimed blow from the biker sent the man hurtling sideways to fall over the upended table where he stayed and watched as the biker applied some more powerful kicks to his intended targets ribs. Stepping back into the vacated space and with his arms outstretched he addressed the onlookers.

"This piece of shit is a wife beater! If anyone wants to stand by him lets have them now!" Still with his arms outstretched he surveyed the crowd until finally he turned his attention back to his victim. Lifting his bloodied head up by the hair he spoke to him.

"You have no friends here and your shitty little secret is out!" With that he pushed the man's head down into the floor and gave him a parting gift of one last kick to his upper arm.

The police group had been making their way through the crowd when the biker said his piece. The Asian woman officer caught hold of the bikers arm and marched him outside as her female counterpart attended the battered and blooded victim. Two male counterparts escorted the Asian officer as far as the door where she refused their intervention and took the biker outside alone. The sideshow was over and people returned to their seats. John and Carls in-depth conversation had dried up and Sean leant forward to divulge his news.

"Do you remember me telling you about . . . the most beautiful woman to ever walk this Earth . . . working at my bank?"

"Yeah!" John answered but looked vague.

"Well, I sent her a Valentine card and today I asked her out and she agreed to meet me for a drink tomorrow afternoon!" Sean's eyes lit up and he smiled at the thought.

"Well done mate I hope it goes well for you!" John took in the news but didn't express any elation on Sean's behalf. Carl had also listened with mild interest. A couple of seconds went by in silence until Carl drew his drink away from his mouth.

"So in all this time your Choo choo still hasn't seen her Foo foo?" Carl followed by John burst into laughter. Sean accepted their fun making with a wide smile and if laughter came to him he would welcome it. As yet the humour escaped him and as he trailed four or five pints behind them he simply watched, listened and waited. John held up his hand to call a halt to the laughter.

"You, mean that you haven't played . . . hide the sausage . . . sorry chipolata with her yet?" the waning laughter started again with Sean accepting their frame of mind with a wide smile but as yet still no laughter of his own. Carl thought as quick and deep as he could to come up with another one.

"You, you, you haven't smashed her pasty?" Carl reeled back in hysterics. John continued to laugh hard and was clearly readying himself for his next offering.

"You haven't even spoken on her furry phone?" Carl added in quick succession.

"You haven't bumped uglies or tried the Trappers hat on?" John managed to add.

Laughing too hard to think of anymore they slowly eased the volume down and with one look at Sean's passive seriousness they laughed loudly again. It was clear that as long as Sean kept an un-amused look on his face, their laughter couldn't stop. Sean played along with this and knew just the right facial expressions to offer and feed their laughter.

It took a while to get things to quieten down enough for John to finish his drink and dry his watering eyes. Carl rose to get the next round of drinks in and was escorted by Sean who didn't trust him to get through the crowd without incident. The operation was a success and three more pints landed safely on their table. Carl made certain he was between John and his stool before slowly lowering himself safely down. Sean drew them both in over the table so he didn't have to shout his unfortunate request. Inwardly he wished he had his sane and reliable friends to call upon for assistance but unfortunately Jason had a big job on working as a stone-mason and Funji was abroad setting up another of Sean's former employers acqui-sitions. He had no choice but to utilise the two friends before him. Reluctantly and with growing misgivings he asked John and Carl to accompany him for his meet-ing with Jess and her work friends the next afternoon.

"Of course it should go without saying but you must be on your best behaviour and please Carl, none of your crass T-shirts! This is a pre-date date and it's really important to me!"

"We'll be there for you mate!" John administered a slow motion punch to Sean's arm.

"Yes we'll be there for you! We could be your Gay friends . . . girls love gays!" Carl's face lit up showing his belief in his brainstorm.

"That's brilliant!" John added his enthusiasm.

"Okay! But first I want you to show me how you'd camp it up all the way to the bar and back the both of you!" Sean kept a straight face and waited for them to decline the offer and retract the whole idea.

To Sean's delight they got to their feet, lined up side-by-side and minced through the crowd toward the bar with exaggerated hip swinging and limp wrists. Carl's effort was close to becoming a full-blown Mick Jagger impression but the finest was yet to come when they made their turn at the bar. They paused, posed, pouted and turned like catwalk divas in almost perfect synchronisity then to the accompaniment of jeers and wolf whistles from the Friday night revellers they minced their way back to Sean. Carl bowed to the crowd in three directions as John stood waiting for Sean's verdict.

"Nice, but maybe too nice! I think I'll stick with plan 'A'!" Sean told him.

"What's Plan 'A'?" John inquired.

"You are two mute and retarded orphans that I look after at weekends" Sean told him and smiled into his beer.

John and Carl sat back down to the table and as time was pressing towards last orders John got another round in and suggested they moved onto a club. As planned Sean declined and as predicted the cajoling started. First John then Carl then John and Carl together pleaded with him to go along with them. Sean stood his ground and insisted that this was his last drink before heading home and get-ting ready for his big day. As time was called Sean finished his drink and double-checked that John at least understood when and where they would meet the next morning. Carl was wavering around on his stool and badly slurred the few words he uttered. Sean doubted they would make it to a club and if they did they'd prob-ably not be admitted. He stood up and reiterated his farewells and left them plan-ning where to go next.

Outside the streets were dark and glistening wet. Taxi after taxi passed him as he made his way home the way he had came, on foot. Molly stayed in her chair as he entered the house. She was in an obvious mood with him for not being walked since the previous morning. He kicked off his shoes and removed his coat before heading straight to bed.

He must've been asleep before his head hit the pillow. He had no recollection of any dream or comfort seeking movements made in the lumpy bed for the entire night. The day was grey and heavily overcast which made his heart sink. It would've been fortuitous to have his first date with Jessica under blue skies. With no sun to illuminate the room he had to reach for his mobile to check the time. Eight fifty, a good time to rise on this special day. He had time enough to give Molly a descent walk get himself ready and to link up with John and Carl.

After a good dose of orange juice and a generous chunk of cheese he was out with Molly straining at the lead. They walked a circuit that they often walked when Sean's time was a factor and work loomed. It was too late in the day for foxes but there were at least a few rabbits for Molly to give chase to. She hadn't the required speed or agility to catch healthy rabbits but every summer when Mix mitosis became prevalent she would catch and despatch one or two a week. Sean accepted this hunter, killer trait in Molly, as they were already dying a slow and painful death and the death dealt them by Molly was a swift one.

Back home he had a coffee before readying himself for the big event. He chose not to shave that morning, preferring instead to keep the designer stubble and shave the next day. He might even grow his goaty back but from now on it was to be Jess's choice to make. If she liked clean-shaven men then she would have it. If she liked the goaties then he would grow it for her. She had seen every combination many times before and now she could choose which look she preferred. Donning his new shirt he promised himself that he would keep it forever as the shirt of his first meeting with his grandchildren's grandmother. All in all he was feeling very positive about the days events to follow and his fears of Carl and John showing him up in some way were forgotten.

Sean marched up to the bar of the George and smelled the unwelcome scent of disinfectant then noticed a large wet patch by the podium. Another wet patch could be seen where the biker had battered the wife beater but what the wet patch to his left was remained an unimportant mystery. Robert, Sue's husband had been sent down to work the bar alone, as she had done the previous night. He was clearly suffering from a heavy night and not at all prone to conversation at such times. Sean sat at the bar with a pint of best and a small whiskey to calm his encroaching nerves. He was nearly half way down his first pint when John bowled into the pub.

"Looking good my man but you should've shaved!" John told him eyeing him up and down.

Sean ordered him a drink and they sat together on the end of the bar like they had done countless times before. John shook his head and told him about the occurrences after he left them the previous night. It turned out that they hadn't made it to a club. On standing to leave the pub, Carl felt sick. He'd attempted to make it to the gents but only got about half way before it happened. John lowered his voice to tell the rest of the story and not have Robert overhear..

"He was like a puke fire hydrant! He knelt on the floor and projected vomit about eight feet across the room. Then like a Dalek with a death ray he turned his head and vomited on a whole group of about eight people by the podium. I don't think there was one person in that side of the pub that wasn't covered in vomit from the waist down." John began laughing hard as he relived the tale. Sean laughed along with him and the large wet patch in the carpet and smell of disinfectant was explained.

"It turned out that most of the people he showered were off duty police. I phoned him just now to remind him that Sue's barred him. She was nearly as mad as the old bill were!" John's laughter increased to hysterics and awarded them a scowl from the distant Robert who was reading a newspaper. Sean thought of the rather rude Asian officer and his laughing suddenly ceased. He wasn't sure why he should feel any sympathy for her but it was there and cut his appreciation of the story dead in its tracks. John noticed his sudden change of heart and gradually quietened down to drink his beer. It was time to make the move to the Red lion. They said goodbye to the ever-cheerful Robert and marched down through the town reaching the Red Lion at exactly twelve thirty six.

John ordered the drinks and Sean scoured the seating area and there she was. She was sitting with two friends, one of which he knew as Karla the other was someone who seldom attended the counters and worked mostly behind the scenes. Jess had her hair tied back in a ponytail revealing the full on beauty of her angular face. Sean took a few deep breaths and with John in tow made his way to her table. With every step he could feel his face and cheeks burn hotter.

"May we join you?" Sean's first words came out as carefree as he could muster.

"Yes, you can!" Jessica inched up and pulled her expansive black leather trench coat nearer her.

The table next to Jess's was empty like so many others at that time of day but it wouldn't be long before this popular, trendy pub would fill. Sean felt that Karla and the mystery plump woman were watching his every expression and faintest tremble. He sat near the edge of Jess's table but set his beer down on the neighbouring empty table. John did likewise and sat opposite him and next to Karla. Sean introduced John to Jess and Jess introduced Karla and Fiona to John and Sean. With the introductions made Jess opened the conversation to be held primarily between the two of them. Sean soon relaxed in her company as she talked and asked endless questions. Every time that he feared the conversation might lapse into an uneasy silence, Jess was ready with another question. She was utterly delightful, her social skills kept the conversation flowing and John kept the drinks coming even to the point of going to the bar with Sean's money so he could sit and continue to talk with Jess. She made no mention of the little old lady incident and was genuinely interested in Sean's answers to her subtly prying questions. She made it known of her dislike of smoking and eyed him suspiciously having picked up the odour of tobacco from his clothing and guessed the probable reason for his minty breath. Karla got on well with John and at times they broke off from the main conversation and held one of their own. Eventually and five rum and cokes later Fiona loosened her stiff self-control began to verbally participate in the session.

24

"Actually what we are all dying to ask you is. . . ." Fiona looked at Jess for permission to continue. Jess shrugged her shoulders to say that it was fine with her to continue.

" . . . Did you send Jess a valentine card?" Fiona stared at him. Karla stopped mid-sentence in her conversation with John and looked to him. Joined by John all eyes except Jess's were on him. Sean savoured his moment of power in the spotlight. He made them wait with nothing but a wry smile to hint at his answer. He came up with the idea of reciting the poem from the card as his answer but decided to give them just an excerpt from it. The least embarrassing portion to save both him and Jess from too from too much embarrassment.

"Not Helen of Troy nor Roxanne its true, could ever come close or hold a candle to you!"

Karla slapped the table. "I knew it, I knew it had to be you!"

Jess just smiled and for the first time in what must've been coming on for ninety minutes words escaped her. John's expression was puzzled and Karla brought him up to date not knowing that he always looked that way on his fifth pint. Fiona took herself off to the ladies room timed to give Jess and Sean some privacy.

"Well, thanks for the card it was really nice. Actually it was the best I've ever received!" Jess turned to sit askew and face him.

Sean feared that he was in for a gentle thanks but no thanks speech. His blood ran cold and he readied himself to hear the words that would condemn to death all the hopes he'd built in his heart for the past year. When they came, they came softly. Jess tried to make their conversation private.

"The words in your poem, did you mean them or is it just a poem you pulled from the net?"

Sean rushed with elation that for now his fear hadn't become a reality.

"It took me three days but it's all mine. I meant every word!"

Jess looked unblinking at him and deep into his blue grey eyes. She'd seen enough and in a single sentence she took the pressure off him and elevated his spirit.

"We can go to the cinema tonight if you like?" She drained her glass and set the empty glass on the table with a thud then rooted through her handbag and jotted down her address and telephone number. Leaning over to speak into his ear she told him. . . .

"They might've thought it was you who sent the card but only I was certain!" She told him and pressed the piece of paper into his hand.

Fiona returned from the ladies and Jess stepped out to where there was plenty of floor space. With a certain degree of showmanship she swung her long black leather coat around her shoulders and slid her arms into its sleeves as it still glided through the air. Joined by Karla the three women weaved their way through the tables and chairs and out of the pub. Sean watched her going until she was out of sight. He was completely awe struck by her. If he worshipped her yesterday, this day he'd come to worship the very ground she walked upon.

Deep in thought and still staring in the direction of the door he didn't notice that John had returned to the bar for another refill. He now doubled Sean who was only half way down his third with no intention of having a fourth. He was still lost in thoughts of his rapid promotion to a world of granted wishes when John returned with two more pints.

"I'll have to make this my last one because I don't want to be all groggy when I pick Jess up tonight!" He told him knowing that John would like nothing more than to turn this dinnertime drink into a full-blown session.

"Good luck with her she's a nice lass!" John paused. "Karla's nice too!" He added to make his interest in her known to the person now in a position to pass the comment on.

"She is yes! She's really pretty isn't she?" Sean thought of the vast incline of difference there was between the pretty Karla and the divine Jess. Certainly Karla with her long blonde hair, sky blue eyes, high cheekbones and athletic build would be near the very top of the beauty chart. Jess however was so far off the chart that she'd soar high above its peak like a satellite over a mountaintop. A rush of adrenalin surged through him and he felt as if he'd just stepped onto a roller-coaster ride of dreams come true. Surely now he would finish his novel, deposit a big, fat cheque in the bank and offer Jess a blissfully contented life of leisure and travel. They'd sleep in four-poster beds in country hotels and Emperor sized beds in city hotels. They'd sleep in hammocks on white sandy beaches and when they tired of travelling they'd relax at their country cottage in the Cotswolds. He'd write a sequel then do it all over again. They'd visit every Cathedral, castle and stately home. Scraping frost from car windscreens before the sun came up and looking out of factory or office windows at the blue summer skies would be distant memories. They would retire to bed when they were tired and wake up when they were hungry either for food or each other.

"Well I can see that I'll be getting no more joy from you today!" John said as he waved his hand in front of Sean's staring, unblinking eyes.

Sean kissed the piece of paper and folded it into his wallet. He declined Johns offer of continuing the session at Carl's house and headed steadily off home still dazed by his success with Jess.

Not knowing why, he followed Molly out into the garden. There was nothing to do there then he remembered his strange dream. He was standing on the spot where he'd been secreted away in the belly of the dragon. His concentration was broken when Molly collided with the half open timber gate and continued her run with her tail between her legs until she got to safety behind him. A big ginger tomcat with its tail bushed out had given chase to her and only broken off the attack on seeing Sean. He couldn't help but to laugh at her cowardice and how she only now barked at the animal knowing she was safe with him. The cat turned about 180 degrees and made a slow, dignified exit with its tail raised high giving them both the view of its rear end. Molly glanced up at him with sad, shame filled eyes and a head that hung as low as her confidence.

To fill in the time before he was due to take Jess to the cinema he cooked up a reasonable meal. It was the first proper dinner he'd cooked in a week. The last meal he had cooked had been a cottage pie that lasted him two days and the rest of the time he'd been contenting himself with pot noodles, cheese on toast and bacon sandwiches. This time he cooked up some cod in butter sauce with pasta shells and peas, with a liberal helping of grated cheese on top it made a tasty and filling meal. Joined by Molly he stretched out on the sofa and in the quiet of the front room and an emerging fantasy with Jess in the lead role he drifted into sleep.

CHAPTER FOUR

Awakened as the Sun made its first appearance of the day slipping below the cloud line on its way to the horizon. He rose from the sofa and stood looking out the back window as the illuminated clouds took on the colours of fire. In a few more moments they were given a fantastically defined silver outline. Rays of searching light that reached out to the heavens made him run to get his camera and keep the moment forever. Unfolding the piece of paper he dialled the number on it.

"Hello Jess!"

"Oh, Hi yuh!"

"Can you see the Sunset from where you are?"

"No, but I will in just a moment!" Sean waited as Jess went quiet. "Wow! Yes I can see it now. Its beautiful!"

"It certainly is!" He agreed. The quality of the moment suddenly impacted on him and he struggled to find words. "I've just snapped off some photographs of it so I can put it in a painting!" He informed her.

"That sounds like a good idea. The colours are spectacular! I'd really like to see it from the top of a hill with the English countryside in the foreground. I know just the right place and I'd love to take you there . . . one day!" Jess paused to allow a more gradual transition in the conversation to the more self-indulgent. "Are you still set for the cinema tonight?"

"Yes, yes I am!" Sean took another photograph. "What time shall I call round?"

"Well no later than seven thirty!" She replied.

"Okay see you in . . . ninety minutes then!" A huge rush of excitement surged through his entire body and consolidated in the hand that held the phone that bore her voice.

Staring out at the greying sunset he said a silent Thank you to God, to Venus to his and her ancestors, to whoever it was helping them to connect with such def-

28

inite and unforeseen ease. He had an excess of energy now so took Molly to the nearby park to chase some tennis balls hit a good distance with the use of an old wooden racket. Hitting the balls for Molly worked out well, it tapped his excessive energy level and left him feeling calm and focussed. Showered and changed he had ten minutes to get to Jess's house just three streets away. The keys to his Land rover jangled in his hand and he was on his way.

He pulled into her street and had no problems finding the house. With no spaces left to park in the street he parked up on the driveway behind a silver Audi TT and began to experience a mild attack of nerves. He walked to the front door of the large detached house hoping that Jess would be ready to come straight out. The thought of walking into the front room and meeting the entire family as she finalised her preparations was an un-nerving one. The idea of two overprotective big brothers wearing brilliant white T-shirts and standing with their bulging arms folded on their pigeon chests haunted him. They'd be staring daggers at him as they waited permission from the father to eject him from the house. The father would judge him at a glance and with two taps of his walking stick the brothers would up-end him and throw him out the house via the wide, lounge window. Jess would protest but be powerless to prize her determined brothers off and end up being forbidden to see him again appeared to be more of a premonition. Sean stepped up to the front door and rang the bell. The waiting did nothing to calm his nerves. Eventually Jess came to the door.

"Hi yuh! Come on in I'm nearly done!" Jess held the door and he stepped inside his eyes immediately feasting on her beauty. She was wrapped in a dark blue towel and had a purple towel wrapped high around her head. Holding the towel in position with one hand she pulled him down and let him kiss her on the cheek whilst also checking him for tobacco smoke. He passed he stealthy sniff test and she gave him a quick closed lips kiss on the mouth, which took him by complete surprise.

"We've got time for a cup of tea before we go, the next showing starts at eight thirty! Go on through!" Jess motioned to the door of the lounge.

Sean's heart began to pound as Jess left him to enter the room alone. Slowly he pulled off his shoes and took hold of the big brass doorknob but didn't turn it. He had to open the door and walk in to meet the family there was no other option open to him. Slowly he turned the doorknob and stepped inside. The room was empty, lights were on but there was no one present. He walked deeper into the room that was so large that it was furnished as two separate lounges. Both areas being very tastefully furnished and decorated to a high standard. Two large modern beige sofas faced inwards to a huge oval walnut coffee table. An armchair accompanied each sofa but at a slightly inwards facing angle. There was a large stone fireplace that was in use though not at this time. The T.V was directed at the coffee table and either side of it were shelves of books. The rear lounge area looked to have an even richer feel taking its style from a gentleman's club. One large black and tan leather sofa and two matching armchairs were centered round a dark oak coffee table. Against the walls was a teak sideboard and wall unit. Displayed on the sideboard were two valentine cards. One of them was his and the other was a shop bought highly unimaginative card with a picture of a kitten peeking out of a basket of flowers. He couldn't resist reading it and thankfully it was addressed to an Amber. There was a painting of two leopards that he found serious fault with at first glance. One leopard had a face that appeared too elongated and that for him ruined the whole effect. He wandered around the second lounge area. On another wall hung a large oil painting of sheep on the moors with an approaching storm. He stared at the picture and knew that he couldn't match it but it was the kind of painting that he liked to attempt and some day would achieve. Just then he was made aware that someone was at the rear of the house. He looked down the passageway that had a door on either side and a door at the end. The door at the end of the passage opened and a female figure walked briskly towards him. She entered the lounge and halted to stare at him. It was the Asian policewoman from the previous night.

"Oh, hello . . . again." She said. Her look of surprise transformed into a look of contempt as she proceeded to walk around him looking him up and down. "So you're Sean? Come and sit down!" She said leading the way to the front lounge.

"Do you drink in the George often?" She asked perching herself on the arm of the sofa opposite the one he sat on.

"Well I used to some time ago! Last night was my first night out for months and I happened to meet up with some old workmates from way back. I haven't had a night out for months." Sean welcomed the chance to distance himself from his hard drinking acquaintances and in particular from the vomit incident.

"Oh really! Why is that?" She asked with an occupational curiosity.

"So that I can get on with my book amongst other things!"

"Oh really? Reading or writing your book?" She quipped.

"Writing it!" Sean said smiling at her question.

"What's your book about?" She asked scanning the room for something that might be out of place or possibly missing.

"It's a historical romance set in the time of the Roman invasion. The second Roman invasion under Claudius!"

"That sounds very interesting! I'm sorry I haven't introduced myself. I'm Amber, Jessica's sister!" She held her hand out to him and left it to him to close the gap and come forward to shake her waiting hand.

"Older or younger?" Sean wished he'd not asked the question before he'd completed it.

"Hmm" was Amber's faint response to his unconvincing flattery. "Would you like a drink?"

"No, no thank you I'm driving!"

"I meant tea or coffee!" Amber snapped back.

"No, no thanks I'm fine but Jess mentioned that she'd like a cup of tea before we go!" With that Jess came into the room. Sean stood up as she entered.

"My God . . . this man has manners!" Amber stated with her first sign of approval.

"Shall we go to the kitchen and I'll make the tea!" Jess said and led the way.

"So it was you who sent Jess the valentine card. Well done, it was beautifully made! I had to give my boyfriend what for after seeing that one. We've been together five years and he's never given me one nearly so good. I keep them up so as not to allow him to forget!" Amber patted Sean on the back.

The kitchen too was huge with a breakfast bar and another door leading to a conservatory that ran the full width of the house. As Jess busied herself with making the tea Sean and Amber were seated at the breakfast bar.

"Where is everyone?" Sean asked Amber.

"Everyone? Who's everyone?" Amber questioned him.

"The rest of the family!"

"You mean to say that two Asian women can't possibly live alone and independent?" Amber became indignant and again found her scowl.

"No! Of course they can but the house is so big I just assumed that this was THE family house!" Sean explained.

"No, this is my house! The only missing person is my boyfriend, Andrew who's away at the moment!"

"Sorry! So there's just the three of you in this big . . . what four, five bed roomed house?" Sean continued.

"Five bedrooms, and yes there's just the three of us!" Amber was still agitated by him.

"Well it's an incredibly beautiful house inside and out." He told Amber, hoping to defuse her irritation at his pigeon holing assumption.

"You haven't seen the back garden yet. It's an embarrassment and needs some serious sorting out but we haven't, none of us got the time or the inclination!" Amber softened her tone.

"Maybe I can do something with it? I love gardening and there's precious little to do in my own garden at the moment. I'd welcome the chance to spend some time gardening again especially with a blank canvas to work from!" Sean took the opportunity to further appease Amber and as a bonus have reason to be near Jess on a daily basis.

"Come along and I'll show you!" Jess interrupted the conversation and led him through to the conservatory and pressed her head against the glass. Sean did likewise and in the darkness he could just make out an overgrown lawn and battered wooden fence.

"You'll need a new fence. The lawn won't be a problem it just needs time spent on it!"

"How much do you think it'll cost?" Amber asked from behind.

"Not as much as you'd think! If you buy the materials my labour comes free!" Sean announced.

"Slave labour sounds good to me!" Amber glanced at Jess who returned her knowing glance accompanied with an excited smile. "When can you start? She asked and placed a hand on his shoulder.

"Tomorrow if you like!" He answered.

"Okay then! There's a side gate at the end of the drive you can use that if we're not in okay? I think we've got some tools in one of the sheds but I can't be sure of that!" She told him.

On checking the time Jess told him they'd better be setting off. She led him to the porch and he led her to the car and opened the door for her to embark. He reversed out the drive anticipating some remark from her about the cold draughty interior but none came. Instead he found her to be as bubbly and talkative as she had been in the Red lion. Inside the cinema he followed close behind her to where she chose to sit. The film commanded her full attention to the screen from the very start. Every time Jess laughed or jumped she would find without looking and squeeze his arm. Sean observed for the first time her silhouetted profile and sank into his new, charmed life. The next time she reached for his arm he made certain that her hand found his and he clasped her hand firmly to keep it.

The homeward journey was filled with talk about the film and as they neared her home Jess wanted to tell him her hopes and ideas for the garden. He denied her nothing. Yes she would have a larger patio a flat lawn bordered by flowerbeds and a path that meandered to the end where there would be a very private picnic area hidden from view. They pulled up onto her driveway and she leant over to give him a kiss on the cheek.

"You know that if we're to start seeing each other the smoking has to stop! I'm dead set against smoking so it's up to you!" She told him with a concerned smile and air of expectation.

"Consider it done!" Came his instantaneous reply certain that he could perform anything and everything she wished. With that she widened her smile, slammed the door shut and stood back to wave him off.

Back home he found it necessary to retire directly to bed only offering Molly the briefest of acknowledgements.

The alarm on his mobile woke him at seven fifteen. As far as he could tell, he'd slept smiling the whole night through. He was eager to get to work on Amber's garden so had breakfast on the move. Two slices of toast and a coffee had breakfast over with apart from one major thing. He needed a cigarette. There were five left in his packet and he lit one. Jess's last words came to mind and he ran the lit cigarette under the tap and with the scrunched up packet dropped them into the bin. His lighter followed and was then joined by the ashtray. He would turn his back on being a smoker and be the man that Jess wanted him to be.

On route to her house with Molly and an assortment of gardening tools on board he called in at the corner shop and bought more sweets and mints than he'd ever bought at one time in his life. Amber's Audi was on the gravel in front of the house freeing the driveway for him to get his Land rover right up to the side gate. It was ten past eight and he took his first daylight viewing of the rear garden. The lawn would have to be dug over and re-seeded. The left side fence had been blown by gales and battered by falling boulders loosened by tree roots on the high, rocky embankment. Certainly a brick wall would offer a better defence and a more permanent solution. The small patio was sunken in some areas and being pushed up by unchecked sapling trees in others. Taking into consideration all the problems with the garden he was determined he would have it serving all of Jess's specifications in a matter of weeks.

There were no signs of life in the house as he began to demolish what was left of the fence. The fence was so rotten he was able to pull it down in huge sections by hand. Molly had become bored and retired to stretch out on the back seat of the car as Sean worked on. Wasting no time at all he began to dig a trench along where the fence once stood.

Towards the end of his first leg a man appeared in the garden walking towards him. He was wearing a white shirt with black trousers and a dark blue, butchers apron. He looked to be in his mid to late forties with a receded hairline and his longish hair pulled back tight to allow it to form a pointless ponytail.

"Hello you must be Sean?" The man said as he shook Sean's dirty hand. "I'm Andrew, Ambers boyfriend! I've been sent to ask you if you want some coffee and toast, or tea if you prefer?"

"Great! A coffee with two sugars would be uh . . . great!" Sean slammed his spade into the ground and popped another mint in his mouth.

"Come into the conservatory I've got a chair waiting for you in there!" Andrew led the way back to the house leaving Sean wondering whether he was a boyfriend or butler. He had the stiff politeness of a butler he was dressed like a butler he even walked like a butler.

In the conservatory Andrew had put up a deck chair so Sean didn't dirty any of the permanent furniture.

"This is for you!" Andrew pointed out the chair in case Sean missed the obvious. "Would you like some freshly squeezed orange juice to start?" He added.

"That would be nice!" Sean accepted.

Sean sat in the deckchair looking out over the garden and as he was alone and not working, smoking or in company he began muttering to himself putting on the voice of Parker from the Thunderbirds. "Oh yes Mi'lady! No Mi'lady that won't do at all Mi'lady!" He chuckled to himself and muttered it again, louder and adding the puppet head and arm movements.

"Would you like some orange juice? It's freshly squeezed just like Mi'lady's tits!" Andrew cleared his throat and spoke from the kitchen door. The resemblance in the voice he had just put on and that of Andrew's was remarkably similar and the fact that he'd been overheard made him laugh aloud.

"Yes please Andrew that would be . . . super!" Sean's voice still hadn't shaken off the Parker impression. He was having a funny five minutes and in Andrew's renewed absence he returned to his exaggerated Parker impression.

"Can I take your knickers off now Mi'lady, they're really chaffing my testicles?" Sean laughed even more audibly as Andrew returned and gave him a strange look that questioning his sanity and needed no words. Sean took the glass and had to set it down on the floor beside him in case he spilled it before he could quell his laughter. Andrew returned to the kitchen shaking his head. He returned to him a minute later with two coffees and a plate of marmalade on toast cut into triangles. He sat himself down on a wicker chair next to him.

"So what is your plan for the garden?" Andrew asked in a far less stuffy tone.

"Re-dig and re-seed the lawn, re-lay and extend the patio, add a couple of flower beds and if Amber agrees I'd like to build a wall along where the fence was!" Sean answered seriously, his warped humour under control.

"Amber will be down shortly! She and Jess like to have their breakfasts served in bed on a Sunday!"

Sean felt a twinge of jealousy at the thought of Andrew having access to Jessicas bedroom. Only the idea that she would soon be down put him back on par. He complimented Andrew on the coffee and popped another mint into his mouth.

"So what do you do Andrew?" Sean sipped from his mug and brought it down to rest on his knee.

"I'm a struggling Architect! What do you do?" He replied.

"I'm a South Patagonian, Electric eel belly tickler!" Sean replied dryly.

"Oh! You're on the dole!" Andrew replied distastefully.

"No! No, I'm sorry! I think that the lack of nicotine is warping my mind! I'm a wannabe writer!" Sean told him taking the conversation more seriously.

Andrew nodded his head as if he understood and forgave him his eccentricity.

"Published yet?" Andrew asked.

"Not finished yet!" Sean told him.

A clattering of crockery sounded from the kitchen and Ambers presence in the conservatory was announced by Andrew's polite standing. Sean too stood and proceeded to tell her about his idea of a wall instead of a fence. Amber was concerned about the cost but he allayed her fears and told her that he knew of an abundance of some perfect building stone from a long demolished and forgotten farm. It had stood in the way of a bi-pass constructed in the seventies. The current farmer if he even knew of its existence would probably let it go for the sake of its own clearance. A copse had grown up and matured around it and it served no purpose. Amber agreed whole-heartedly when he assured her that its cost would be half that of a replacement.

"In fact I'd like to build the wall to look like an old ruin!" Sean continued fused with enthusiasm to build her something unique.

"I could incorporate arches into it and have it take on the appearance of a ruined abbey! With some ferns, ivy and roses attached it would look fantastic!" Sean's enthusiasm was contagious and Amber was swept along with the idea. Andrew however remained quiet and unmoved by the topic until Amber drew him into the conversation.

"What do you think Andrew?" She asked.

"I think what Sean has in mind is something akin to a Folly! It all depends on the quality and quantity of the stone! I've no doubt Sean can build but whether or not we're still living here when he finishes I just don't know!" Andrew spoke in a dreary monotone that dampened the mood into an uncomfortable silence and earned himself an angry stare from Amber.

"I'll get going on the footings then!" Sean told them as he zipped up his work jacket and returned to the cold.

After another hour of digging he heard a banging coming from the conservatory. It was Jess who wanted to wave hello and give him the thumbs up. He waved back and leant on his spade, his energy was almost spent. With Jess gone from view he returned to his labour until he began to suffer the effects of wavering around and almost losing his balance through exhaustion. It was time for a long, comfortable rest and a meal. He walked into the conservatory and leant into the kitchen where on getting Jess's attention told her of his plan to go home and maybe return that afternoon or maybe early the next day. Jess in turn told him of the Sunday night ritual of having a meal delivered and wanted him to attend and be back for it by eight. Sean happily agreed and she noted him down for lamb madras.

Sean returned home to shower, shave and change into some clean clothes. After a full English breakfast he led on the sofa as his aching muscles relaxed as he dozed with the radio on low.

When he woke it was too late to get to the supermarket to re-stock his depleted cupboard and freezer. There were four more empty hours before he could see Jess again and he settled down with his sketchpad to attempt as he had done so many times before, to capture her likeness. The result after an hour was the closest he'd ever got to something that resembled her but it was still far from being an accurate image. Her face had so many angles that to get them all in proportion was proving impossible. He doubted that even a camera with a professional photographer behind it could capture her intense beauty.

He loaded the land rover with all the spare bricks and boulders from his rockery and returned to his sketchpad drawing what he hoped to achieve with Amber's wall. Arches would save on building material allowing him to increase its height. A fake, bricked up doorway would add to its appeal and with a couple of flying buttress's, some flagstones and gravel at the base the effect would be complete. He was pleased with this drawing and decided to show it to Amber and Jess that evening. Still with time a plenty he made another sketch of the same design but this time added the ivy, ferns and climbing roses.

At last it was time to have a last wash, freshen up and head off to Jess's. This time he would take the bike. He folded the drawings to his chest, zipped up his leather jacket and pulled on his crash helmet. His Triumph Daytona roared into life at the first press of the button and a surge of love for its deep rumbling growl passed into him. He roared up onto Amber's driveway and couldn't resist revving it before silencing it with a turn of the key. Kicking the side stand down he leant the bike to rest. Jess was at the door and leaning out to see who it could be. On removal of his helmet she smiled and opened the porch door. Sean placed his helmet on the floor next to the choc-a-bloc shoe unit and pulled off his boots. This time Jess stayed with him and held the door for him to enter the front room.

"We're all in the kitchen the food will be here shortly!" She told him and rubbed his arm a few most welcome strokes as they walked the passageway. Sean said his hellos to Amber and Andrew who was at the rear of the kitchen preparing the plates and cutlery. He and Jess joined Amber at the bar where he proudly produced his drawings.

"My God that'll be lovely!" Jess exclaimed and passed them across to an impatient Amber.

"Wow! That's rather more elaborate than I expected, but I love it, it's great! Andrew come here and take a look at these!" Amber summoned him commandingly. Andrew came directly over and took a drawing in each hand. He held the silence as everyone waited for his comments.

"Well. . . . Are these supposed to be flying buttresses?"

"Yes!" Sean said wondering what else they could be mistaken for.

"Well good luck with it! There's a lot of work there, carpentry too!" He folded the drawings and handed them back to Sean and went to answer the timely doorbell.

Andrew carried the three brown paper bags of food to his end of the kitchen and emptied the foil containers onto plates and into bowls. Rather than offering any assistance both Amber and Jess retired to the dining room empty handed.

"We should let Andrew organise the food." Jess told Sean and beckoned him to follow them. Sean stopped trying to work out what was going on with Andrew. He hadn't warmed to him and believed that maybe he and Amber had recently been in dispute. However the atmosphere was relaxed enough and apart from Andrew's curtness regarding his drawings there was no sign from either Amber or Jess that anything was out of the ordinary.

Andrew ferried the plates to the table in the dining room two by two then brought the sundry dishes and bowls. Even then he wasn't finished. He then fetched a bottle of chilled water and starting with Amber poured it into each persons glass filling his own glass last. He was more of a butler than most butlers Sean thought as they settled down to what was an exemplary meal. Sean remembered to ask Amber what had happened to the biker who'd launched the attack in the pub on the Friday night.

"Oh I took his name and address but the other man wasn't keen to press any charges so I had to let him go with a caution." Amber said dismissively and turned to converse exclusively with Jess about that afternoons jogging.

Jess brought the topic of holidays to the table and quizzed Sean on his most recent, best and worst of holidays. Later she revealed that she and Amber were planning their next holiday together. The previous year they'd been to New York but their vow to return the very next year had been usurped by the lure of the Inca's and Aztecs. Amber suggested that they retired to the front room allowing Andrew to clear away. Sean became ever more baffled by the relationship between them and used his thanks for the meal to offer some appreciative assistance with the clearing up. Amber accepted his offer on Andrew's behalf and as she and Jess went into the front lounge, Sean and Andrew began the clear-up operation. Sean washed as Andrew dried and put away and for the first time Andrew revealed that he did after all have something of a personality. To Sean's surprise Andrew showed appreciation for his willing help in the business end of the kitchen. Andrew quizzed him on his kitchen skills and why he'd left his last job after he'd been there for so long.

"It was a great job with great people but when we were given a new managing director he created problems where none previously existed! He was an egomaniac and knew nothing of the people behind the firm's initial success! After a year of incredible stress I'd had enough and decided to make my bid for freedom and write my book!" Sean told him still feeling bitter.

They finished the dishes and Andrew told him to go through to the lounge and let him get on with the coffee. Sean walked into the lounge where Jess and Amber were sprawled out on a sofa each. Jess sat up and patted the newly vacated space next to her. He sat on the spot indicated, his legs stretched out in front of him and he was fully contented. The hatchet he felt Andrew had for him had turned into an olive branch; he'd appeased Amber and was sat next to the most beautiful woman in the world. They watched the television in relaxed mode and relative silence then Jess asked Sean if he would mind giving her a foot massage. He had been hoping that they might get to have a cuddle but this was a more personal act of familiarity and he welcomed it. He turned to face her and rested his back against the arm of the sofa. Jess swung her feet onto his lap and led back plumping a cushion behind her head. Taking each foot in turn he pressed his thumbs into the soul of her foot and moved them to the sides. He pulled each toe individually and gave it a little wiggle. He was determined to do the most professional job for her and plied his fingers and thumbs to bring new life to her achy feet and equally importantly for her personal pleasure. Andrew brought the coffees in on a tray and set them down on the coffee table. Sean kept his hands busy and stared blankly at the television with his mind becoming numb with encroaching tiredness. Then he noticed that Amber too was reclined on her sofa having her feet massaged by Andrew. They were like a mirrored image of each other. He began to realise that there was more going on in that house than what he knew of. His uneasiness passed into nothingness when he saw the contented look on Jess's face. He took the occasional sip of cold coffee and continued to rub her feet with one hand so as not to break her enjoyment. No one spoke. No one was even watching the television anymore. Both Amber and Jess looked to be asleep as he and Andrew massaged their respective girlfriends feet. The documentary had finished and the news was on; still no one spoke indeed Jess and Amber appeared to have drifted off to sleep. Jess's smile had relaxed but he continued to gently press and rub. He let his mind wander. He was responsible for her current state of relaxation and she was responsible for the pride he had coursing through his veins. Amber dug a foot into Andrew's side and he ceased his massage. She swung herself to sit upright and held her head in her hands and yawned. Andrew cleared the coffee cups away and with the clanking of china Jess too opened her eyes. Sean felt as if he'd been somewhere in the twilight zone and now normal service was resumed. Jess like Amber sat up and Sean's intention of waking her with a well placed kiss above her toes was not to be. Unlike Amber Jess thanked Sean for the massage.

"You can do that for me whenever you want!" She told him with a smile.

"Jess, I'd do that for you every day if you like!" Sean tried to say the words without appearing over keen but inside he was willing her to take him up on the offer.

"Okay! Every Sunday after jogging and every weekday after work you can do me a foot massage! How does that sound?" Jess looked at him with no discernible expression.

"That sounds great! But why leave out Saturdays?" Sean asked.

"Okay! And every Saturday when I get back from shopping." Jess said widening her smile.

Amber was sitting and listening to their conversation in silence. Sean gave her a quick sideways glance then turned back to Jess. Jess yawned and covered her mouth with her hand.

"Come on I'm off to bed now!" She told him. Sean immediately thought of the wonderful possibilities and his eyes must have lit up.

"Alone!" She added noticing his expression.

Sean followed her to the porch and as he was about to put his crash helmet on she prevented him and pulled his head down to kiss him on the lips. Her kiss went deep and in the surprise he dropped his helmet to the floor with a loud thud. Jess jumped at the sound, smiled then returned to the kiss. Taking firm hold of his hair she pulled him away from her lips. Sean was enflamed and put his arms around her, pulling her into him and leaning to kiss her again. This time she turned her head but he wasn't going to abort the mission without some accomplishment and defused his passion by kissing her neck. Again she grabbed him by the hair and roughly yanked his head back. This time she held him at bay and stared through his eyes deep into his soul.

"I asked you before if you meant what you said in your card and you said yes!" She took a firmer grip of his hair.

"Well then, if I want to kiss you I will! What you've just done implies domination and I wont be dominated! If you want to be with me you will fully respect me or there is no us!" Jess released her grip. He heard and understood her words. Her eyes now held him as surely as when she'd held him by the hair.

"Do you want to be with me?" She asked softly.

"Yes, I do!" He replied.

"Are you willing to be mine?" She said, her voice little more than a whisper.

"Definitely yes!" He replied.

"Kiss it!" Jess led him with her eyes to look down to the floor where she'd put one foot forward.

Sean knelt and lowered his head to press his lips to the cold flesh of her foot just above the toes. One long kiss led to another and she remained silent. Clearly contented to have him continue his kisses roamed freely and purposefully over her proffered foot.

"Enough now!" She said with the softest whisper ever to reach him. He let the last kiss linger a little longer before he raised his head.

"I'll see you tomorrow at five twenty. I'll tell you more of what I expect from you then!" She told him.

Sean stood keeping his eyes on her a moment longer than she was comfortable with. The moment didn't call for words only compliance mattered. He picked up his helmet and left.

Jess returned to the lounge in jubilant mood. She had exercised her power over him perfectly. It was real. She had connected with him so definitely that she had commanded him with whispers and he'd responded to her dominance flawlessly. She now had her man like Amber had Andrew. He was to be entirely hers and she in turn would love him for it.

CHAPTER FIVE

Amber's alarm sounded at seven fifteen the next morning. Andrew was the first to rise and shower. Dressed in his black trousers and white shirt he trotted down the stairs. As he descended Jess's alarm rang out, the weekday morning ritual hinged on perfect timing. In the kitchen with the radio on low he busied himself preparing breakfast. By the time the first round of toast popped up Jess and Amber were sitting at the breakfast bar in their slippers and bathrobes.

Jigging around in her chair and drumming on the table with her knife and fork to the music on the radio Jess was in buoyant mood. Amber, quiet at first was soon jollied up by Jess's contagious high spirits. She pulled Andrew down by the shirt collar and kissed him on the forehead then smacked the spot she'd kissed with her jam-laced spoon.

"There now Andrew what do you say?" She asked.

"Uh, thank you mistress?" He replied dryly.

They laughed as he wiped his forehead with a piece his toast but they weren't finished with him yet. Amber looked at Jess motioned toward their toasts. As soon as he'd finished wiping the jam from his head they simultaneously stuck a triangle of toast to the sides of his face.

"Do you know? I think you'd look really good with long sideburns!" Amber said patting his hand on the table. Jess quickly blobbed a spoonful of jam on another piece of toast and pushed it onto his chin. "And a goatie!" She added laughing loudly.

Amber intercepted his hand and prevented him from removing the toast.

"Keep it there until we have finished your new look!" She insisted. She quickly laced another piece of toast with jam and pressed it to his forehead. She produced her mobile and snapped a couple of photographs of him. Jess too insisted that he wore the toast until she returned with her mobile. Laughing along with

Amber she got him to turn his head to the side she too took a series of pictures of him.

Running several minutes behind schedule due to the fun making Jess thanked him for the breakfast and danced her way out of the kitchen taking the last of the replacement toast with her. Amber commented that she'd never before seen her so jolly first thing on a weekday morning. Andrew agreed but his doubts about Sean's sincerity kept him from sharing in Jess's joy. Amber to a lesser degree shared his concerns and had a plan to find out more about her choice of man.

"I'll run a check on him at work and see what I can come up with!" She told him. "However I think you should get close to him and see what you can find out!" After a few moments thought she suggested Andrew gave him a coffee when he arrived that morning, put him at his ease and help him in the garden. At around mid-day get him to have a long break, play some music he likes and subtly probe him. Whilst having a man-to-man talk, he was to ply him with whiskey and find out his true, unguarded feelings for Jess. Why did he split with his wife? What his idea of an idyllic lifestyle was? It would also be a good idea to find out his response to some of their basic philosophy.

At eight forty Amber and Jess drove to work. Andrew busied himself with the household chores and listened out for Sean's arrival. When he finally pulled up at nine-twenty he called him into the conservatory for a coffee. They sat looking out into the garden and Andrew began by apologising for his stuffy behaviour the previous day. He put it down to becoming a bit stir-crazy since leaving his old premises and setting up office in one of the bedrooms upstairs of the house. He missed his little office and his daily trip to the bakery next door. He missed his lunches in the quaint café opposite and the pint of beer he'd have in the Saracens Head with other business proprietors after work.

"If it was so idyllic why did you give it up?" Sean queried him.

"Well my wife had run off with my business partner and I was, I suppose, heartbroken, angry and at a very low ebb. That's when I met Amber, she took charge of my life and completely re-organised me turning my life around!" Andrew's eyes welled up as he revealed his bad old days.

"Well, you must consider yourself really lucky to have found someone like Amber at any time! " Sean told him.

"I was indeed lucky! I was commissioned to do some work at the farm where Amber has a horse and I met her there or she met me, either way I was blessed." Andrew perked up and smiled.

"Blessed! I think that's how I feel to have found Jess! They both do have a tremendous sense of presence don't they!" He told him.

"Charisma! Yes they do! Being around them is an honour! Living here with them is like . . . living life inside a perfect dream you don't want to awaken from!"

They both fell silent, as Andrew's statement impacted on them. The atmosphere in the room changed and demanded that they took a moment to reflect on Andrew's words. It felt to Sean as if a ghost had entered the room and a chill ran up his spine making him shudder.

Andrew took the cups into the kitchen and Sean set to work deepening the foundations for the wall. Ten minutes later Andrew dressed in brown over-alls and green wellies joined him.

"Mind if I join you?" Andrew asked.

Sean was put on the spot. He wanted to do the job from start to finish alone and unaided. The final creation would be entirely of his making unsullied by outside help. However here he was especially dressed for the occasion.

"No! Not at all! Jump in!" He told him and suggested that he loosened the soil with the fork whilst he himself dug it out. Andrew set to work with gusto like a man possessed. Sean worked his way along behind him until they'd reached the end of the trench-line. They worked back along the trench reaching the required depth and chatting like old pals. Andrew asked him what the first record he'd ever bought was and who he'd seen in concert. Andrew plied him with snippets of information about his own life and was able to keep Sean engaged in telling his stories from his school days to his year long infatuation with the unobtainable Jess. They worked hard and sweated in their toil until they reached the final spade-load of soil.

"I think we've earned a break and a glass of something special, have we not?" Andrew announced breathing deeply. Sean agreed and they trudged back to the house for refreshment. Andrew insisted that they sat in the rear lounge and Sean took off his muddy boots and rolled up his muddied trousers to the knee. Happy to have his choice of music he perused the formidable collection of c.d's finally settling on some Steve Winwood. Andrew brought in two tumblers and pulled out a bottle of whiskey from the well-stocked cabinet. Together they knocked back the first two glasses in quick succession and then settled down in their chairs to take their drinks at a more civilised pace. As advised Andrew began to hold back and pour less into his own glass than he gave to Sean. Sharing anecdotes about friends and family and telling a few jokes they were soon falling around laughing. Ensuring that Sean's glass was never empty Andrew got into character and began to reveal his characters dark side. Knowing how far to go at each stage in the conversation exposed himself as a predatory male with a hidden agenda to fulfil and worm his way into Amber's life.

"I know Amber, she'll never allow the stigma of a second failed marriage to blight her character. Once I've got that ring on her finger the tables will turn and I will wear the trousers. She'll do as I instruct her and as for her career . . . well that's the first thing she'll be saying goodbye to!" He expertly revealed drawing Sean to a place where he could either fit and tolerate his stand on the female gender or take a moral stand and alienate his newfound friend.

Sean became more and more agitated at what he was hearing. The funny half hour was over and Andrew was spilling out more and more bigoted opinions. Sean considered returning to the garden but not before he'd vented his pent-up agression.

"Andrew mate! You're straight out of the dark ages! Your ideas are . . . crass and offensive to anyone with half a brain! The really sad thing is that . . . you're an educated, professional man so your ideas just go to prove you're totally fucking warped!" Sean said his piece and stood to leave the room.

"Come on Sean! It's always been that way with women! A man will woo the woman he wants and when they become married and she relies on his providence and protection they take a back seat and serve the man of the house! I'm wooing Amber just as you are wooing Jess! When it all works out we, as men will take our time-honoured place as the head of the house! We have to show them what we're capable of and seep it into their predominantly dormant brains that they need us more than we need them! A woman's primary role is to carry on the bloodline, to bare and rear the children of men! Their secondary duty is to provide us with sustenance and sex! The rest of the time they are better off looking good and staying quiet surely you can see that? You're not a stupid man. You know I'm right!" Andrew argued and found it difficult not to laugh at his characters massive effect on Sean.

Sean had heard enough and became so agitated by Andrew's presence that he was starting to shake with anger, a sure sign that he was going to lose his temper. He was considering smacking him in the mouth but reasoned that Andrew had his feet firmly under Amber's table and that he was the unproven newcomer. Undoubtedly they would believe Andrew over him so held back his overpowering desire to batter the evil from his body. Slamming his glass down on the table he walked to the conservatory.

"Don't say anymore, I don't want to hear it! Christ no wonder your wife left you if that's what you actually think!" Sean put his boots on and walked out into the garden with his trousers still rolled up to his knees.

Unseen by him Andrew was struggling to regain the cold-hearted composure of his character in the rear lounge. After a few deep breathes he went to rejoin Sean and see how much further he could take him.

"What's the matter with you? Be a man and admit I'm right! The girls just need it bringing gradually to mind how a functional household actually works! I'll support you and you'll support me! Together we can get this house in order and the girls in line. We'll all be happy, so where's the problem?" Andrew wondered how long he could keep it up without a resurgence of his laughter giving him away.

"The problem's with you my friend! It's in your head! You might be a clever man but you've got some serious mental issue!" Sean shouted at him pointing his finger and swaying around like a tethered balloon.

Andrew walked un-shoed into the garden. "Come on! I've pushed you far enough! Well done! I just had to test you, I'm sorry, now come in and sit down before you fall down!"

"No! I don't think so. You're a snake! A sad, crass, twisted, pigot! I'm gonna get Amber to give you a tie delector test. She'll soon see through you, you're not as clever as you think!" Sean staggered a few feet to his left then to the right before finally tripping over his untied laces and falling forward.

Andrew approached and tried to lift him to his feet.

"Fuck Off! Don't touch me. I don't want to be contaminated by your loathsome molecules!" Sean insisted and pushed him away hard.

"Sean I was testing you! I had to know what kind of man you were if I was to let you anywhere near Jess! I'm sorry to have tested you in such a childish way but lets face it . . . you've passed my test with flying colours my friend!" Andrew explained and motioned him to come inside.

Sean cautiously followed him back inside.

"Who the fuck are you? Are you Amber's butler or some kind of Sprucer? I want to know now so make your mind up!" Sean told him as he walked on through to the kitchen.

Andrew filled the kettle and turned to face a wavering Sean.

"I'm Amber's slave. I love her and have vowed to serve her . . . selflessly!" Andrew told him and fixed his eyes on Sean's. "There . . . I've told you! Make of it what you will but I love her more than words so this is how I show her what she means to me!"

Sean walked back out to the conservatory and plonked himself down on the wicker sofa then remembered that his was the deck chair. Andrew prevented him getting up and pushed him back down with a firm hand on his shoulder.

Drinking their coffees Andrew again congratulated him on passing his underhand method of testing. "I had to be sure of you because I think Jess has fallen for you too! I don't think I have to tell you how very special the girls are to me!" Andrew said and observed that Sean was in no state to hold a conversation. He leant over and took the cup from his hand.

Two hours later Sean awoke and Andrew was hand to make him another coffee. Sitting with him in the conservatory they shared a plate of tuna fish and cucumber sandwiches.

"I gave you a bit too much information earlier. It wasn't my place to tell you what I did but it's done now and I'd like to know what you make of what I said?" Andrew asked him in a gentle almost sheepish tone.

"Fair play to you for at last being honest. All I can say is . . . if it works for you then where's the harm in it?" Sean wasn't prepared for the question and hadn't formed an opinion on his revelation.

"You know that if you can't do the same for Jess as I do for Amber . . . there'll be no future for you . . . with Jess anyway!" Andrew told him and immediately regretted divulging that information. "I'm sorry, I shouldn't have said that!" He added

Sean looked him in the eye. "I know that already! If Jess wants to make a slave of me then I've got news for her!" Sean stopped and waited for Andrew to ask the inevitable question.

"What news is that?" Andrew asked.

"I've been hers to do with what she wants from first time I saw her!" Sean admitted.

Andrew exhaled and smiled. "Okay! Let's please keep this conversation to ourselves. Jess will want to be the one to fill you in as and when she feels comfortable with it. Okay?" Andrew told him.

"Yeah! I understand!" Sean submitted.

"Gosh! Hark at us. It's nothing sinister. In fact I've never been happier. It's a tremendous thing and I envy you about to embark on a whole new exciting way of life and I promise you, you'll be as happy and contented as the rest of us!" Andrew told him and brought his hand down firmly on Sean's knee.

"The rest of us? How many of you are there?" Sean inquired.

Andrew immediately cursed his slip of the tongue. "Hmm, well I'll tell you this and let that be an end to it! We . . . are many! We have formed a society and it's flourishing. We're all like-minded folk from every walk of life. Now let that be enough for you. Be patient, Jess will tell you all as and when she chooses to do so. Okay?" Andrew told him firmly.

Okay! So just tell me some things about Jess. What about previous boyfriends?" Sean inquired.

"Well, in the fifteen months she's been with us she's not expressed an interest in anyone that I know of. I don't know about when she was at her parent's house but I suspect not! Her father ran a strict, and I believe very strict household!" He told him and continued. "Sean, Jess is very particular about who she will tolerate around her and so far you've impressed her no end! That said, she still has very high standards and expectations!" Andrew paused. "Now let me ask you a question . . . In your card you used the words Love, Adoration and most noticeably Worship! Is that what you actually feel? Do you worship her?" Andrew asked looking him square in the eye.

"Yes! Yes I do!" Sean said without hesitation.

"Then just be yourself and you and she will go far!" Andrew smiled and patted him on the shoulder.

Sean suddenly remembered his appointment to give Jess a foot massage after work. He had to get home showered and changed and back again in little more than an hour. He said a hasty goodbye to Andrew and put Molly's lead on for the walk home. Time was short so he rapidly showered and made himself presentable. He said his time- honoured goodbye to Molly and walked at speed the twenty-minute journey back to Jess's house. He arrived at the base of her driveway just as a white Vauxhall Corsa drew up.

Jess called out to him as she disembarked and waved goodbye to Karla who tooted and pulled away. The unique sound of her high heels on the tarmac drive reached and pleasured his ears. She was smiling widely and took hold of his arm as they went in together. Inside the porch she clasped her hands around the back of his neck and kissed him. She kicked off her shoes and pushed her feet into her black sequined slippers. Sean was bent double untying his boots so she patted him on the head and told him to come through to the kitchen when he was ready. When he reached the kitchen she was having a coffee with Andrew who pointed out that the cup on the end was for him. Sean sat on the stool at the end of the bar and sugared his drink.

"Are you ready to work your magic?" Jess asked him and sipped her coffee.

"Ready when you are!" Sean replied getting to his feet and picking up his mug.

"No! I want you to do it now. In here!" She told him watching his face for any fleeting expression that would reveal an inner reluctance or indignation.

Sean set his cup down and with a simple smile sat himself down on the cold kitchen floor. Jess took one foot off the footrest of her stool and offered it out to him. He pulled the slipper off and began to press and rub.

"Andrew, get Sean a cushion to sit on would you?" She requested.

Andrew did as asked and returned with a deep red corduroy cushion from the second lounge. Sean raised himself up slightly as Andrew dropped it to the floor and slid it under him with his foot. Sean felt certain that Jess wasn't only testing his obedience but also displaying her dominance over the world around her.

Jess leaned back on her stool and rested her back against the wall. Sean's mind emptied as his heart rate slowed as he rubbed each foot in turn. The only sound to fill the air was that of Andrew's knife chopping through carrots. Sean's eyes closed as he repeated his perfected hand and thumb movements into a recurring pattern. He opened his eyes when he felt a rush of air pass over him. Andrew had walked by him at speed to answer the door but Sean hadn't noticed the bell. Moments later Andrew and Amber entered the kitchen. Amber sat opposite Jess and Andrew returned to his cooking. Still nobody spoke. It appeared as if he was in a film with the sound muted. Only Andrew's stirring of Amber's tea let him know he'd not gone deaf.

"You've got him trained up quick!" Amber's voice broke the marathon silence.

"There's no training involved! Sean offered and I accepted!" Jess spoke as slowly and relaxed as she felt. Amber didn't reply. Maybe she'd given a facial expression but from where he sat he couldn't tell.

Jess lifted her foot from Sean's hands and lightly touched the ball of her foot to his lips. The only give-away sign that he'd kissed her foot was the tutting sound from his lips. She withdrew her foot after just one kiss. Using the footrest of the stool she slid her other foot free of her slipper and offered him that one to kiss too. Again it was just one kiss then she withdrew it. Sean refitted her slippers and stiffly rose to his feet.

"I'll be going now. Molly will need walking and. . . ." He had no other reason to leave but felt it was time for him to go. He said goodbye to all and Jess followed him into the darkened conservatory. He reached the back door and turned to face her.

"On your knees!" She whispered almost inaudibly and escorted him down with her hands placed gently on his shoulders.

He knelt in front of her and she ran her fingers through his hair. Neither spoke. She stroked the sides of his face and ran her fingertips across to his lips. He kissed her fingers as they passed then she pushed them into his mouth. He made no movement; he simply opened his mouth to give them free access. Her fingers went deep inside his mouth and withdrew so her fingertips pulled across his bottom teeth then back deep inside again.

"I'll see you tomorrow!" She said as she withdrew her fingers wiping them in his hair then she lifted his chin to see into his eyes.

Sean stood, his jeans made taught by the presence of his unappreciated, untimely erection. He walked to the car looking back only when he'd opened the loudly creaking door. She was still in the doorway watching him leave. He raised his hand to her and she returned the farewell. He started the car and reversed out of the drive. Half way down the street he pulled into the nearest parking space and turned his engine off. He put his hands to the five to twelve position on his steering wheel and rested his head against them. His head was full of her, nothing but her. He wasn't safe to drive with his mind running only on images of her. His legs trembled and when he took his hands from the wheel to thump the nervousness out of them they too shook. He needed a cigarette and realised he'd pulled in very near the general stores. He opened his door and went in to get ten cigarettes. He decided to smoke just one once he'd reached home and drove slowly off.

Inside he immediately reached for the cigarettes in his pocket and realised he had no form of ignition. He went to the kitchen with a cigarette in his mouth and thought about rooting out the lighter from the bin but decided instead to utilise the gas stove. Bending over to put flame to tobacco he heard a crackling sound. He stood up and felt heat on his forehead and smelt the stench of burning. He slapped the flames on his head out with a rapid series of panicked slaps from both hands. He looked at the palms of his hands and they were smudged and speckled with powdered black carbon that was once his hair. In front of the mirror in the bathroom he saw the aftermath. The flames had claimed a huge swathe of hair burnt down to just millimetres. It looked as if there had been a nuclear bomb dropped on the edge of a forest. He returned to the kitchen and disgusted with himself threw the cigarettes into the bin.

Back in Amber's kitchen Jess returned to her place at the bar. Amber was flicking through a magazine and finally closed it.

"I ran a check on Sean today!" She announced.

"And?" Jess asked suspicious of why Amber felt it necessary and curious of what she had discovered.

"He was arrested for drunken disorderly and found to be in possession of a banned substance in the grounds of the Admiralty building on the Thames embankment in 1990. Drugs class B. No charges were brought against him. He was fined for speeding at 110 miles per hour on the M4 in 1995 closely avoiding a ban! Since then he's been a good boy! He was involved in a collision between his motorcycle and a stolen vehicle in 2002 and acting on information given by him traffic division were able to pursue and apprehend the thieves!" Amber announced to Jess loud enough to involve Andrew.

"So he's not a murderer and he's not a thief! There's nothing at all sinister about him!" Jess deduced on everyone's behalf.

Andrew announced that dinner was about to be served and the girls retired to the dining room. Amber opened the mealtime conversation by asking Andrew how he'd got on with Sean that day. He smiled across to Jess and gave them a minute-by-minute account of his day with Sean. Amber and Jess listened intently as he told them of Sean's enraged response to his bigotry and admitted telling him more of their society than he'd intended. However, Sean had taken the divulged information in his stride and saw nothing distasteful about it.

"Indeed he submitted to me that he was; from the first moment her saw Jess . . . hers to command!" Jess was grinning from ear to ear at the news then Amber asked to hear a personal summary of his findings.

"He has a chivalrous nature that stems from his romanticised love of history! He is . . . I believe; completely taken with Jess. . . . And I believe that we have a perfectly acceptable addition waiting in the wings!" Andrew completed his appraisal and looked again to Jess.

Jess was so pleased to hear his shining assessment that she brought her hands together in one loud clap. Amber slowly shook her head from side to side.

"There is no fast-track to the farm! He must serve his time! What we expect of him is more than mere words and a foot massage!" Amber's level minded judgement took the smile from Jess's face. Andrew felt that Amber had ignored his opinion but didn't challenge her cautiousness. Jess had no argument to put to her beyond what she felt inside. They returned to their meals in silence as their thoughts lingered on the Sean question.

"What if I did . . . fast-track Sean? I honestly feel that he has all the qualities I require of him! I've looked into him and I like what I see!" Jess broke the silence and voiced her heartfelt opinion.

"Yes okay but don't rush him through things! He will need time to adjust! Use your time to bond with him, enjoy him and let him get to know you! He . . . is . . . not . . . ready for the farm!" Amber was adamant.

"Tell me what I have to do to prove to you that he is no threat to us!" Jess raised her voice.

"Give him time! You've known him what three days and you want to take him to the farm. Let's do things properly shall we . . . in stages!" Amber explained forcing herself to speak calmly and not show her anger at being challenged.

"Yes I understand that but with the words he used in his card, with what Andrew found out today and with what I know feel so strongly about him . . . I just want him to know everything about me! About us. . . . They say how hard it is to quit smoking and he's done it for me straight away! He's not just willing to obey, he's eager, even at this early stage!" Jess revealed.

"Jess, Jess, Jess, you are falling for the idea of him WITHOUT knowing him! You should take a step back and see the whole picture. He will get to know you but just think . . . there is such a thing as too much, too soon!" Amber reached over the table to squeeze Jess's hand.

"Tomorrow I will show you just how suitable he is. I'll leave you in no doubt about him. He's more in my power than Andrew is in yours! Sorry Andrew but that's how I feel!" She insisted.

"Why wait until tomorrow? He's yours to command! Phone him up and get him back here now!" Amber suggested.

Without taking her determined eyes from Amber's Jess sent Andrew to bring the phone and dialled his number.

"Hello Sean! I want you to come over straight away okay!"

"Um Hi Jes.s. . . ." Sean couldn't bring himself to question her and making up an excuse not to attend her was out of the question. "Yes okay I'm on my way now!"

"You've got ten minutes!" Jess hung up to let him begin his journey and handed the phone back to Andrew.

Sean grabbed his keys and flew out of the house. As he drove he searched for an alternative reason for his hair to be so severely singed but nothing came to the fore and in any case she would know if he'd lied to her. He pulled up behind Amber's car and reached into the glove compartment for his black woolly hat. He stretched it over his head and before he got to the door Andrew was there to meet him. He escorted Sean into the dining room and asked what he'd like to drink. Sean requested a tea and stood just inside the door waiting for Jess to tell him why he was so urgently required..

"Come in, sit down and take your hat off!" She told him.

Sean did as he was told in the order of which he was told. He slowly removed his hat and waited for the inevitable question. He wasn't prepared for the laughter that ensued. Jess and Amber alternated their looks at him then at each other in a fit of mocking, hysterical laughter.

"What on earth have you done to your hair?" Jess asked.

He took a deep breath and began.

"When I got home I needed a cigarette but I didn't have a lighter so I tried to light the cigarette over the gas ring!" Sean explained in the saddest and most humble voice he could muster. Jess's smiling face turned deadly serious. Her eyes searched him for an explanation but there was only one. He'd not stopped his smoking as promised. Sean saw the seriousness in her face and told her about his drive home and his attack of nerves brought on by trying to give up his addiction on will power alone. She let him explain further that he hadn't actually lit the cigarette and he'd thrown them straight in the bin. Jess remained silent so he continued to tell her that he'd intended to get a packet of nicotine patches for the hard times when he wasn't with her.

The following silence seemed to stretch out to minutes. Andrew came in and delivered his tea. He looked at Sean's hair and sensing the atmosphere held back his desire to mock him. Andrew left the room followed by Amber. As the door closed Sean went uninvited to kneel in front of his Jess.

"Jess, I didn't smoke! It was a moment of weakness but it didn't happen!"

Jess put her elbow on the table and rested her head in her hand. She looked at him, her little finger stroking her brow like a windscreen wiper.. Her silence continued as she thought on her response.

"It doesn't matter! I want you to go now!" Jess told him solemnly and lifted her head from her hand.

Sean had a choice. He could blindly do as he was told and risk her miss interpreting him or show his need of her by other means.

"Please Jess I don't want to leave with you angry at me!" He chose the latter option.

"I'm not angry I'm just disappointed!" She said flatly.

"Then do I come back tomorrow?" He asked reaching his hand slowly out to touch hers and quickly withdrawing it before the contact was made.

"I can't be mad at you!" She said breaking into a smile "And I don't want you to go. I should be cross as hell but I'm not!" She told him forcing the smile from her face.

His relief was as apparent as hers.

"I am however going to make some kind of statement. I'm going to have to punish you!" She said dryly. "Wait here!" Jess went to speak with Amber in the front lounge.

"I'm going to punish him and I wondered what might be appropriate?" She inquired.

"He's your man. You decide how he'll be punished!" Amber delighted in Jess's decision rose from the sofa.

Jess lowered her head in thought then raised it to make her announcement.

"It'll serve two good purposes if I beat him. One; it'll show him that I won't be deceived and two; it'll show you that he is fully accepting of my right to rule!" Jess told them.

"So when is this punishment going to happen and what form will it take?" Amber asked.

"Here and now! I'll . . . use his belt to beat him in the kitchen!" Jess told them her eyes avoiding theirs and showing that she already had reservations about the severity of the said punishment.

"Okay if we're going to do this we have to do it properly. I don't think you have the experience to wield a thick leather belt effectively. You should use something else." Amber announced and asked Andrew to come up with an alternative.

"I can only think that he goes outside and obtains his own implement from the garden!" Andrew suggested.

"Perfect! Well done Andrew!" Amber declared. "Well Jess, is that acceptable to you?"

"Fine!" She told them raising her head and purposefully seeking out their eyes to show her confidence in him. Then in the next second her resolve broke. "No this is too harsh! He didn't actually inhale and he's already sorry for weakening."

Amber raised her gaze to the heavens. "You said this punishment served two purposes. He'll have to take a beating from you soon enough anyway. It's a part of his rite of passage into the society and your life. Of course if you're not sure that he'll accept corporal punishment then by all means make a joke of it and give him the slipper across the ass. However that will only go to mock your own authority and his commitment to you! The choice is yours!" Amber stated sternly.

Jess thought for just a few short seconds. "I'll do it! I'll show you what calibre of man he is. He is true to his word and he is totally mine!"

Jess was heartened to go through with it and returned to Sean in the dining room. She closed the door behind her and leant against it to ensure their words were private.

"I've decided that your punishment will be physical! I want you to get me something to beat you with from the garden. . . . Of course if you think this isn't

50

for you then you can always leave!" Jess stepped away from the door and put a hand on the doorknob in readiness for his potential exit.

"No Jess I won't leave! I will stay! You can do whatever you want to me, I broke my word!" He said with conviction.

Jess opened the door and walked out behind him. She remained in the kitchen and was joined by Amber and Andrew. Sean searched the patio area for a reasonable sapling as Amber instructed Jess on the ritual to take place. Moments later she sent Andrew out to the garden with a torch to hurry Sean along before Jess's resolve could diminish.

"This will help!" Andrew called out to Sean shining the torch into the overgrowth.

"Cheers!" Sean said as he followed the beam of light to a young sycamore tree. "I take it you know what's happening?"

"We've all gone through one form of corporal punishment or another from our women folk! Look on it as opening a door to her heart! Once you've gone through it you have really began to get her trust! Amber's too for that matter! Prove your worth and your steel. Trust her to take you forward!" Andrew told him. "It's all new territory for her too you know!" They walked together back to the house as Sean stripped the sapling down to a single, slender length.

They removed their shoes in the conservatory and stepped into the kitchen where Jess and Amber were waiting. Sean handed Jess the stick and asked if it would do. She took it from him and swished it through the air.

"It'll do just fine!" She told him with a wavering voice that revealed her misgivings. "Now strip to the waist and touch your head to the floor!" She added with as much authority as she could muster.

Sean had been expecting to be caned across the backside and was taken by surprise at the seriousness and severity of the imminent punishment. His eyes sought hers but found only her steely determination.

"DO IT NOW!" She shouted her demand at the first sign of his hesitation.

Sean lowered his head and unbuttoned his shirt in the silence that ensued. Andrew held his hand out to take the shirt from him and Sean lowered himself to the floor at her feet. Jess swallowed hard and cast her eyes to the ground beside him as the strength left her arms and her blood ran cold. Amber cleared her throat and immediately got Jess's attention. Giving her one stern stare that implored her to continue she hardened her stare and motioned to the waiting Sean.

Jess slowly sidestepped Sean and again swallowing hard she summoned the will to find the nessaccary words and the strength to strike him.

"This is to introduce you to my authority over your will!" She raised her head to heavens gathering the will and determination to make the blow happen. She raised the cane and brought it speeding down on his back just below the shoulder blades. Sean let out his shock at the pain in a solitary, involuntary "Aah!" His hands turned up and cradled his head, his fingers pressed hard into his scalp. Jess lifted the rod from his back revealing the dark red stripe it left on him and raised it again.

"This is for your disobedience and defiance!" She raised the cane again and brought it down just below his first stripe. "Aargh!" All his strength accumulated in his hands and he gripped his skull crushingly tight. Without words and warning the rod again came down on him and he was taken by completely by surprise and yelled out his shock and pain. The room fell into silence as they all waited for Jess to speak or strike again.

"That will do!" She announced and handed the cane quickly over to Amber glad to have it out of her care. Jess covered her mouth with both hands and stared wide eyed at the marks she'd made on him. "Get up now." She told him wanting the house to return as quickly as possible to something that resembled normality. Sean stiffly rose as Andrew handed him back his shirt and reassuringly squeezed his shoulder. He took his time putting his shirt back on and kept his eyes cast down trying to come to terms with what he'd just experienced. He understood that nothing would be normal from then on and Jess too was silently contemplating the possibilities of losing him in the next few hours that would follow.

Amber defused the sombre mood and injected her unique take on the scene now unfolding between them.

"Well done Sean, I didn't think you had it in you but you've certainly showed your colours here tonight . . . what was worse . . . the punishment itself or the embarrassment of having onlookers?" Amber asked walking to him and lifting his chin to see into his eyes.

Sean thought quickly to answer wanting to become free of Amber's prying eyes. "The being watched." He declared.

"That is the correct answer. If the punishment were cause for your distress then your commitment to Jess would be in question. As for the audience being a problem, I think you'll find that from now on you can share anything with us. Your pain, punishment and degradation is all of ours to share and delight in!" Amber continued to stare into him with eyes that read his immediate thoughts. In the hush that followed he breathed in low and let his unblinking eyes give her free range to his mind. Nobody in the kitchen moved. Time itself was standing still awaiting Amber's permission for it to tick again. Sean knew that Amber's mind was presently inside his own and nothing could be kept from her. Was she about to kiss him he couldn't tell, the mind reading was a one-way street. If that was true then she already knew that he thought she might.

"You'll do well!" Amber spoke and released her grip and her gaze. "Behave yourself, surrender yourself and thank Jess for the beating!" She commanded him and motioned toward Jess.

Jess was about to protest but as quickly as lightening Amber held a silencing finger to halt her before the first syllable came out.

"Thank you Jess. I shan't let you down again." Sean uttered raising a smile and feeling the weight of Amber's oppression lifted from his mind.

Jess too felt the atmosphere lift and smiled back to Sean. She went to him and careful not to touch his wounds she cupped his head in her hands. Amber and Andrew withdrew quietly to the lounge as Sean held Jess in his arms. With her head buried in his chest Jess let the moment overwhelm her and filled with tears.

"Shoosh now. We've done it! We've both proved something to one another. We can go anywhere with this now! Jess I'm totally yours and I wouldn't have it any other way!" He told her softly.

Jess bit her lip and pressed her head harder into his chest to hear his heart beating.

"I'm as much yours as you are mine! That's the secret!" She told him holding back the floodgates to her tears.

Jess found her strength and dignity. She stepped away from him and taking him by the hand she led him into the lounge. Seated on the sofa she patted the sofa for him to sit beside her. They sat holding hands with their fingers interlocked and it was know by all that Jess had something to say.

"I think he's earned the right to know something of us now hasn't he?" She asked Amber.

Amber sat forward and acknowledged Jess's request with a compliant nod.

"Where shall I start?" She breathed in deep and glanced at Andrew to draw inspiration. "In our little society women are revered, respected and prized above all things. Our men-folk are sworn to serve, defend and uphold our right of total freedom. You have seen how Andrew serves me, so it is with all of us in the society. He frees me to pursue my career and live my life to the full." Amber stood and began to slowly pace the room to deliver her lecture. We perform certain rites and rituals but that is not an intended part of our society's future. We feel there is a need to purge our souls and minds of the conditioning we have lived under outside the society. The second generation born to us will decide for themselves the next stage on the way forward and will not see the purges that take place such as you went through tonight. They will develop in a truly responsible, matriarchal society and armed with that new knowledge and culture and compare it to the way of the world beyond. This world has had thousands of years of so called civilisation to find the way ahead and in truth knows it well. It does however refuse to put its hands up and admit the rights of half the world's population, indeed it often seems to relish in denying them their freedom. The enslavement of women through fear and conditioning is continuing on a huge scale and is abhorrent to us. We are going to grow and expose its crassness! We will fight it tooth and nail until it is forced out of existence." Anger grew in her voice and forced her to take another moment to calm herself. "Well we are making a stand and allowing the basic truths into our lives. We are all free to develop and evolve led by the heart to something fine and pure. It is your heart that has chosen to honour Jess with its gift of you. Our rites and rituals are designed not only purge you of what has gone before but make your love of Jess plainly visible and so very real." Amber returned to her seat and after a short pause for thought she continued. "When I saw you at Jess's feet today, I felt the actual presence of love. If the scene were reversed it would have spelled a very different story. Have I said anything so far that you disagree with?" Amber asked.

"No, not at all!" Sean's reply came swift and sure.

"Our society is very new and we are not working from any book. We are writing the book as we go and learning from each other. I believe that you have something in you to teach us but so too have you a lot to learn from us. So far I have avoided the 'S' word but you yourself freely used it in your card to Jess. Do you intend to become her slave and serve her selflessly?" Amber asked knowing the answer to come.

"Yes I do! I mean . . . I am already and very happily hers!" Sean admitted.

"You may well become her slave but you haven't yet earned that right!" Amber informed him ending the conversation with stern words. Clapping her hands twice she made herself comfortable on her sofa and lifted her feet for Andrew to rub them on his lap.

Sean sat staring into space torn between two very different opinions on Amber. Was she simply a pretty, upwardly mobile, control freak with designs on becoming a despotic leader of a fledgling cult? Maybe she was exactly what she portrayed herself to be, she had indeed had got inside his head and read his thoughts. That was as real as the caning and every word she had spoken rang true leaving no room for argument. Everything around him was perfectly real and he didn't wish to be anywhere else but where he was. He was with Jess and proving his worthiness to her at an unprecedented speed and wanting more.

Jess touched his shoulder and motioned him to follow her into the dining room. Again she closed the door behind her and leant against it.

"Don't let her frighten you Sean. She's painted a pretty bleak picture of what we're about. I just want to assure you that . . . I will look after you." Jess forced a simple smile and waited.

"She said I'm not yours yet but I am! Jess you could have the coldest and blackest of hearts and I would still be honoured to call myself yours and . . . serve you. Being with you is all I want." He submitted and stood nearer her.

Jess embraced him still thinking on his words.

"Is that how you see me now? A cold hearted and wicked woman?" Jess pushed him away at arms length to read his thoughts through the windows of his eyes as he answered.

"No, I don't see you as anything but . . . perfection itself!" He replied with a smile.

Free of the fear of losing him Jess smiled a radiant and almost overjoyed smile and led him by the hand back through to the lounge. The evening had been an eventful one and now normal service was resumed. Amber told Andrew to make a pot of tea and Sean to turn the television on. Sean couldn't sit comfortably on the sofa so plonked the three spare cushions to the floor and was about to sit on them when Amber threw one of her cushions to him. Now he could sit with his lower back rested against the sofa and his burning stripes above and beyond any potentially painful contact. Jess laid herself out on the sofa and gently ran her fingers down the side of his face and occasionally through what was left of his hair. Andrew returned with a tray of tea and biscuits. Sean made an effort to get up but Andrew waved him back down. From time to time he became aware that Amber was staring at him and his mind tripped back to when he first saw her in the pub. There was something more at work between him and his new family than he was currently able to comprehend. Amber and Jess's awe-inspiring presences couldn't simply be argued away as charisma. They had something more to them, there was a spiritual side to them that he craved to know more of and watching the television with them was just killing time until the next revelation was to be revealed.

"I should be getting back, Molly will be needing to be let out!" He whispered up to her.

"Okay but don't take long!" Jess told him and tugged a tuft of his hair.

"So . . . you want me to come back?" Sean looked surprised.

"Yes! You live here now! We'll talk more about your little dog tomorrow!"

Sean took the look of surprise from his face and replaced it with a look of bewilderment.

"Don't you think we've waited long enough?" Jess asked with a perplexed look of her own.

"Yes, yes I do! I'll be back inside an hour!" He replied flushed with excitement and adrenalin surging through his veins. As the conservatory door closed Amber sent Andrew away so that she could lecture Jess.

"Jess, I've just told you about your impatience and you've just jumped the gun again. For God's sake slow down. You rush at everything lately and it un-nerves me!" Amber was clearly very cross with her. "I didn't intervene because I didn't want to challenge your authority in front of him! Yes he can move in but I intended it to be within a few weeks or so! Anyway it's done now so I'm going to tell you something and you'd better listen and adhere to it!" Amber paused to make certain she had her full attention. "There will be no full on sex! No penetration! You will assert your dominance at all times! Sex is a very powerful tool so use it for your pleasure and stay in complete control of both yourself and him! Satisfy your curiosity by all means but just remember who's in charge. . . ."

"I get it, I get it! Enough already! Thanks for your advice but I am not you! I will do as I please!" Jess retaliated with real venom in her rising anger.

"Yes that's it! Just make sure you do as YOU please! Sex is the biggest, most potent power game of all. . . . Apart from that . . . enjoy him!" Amber softened her tone dramatically and an uneasy peace was declared. She called for Andrew and suggested that he was to bring three glasses of whiskey to make a respectful toast and mark the occasion properly. Jess was won over in an instant and though she wasn't a whiskey drinker she happily toasted her possession of her very own human being. She drained her glass in one and inevitably coughed and spluttered as the burn hit her throat and warmed her belly. Amber ordered the glasses to be re-charged and offered a toast to Sean. "May he prove himself loving and obedient to your every word!" They all toasted Sean and Amber was ready with another toast. Andrew re-charged the glasses again. "Here's to the end of the terrible trio and the beginning of the fantastic four!" Jess smiled and eagerly raised her glass and again downed it in one. Amber had yet another toast to propose and get Jess to have a fourth whiskey. Andrew charged the glasses. "Here's to the society, may it grow and influence the consciousness of the world!" They drained their glasses and Amber asked Andrew if he could think of anything they'd missed.

"No my mistress, I think you have covered everything adequately!"

"I've got one!" Jess said eagerly and Andrew dispensed more whiskey.

"To slaves, may they serve us and love us as we deserve and desire!" Jess downed her fifth whiskey alongside a delighted Amber and a quietly amused Andrew.

Andrew took the near empty bottle and glasses away and Jess stretched out her arms and spun on the spot like a whirling dervish. She managed a fair number of turns before she collided with and collapsed onto her sofa. Amber sat next to her and ignoring Jess's reluctance to have her space invaded she pulled her close and held her in position with an arm around her.

"I'm so proud of you my little sister! You've waited the longest and got what could be the best! Our lives are so different now aren't they? The happier we become the more I resent our wasted years in the old life! Now our lives are filled with contentment, relaxation and fun. Now we have a loving and devoted slave each. How many women actually achieve this level of satisfaction? Not many, not yet! You know, when I think what we were expected to become . . . well that's men for you . . . controlling us for their own needs with hypocrisy and lies wrapped up in tradition, machismo, culture and religion. Even here it happens and women grow up believing that they are born to serve! To take second place! To take without complaint whatever he dishes out and believe that it's a natural function, the way of the world and what God wants for us. My God! Do you know the rape laws in the old country?" Amber didn't wait for the answer. "For a woman to report a rape it has to be witnessed by FIVE independent, MALE witness's who are prepared to make a statement that they SAW the rape taking place! FUCKING HELL! Men eh? Laws written by men for men" Amber gently moved Jess aside and stood up to pace the floor and encourage Jess to feel the injustice, bitterness and rage she portrayed so well.

"BASTARDS!" Jess vented her rising anger with the one word said loudly. "But we can't let them blight our lives now! We can't take on all of the world's shit! Hate them yes but I don't want to think about them tonight! Not tonight? Jess requested.

"You're right! We'll take the fight and the light to them in our own good time! The farm will bring peace to a lot of troubled souls!" Amber lowered her tone. "It is a special night for you! I'm sorry! You have got a good head on your shoulders and I know you'll always do the right thing!" Amber spoke softly and embraced her again her rouse having worked perfectly and re-awakened Jess's mistrust of men's intentions and her loathing for machismo.

Sean returned and entered through the conservatory. He had his boyish excitement pretty much under control apart from a constantly reappearing expectant grin. He had with him two carrier bags, one with his toothbrush and clean underclothes and the other with his work trousers and paint splattered fleece. Jess stood from the sofa and swaggered toward him kissing him passionately on the mouth. Holding the back of his head with one hand and supporting herself with the other on the sideboard she dominated the kiss as her passions rose forcing her to lead him to the bedroom. She needed a hand on each rail to ascend the stairs and stopped near the top.

"Go back down and get the whiskey from the cabinet!" She told him. Sean turned about and began his descent. "Don't bother with glasses!" She shouted to him.

Whiskey in hand Sean called out to her to hone in on her voice and find her room. On entering he saw her sat at her dressing table staring straight at him. The room was large and the bed a single divan. There was a solid oak chest of drawers and matching wardrobe. There was a bedside lamp on a bedside table next to the small bed that meant they would be constantly close through the night ahead.

"Come here and kneel at my feet slave!" She told him firmly and as he knelt she stood and with a gentle swaying motion issued her next command. "Take them down!"

Sean unbuckled her belt and freed the button before slowly unzipping her listening and enjoying the sound made by every freed tooth. Finally he tugged at the sides of her trousers and pulled them past her hips. She became seated again as he completed their removal. "Give me the bottle!" She commanded him.

He handed her the bottle and she pointed her toes to his mouth and carefully tipped the bottle but hadn't removed the cap. Sean with his gaping mouth ready to catch the liquid from the tips of her toes laughed with her. She removed the cap and flung it carelessly to rebound off the ceiling. Steadily she tilted the bottle a second time as the golden liquid trickled down her shin to her calf and off her heel to the floor. Sean had to move quickly to lie on his side and catch the flow. Jess stemmed the flow and repositioned the neck of the bottle as he watched her and readied himself at his original position. This time she poured the whiskey directly onto her foot and as it trickled and ran in three separate streams he ran his tongue over her foot as fast as he could. All too soon the bottle was empty and she lowered it to the floor beside her.

Lick my feet slave!" She commanded relaxing further back into her chair and offered him the un-anointed foot to lick at. His passion for her dry foot overwhelmed him and enflamed his desire to a new, vigorous intensity. Jess watched him at work basking the knowledge of the power she had over him. He cradled her foot so gently in his hands and occasionally angled it to explore its every contour. Not wanting to even blink she watched him and occasionally pointed her foot signalling him to take her toes into his mouth. She rested one foot on his shoulder as he worked on the other and alternated a rested foot for a wet one many times over.

"My slave likes to lick my feet, I might have the best of all!" she said closing her eyes as relaxation and tiredness took her over. Pulling her foot from him she told him it was time to sleep. She staggered over to the bed and Sean climbed in beside her. With one arm draped over him she was asleep and he was left to watch her and feel her every breath on his face.

CHAPTER SIX

Jess's alarm sounded and she leant over him to quickly silence it. Without a thought for Sean's presence she took her full weight on her elbow and rested her elbow on Sean's chest. Her knee came dangerously close to causing him further discomfort as it came to rest on his pelvis. Protecting his bits with both hands he waited for her careless return journey to her side of the bed. The alarm silenced she straddled him and removed his protective hands. She felt the heat of his morning glory against her thigh causing her to give a whole new facial expression. Her sloe eyes rolled from top to bottom then to the side and she was smiling an innocent, slightly embarrassed and thought filled smile. Her eyes continued their search, roaming from high to low and from left to right as she nestled down on to him. He stroked her sides with his fingertips and with a shake of her head her hair fell around his face screening them off and cutting out all images but each other's faces.

"There'll be no work for me today I'm staying here with you!" She said softly. "First though you can tell Andrew to phone work for me and get me a tall glass of orange juice!" She rolled off of him and led on her side to watch him dress and carefully close his zip over his prominent appendage.

Down in the kitchen he informed Andrew of her intention not to attend work and asked him to phone it in for her. He had some orange juice for himself and took Jess's up to her. Jess drank it eagerly until the glass was empty and handed it out Sean to place it carefully on the bedside table.

"I should get my head shaved today!" He told her.

"Not today you won't! I want you with me all day. Now undress I want to see your . . . thingy!" She said waving her finger in the direction of his groin.

He done as instructed and stood naked and to attention at her bedside. She swung her legs out of bed and sat facing his growing, nodding erection. She took it in her fingers lifting it and moving it around to inspect it. She put her closed lips to it and kissed it. Her fingertips moved lightly over his testicles and she ran the back of her hand under them, turning her hand she lifted them and felt their weight. Sean put his hand on her head and began to stroke her hair but she pulled her head away and giving him a look that told him not to continue with that line of action she gripped his cock hard.

"Keep your hands off me!" She told him and fixed him in a stern, almost angry stare. She stood and pushed him by the shoulders to his knees. Drawing his head forward she had him to take down her knickers and stepping free of them she took firm hold of the back of his head and with both hands pulled him to her. Sean began to kiss her inner thighs and between her legs. She fell back onto the bed and he followed her as if connected to her by a short and invisible cord. Repositioning herself to lie comfortably on the bed he followed her keeping his head between her legs. His hands held her buttocks as his passion for her drove him on from her clitoris to run his tongue hard down to enter her with every lap. She began to writhe and gripped his head in her hands her fingernails pressing into his scalp. He lapped at her faster and faster until she tapped him on the head and told him to slow. She directed him back to her clitoris and told him to press his tongue harder and slower against it. Teasingly he took his attention to her thighs, pelvis and stomach. Frustrated by his desertion she slapped him hard across the face.

"Don't stop!" She demanded.

He returned to where he was wanted with renewed passion and sent his hands to cup her breasts his fingers to trapping her nipples. Jess writhed higher and went into a circular motion holding his head steadfast where it was needed.

"Lick me you fucking slave! Lick me!" Her voice spat the words out with a venomous ferocity. "You're my slave. My property. YOU'RE MINE! I fucking own you now!" Sean sped up his loving of her as she allowed and continued to inform him of his new position in her life.

"You will obey me! Only me, Please and pleasure me. You will lick my feet like a fucking dog when I want! Won't you? Won't you? She caught a firm hold of his hair and pulled his head to one side as she climaxed and pinned him face down on the bed until her orgasm subsided. After a few deep breathes she released him to rise up the bed and lie beside her.

To her surprise Sean began to laugh. She smiled at him and asked what it was he found to be so funny.

"We both came at the same time! When you were cursing and digging your nails into me I went off like a rocket!" They laughed at the welcome release.

Entwined in the single bed they kissed and stroked each other until Jess found the cold wet patch. She threw the covers back and climbed out of bed to tug the sheet from under him. Rolling it up she discarded it on the floor and rejoined him face down on the bed. He straddled her and kissed the back of her neck then rained kisses across to her warm, dampened shoulders and down her spine. He reached her ass and kissed her buttocks ploughing his way between the cheeks of her ass with his stubbly chin. He kissed down the crease of her bum to her vagina. Then suddenly applied his tongue to her bottom and spread her bum cheeks open with his hands. Jess groaned to express her growing pleasure.

"Oh you're so mine!" She told him adding a command to tongue it faster. He sped up his rate of licks and began to apply long strokes of his tongue with it rarely re-entering his mouth. Jess rolled over and pulled him up to lie next to her again. She took his hand and pressed it to her vagina. Slowly he let one finger slide inside her and then another. He pushed them deep all the while looking into her hungry eyes. She bit her bottom lip and shut her eyes tight as she pushed herself on his fingers. With his thumb pushing against her clit on every return of his fingers she told him to go faster and faster until she pulled herself free of his fingers and embraced him crushingly tight in her second orgasm. She had beads of sweat on her forehead, which he open mouthed kissed from her as she lightly ran her fingertips over his shoulders and down his arms.

By the time they'd showered and ventured down to the kitchen Amber had long since left for work. Andrew was nowhere to be seen and must've been holed up in his office room. They prepared tea and toast together and took it in the conservatory. Sitting together on the wicker sofa Jess told him that the best thing was for Molly to move in too. It would have to be agreed to by Amber but she saw no problem as long as she stayed in the conservatory. Jess had everything already planned out and suggested that he used the small box room for his storage and utilised it for his writing and painting requirements.

"You can let your house out or sell it outright it's up to you." She added.

"There is another possibility we haven't thought about as yet . . . what if you move in with me!" Sean saw the change in her face. She wasn't at all impressed by the notion and gave him a point blank "No!" He realised that his suggestion hadn't been well received and on reflection he should've known that he had joined them and it wasn't for him to break-up the unit. After expressing his regret at making the suggestion stood up and took the cups and plates into the kitchen. Jess followed him and put her arms around him whispered in his ear.

"Let's get back to bed. I'm on a terrible guilt trip about work and I need you to take my mind from it!"

They returned to the bedroom and seated at her dressing table she had him kneel in front of her. With one foot on his lap and the other resting on his shoulder she reclined in her chair and questioned him.

"Is this what you envisaged when you wrote the card?"

"No! This outstrips everything I've ever dared to dream!" He kissed the leg of the foot resting on his shoulder and rubbed the foot on his lap.

"Things will settle down in time but I want . . . I need to know exactly how mine you are?" Her voice was quiet and her words were spoken softly as they came straight from the heart.

"Jess, I'm totally yours! There's nothing I won't do for you! Pleasing you pleases me immensely! It's all I want! All I need!" He stared up into her wide eyes and she smiled.

"Yesterday when I beat you I thought I was going to throw up . . . but now I want to explore us to the full! I want to know you and at the same time find out who I am!"

"I think we've got a lot of . . . finding out to do!" He said with a growing smile. "I should go and see to Molly! Come with me and we can have a walk in the fresh air?" He spoke with a lisp that made her giggle. She guessed what had caused the problem with his speech and smilingly agreed to go with him. They dressed for the cold and ventured outside to the car.

Sean unlocked his front door and Jess walked in behind him. Molly clambered off the chair and sniffed at his trousers to know where he'd been. Eventually turning her attention to Jess she wagged her tail expecting to be made a fuss of. It didn't happen. Jess simply patted her too heavily on the head and moved away.

"Hmm wood chip!" She smiled and gave Sean a very disapproving look. She cast her eyes around at his poor taste in home decoration. His miss-matched three-piece suite, flat pack desk, threadbare carpet and ancient television perched on a flat pack corner unit were only her immediate points of disapproval.

"I take back what I said about letting this out! I think you should set fire to it! Better still pull it down, bulldoze it and then set it on fire!" She sat on the arm of the sofa shaking her head in disbelief.

"Wait a minute you haven't seen the upstairs yet!" He told her, leading her believe that it wasn't all so bad.

"Is it better than this?" She asked expectantly.

"Nope!" He replied with a burst of carefree honesty.

They went up the stairs anyway and there was one face saving item of furniture that met with her approval. His chest of drawers was similar to hers and at least had some age to it. She expressed an interest in the double bed but was quickly deterred by his informed distasteful account of it. In the next room she browsed through his paintings and was moved to say that three of them were actually quite good. One in particular she'd like to have on her wall. He told her she could have it and she pulled it from the stack and carried it with handed it to him to carry.

"I can not believe you wanted me to move in here! Your furniture's distasteful, your bed's dysfunctional your décor's disgusting . . . I'm disappointed to the point of dismay!" Jess told him as she moved down the staircase.

"I take it you . . . disapprove!" He added.

"Disapprove? I'm distraught! Your house is a disaster area! I may even have to dispense some discerning discipline to you this very evening! " She told him failing to hold back her smile.

"I am at your disposal just don't disown me or I shall be decisively and distinctly distraught! Discipline me diss evening at your discretion!" He said smiling and showing her seven digits.

"I can see that I am indeed going to have to dispence some disturbing discipline on you to display my displeasure at your dismal display of disgraceful, discount furniture and it's not open to discussion! Ha!" Jess counted the awarded points on her fingers as she spoke them and joyously displaying nine fingers, she danced around him successfully claiming the ultimate victory.

"I couldn't be more disinterested!" Sean had the final word and received a slap across the back of the head for his disrespect.

Sean clipped Molly's lead on and they walked to the canal. Jess held his hand until Molly was unleashed then she leant into him and they walked on with their arms around each other. She knew all the paths and cycle tracks through her jogging jaunts with Amber so Sean took her off the beaten track and through the fields taking in the ponds and derelict farm with its deep well in the middle of a copse. Jess sat on the low wall and waited patiently as he sorted through the loose boulders to make a pile ready to load the next day. With the sky darkening and low-lying clouds blowing in to hide what would've been a colourful sunset they began the homeward journey by the most direct route. Sean couldn't help but be impressed by the way Jess vaulted the barbed wire fence and leapt the swollen stream more surely and effortlessly than he ever had done. She was thoroughly enjoying the walk, the fresh air and watching Molly doing her own thing. She warmed to her and twice, when Molly rejoined the pack she called her over and stroked her under the chin.

Back at Sean's house Jess perched herself on the arm of the sofa as he roamed around packing a suitcase and rucksack. When he returned from the upstairs he found Jess flicking through his sketchpad.

"How long have been doing these?" She asked him referring to his many attempts to capture her likeness.

"About a year! Since I first saw you!" He told her.

"Why didn't you ask me out sooner? I waited months and began to think that you never would!" Jess was annoyed with him. "We've wasted so much time haven't we?"

"To tell you the truth I never expected you to say yes! I was certain you would let me down gently and I would have to get on with my life . . . broken hearted! Empty! Just a shell of a man! In a great deal of mental anguish and physical pain but free of my delusions of ever being with you!" He explained.

Jess flung the pad on the sofa and put her arms around him. Cheek to cheek they cuddled until she kissed him.

"I was so sure it was you who'd sent the card and was reading it over and over willing you the strength to ask me out!" She revealed as she released him and stood ready to go.

Jess phoned Amber and asked her about Molly coming to stay. The response from Amber was quick and positive helped by the fact that she was at work and didn't like to be disturbed. Sean collected a few of Molly's things and put them in a carrier bag. He put her things with his case, rucksack and Jess's painting in the car and they drove home.

Sean asked Andrew for a blanket and settled Molly down in the conservatory. Jess inquired what was for dinner and Andrew explained that he had been too busy with his work to prepare anything more than some chips to add to the fish that Amber was due to bring home within the hour. To Sean's relief Jess was too hungry to wait and decided to make some salad sandwiches. Andrew made a pot of tea and Jess got out all the ingredients she wanted in the salad sandwich. Grabbing him by the shoulders Jess positioned Sean to stand in front of the chopping board where she gave him his instructions.

"All this evenly spread and positioned and cut into triangles please!" He expertly sliced the cheese to a uniformed width and included all the ingredients that Jess had taken from the fridge. He took the plate of triangular cut sandwiches to the bar along with three small plates and returned to tidy the mess on the worktop.

"Lets eat them all before he sits down!" Jess leant over the bar and whispered to Andrew.

He smiled at her and forced an entire triangle into his mouth. Jess did likewise and they chewed as fast as their jaws would allow. Sean walked by them returning the Tomato's and cucumber to the fridge. They both slowed their frantic chewing and acted normally until he was safely past them again. Swallowing hard they both took another round each and stuffed them into their mouths. Jess put the final sandwiches on Andrews and her plates just as Sean passed them again with the lettuce and spring onions. On completing the final wipe down of the worktop and rinsing off the chopping board he stepped up to the breakfast bar drying his hands in a dishcloth. Jess and Andrew had cleared their plates of the last of the sandwiches and both had bulging cheeks. Sean's eyes opened wide at the sight of four empty plates and looked at both the culprits in turn. Jess had to cover her mouth to prevent it opening as she laughed at his pitiful expression of sadness and dismay. Andrew too found it amusing to the point of laughter and dare not take another look at him. Choking on his sandwich he stood up and bent double. Sean's eyes flicked from the empty plates to Jess and Andrew and back to the empty plates, which, only made Jess laugh more hysterically. Still unable to open her mouth she too had to stand and bend double, her hands ready to catch any ejected sandwich. They finally got to swallow their food and let their laughter take on it's audible climax.

"Got any biscuits?" Sean asked sorrowfully sending them into laughter again.

Sean returned to the fridge and retrieved one tomato, two spring onions, three lettuce leaves and the cheese. He made himself a devil may care sandwich and took a hungry bite from it before wiping the breadcrumbs and unwanted green stems from the worktop in his hands.

His and hers hunger pains abated she led him to the front room to watch some television and perform his magic on her feet. After twenty minutes or so he suggested that he might be allowed to go and collect a carload of the stone. He could unload it that evening and be freed to pick up another load first thing in the morning whilst he waited for the builder's merchants to deliver the sand and cement.

"I've got a better idea! Why don't we work up an appetite upstairs before Amber gets home with the supper?" She said raising her eyebrows at him.

"I'm here to please!" He said batting his eyebrows back at her and secretly wondering how his tongue would perform if that's what she had in mind.

"Do you think you're up to it? You're still talking a bit funny!" She said with partial concern.

"I'll do my ve-wee bwest." He joked.

"Then I won't work you too hard. Two orgasms should do it!" she said grabbing him by the hand and leading him up the stairs.

Hurriedly undressing Sean suddenly stopped and stood motionless.

"I think she's here!" He said.

"Really?" Jess stood still and listened hard.

"No!" He suddenly re-animated and had his trousers off before her.

Jess led on the bed and hastened him to get started. In a fast-forwarding action he set to work between her legs at a humorously high speed. Jess began to laugh and told him to either take it slow or take a beating. He obeyed and slowed to an incredibly slow motion. Jess laughed again but this time gave him a few warning taps on the head. Joking over with he quickly found her rhythm and soon had her writhing and gripping his head tensely in her hands. She whispered almost inaudibly to him her voice gaining in volume as her excitement grew and she travelled deeper into a world of her own making. With her increasing pleasure so too grew the ferocity of her words. She progressed further into her private world and took Sean along with her as the means of her entry and exit to her Palace of pleasure and pain. His increased pain meant her heightened pleasure. She dug her fingernails into his scalp and vowed to perform acts of extreme violence on him until the door to her orgasm was flung open and her soul escaped back inside her body.

Sean's face was dripping wet and when she completed his release he reached for his shirt and wiped his face with it. When he looked at her she was staring at him, her eyes wide and wild.

"That was amazingly intense! I don't know where all the swearing came from! I felt as if I was possessed! I felt fantastic . . . but . . . possessed!" She told him lying flat on her back and kicking the duvet off the bed.

Sean took his boxer shorts off on locating his stain used his shorts to wipe it from the mattress.

"You came too?" She asked watching him check the duvet for further stains.

"Well I didn't think I would but when you began to rant at me and pull my hair I went off like an airport foam thrower!"

"So that's the second time we've cum together! That tells me that we're really connected on more than just one level." She told him.

"I'm thinking that we were together before! I don't know when but maybe I was your slave who became your lover. Maybe we were discovered and separated and our souls have searched many incarnations to find a time where we can . . . come together again and complete our . . . union? A time where we can live our lives together free of breaking with convention and taboo's!" He explained his thoughts as they occurred to him.

Jess liked what he said and it became more real to her the longer she thought on it.

"But where does my aggression come from? I was honestly planning to beat you! If I had that cane up here I think I'd have used it on you and as for the swearing . . . that's just not me!" She looked to him for further explanations.

"I became your lover don't forget. To start with I was just a slave that you utilised. It was in brutal times and beating a slave was commonplace. I soon became your lover and it was your aggressive love-making and swearing that led us to be discovered and we became separated!" He looked at her pleased with his story of their former life together.

"And this was when?" Jess asked annoyed at being blamed as the guilty party.

"Ancient Egypt, Greece, Rome maybe I was a captured crusader knight and you a high ranking noble woman on the side of Saladin who bought my life?" He offered her his possibilities.

"I want an answer! Empty your mind and tell me everything you feel and see." She sat up on the bed infused with hunger to hear more. Sean was her vehicle to take her to another place and another time.

Sean knelt in front of her and stared into her eyes. She took his hands and held them on her lap. They became locked into each other's eyes with only the ticking of her clock reaching his mind.

"It was Rome! We first came together in ancient Rome! You were involved in an Egyptian styled cult there! You were one of the priestesses and I was a temple slave. You had me beaten so many times for my daring to look at you but I never stopped. Whenever you walked by I would be drawn to look on you even though I knew the consequences. Certain of the pain that would follow I had to look upon you. One day you came to realise and understand that the disrespectful and defiant slave was in love with you. Instead of having me beaten you would take me to your room to humiliate me yourself! You'd have me lick your feet like a whipped dog and slap me with your slippers and hands. I never felt that humiliation; every second I spent with you made my life as a slave worth living! Eventually it became a nightly occurrence and I would come to your room not for a beating or humiliation but to pleasure you and watch over you as you slept. We never coupled as I was still just a slave but we did many fine things! One night your cursing, born of your frustration at our incompatibility led us to be discovered and we were torn asunder. Arrangements were made to separate us and keep us apart. We managed one last evening together before I was due to be taken away and sold. We walked along a beach and watched the sun set and you finally told me that you loved me too. Listening to the waves breaking over the sand you promised to find me and buy my freedom when you yourself became free. . . . It never happened . . . we never saw each other again...until now!"

Jess's eyes had welled up and a tear began its journey down her cheek. Its coldness trailed down her face and was left to run its course unchallenged. It was quickly joined by another tear racing to catch it. The muscles in her face began to contort and audible crying became inevitable. She burst into action and pulled him close, holding him and squeezing him tight.

"Where on earth did that come from? That was beautiful! Sad but very beautiful." She asked stemming her sobs with an outburst of laughter that proved easier to quell.

"I didn't mean to make you cry! I just said what I imagined helped along with a dose of our own current reality!" Sean rubbed her back looking to smile at her and wet his lips with her tears.

"Don't say imagined! It was too real to attribute to imagination! I think we were those people!" She told him firmly.

"Jess, I just made it up. I told you a story that's all!" He insisted.

There was a knock at her door and Andrew called out that supper was ready. Jess brushed her hair and Sean dressed in only his jeans quickly retrieved his bags from the car and dressed for dinner. They entered the dining room together and Amber immediately picked up on the fact that Jess had been crying. Concerned and glaring across at Sean she questioned her on what had upset her. Jess explained that Sean had told her a story that was so wonderfully sad that it had moved her to tears. Amber concerned that Jess's explanation might be a cover story insisted that he shared his story with them. Sean was embarrassed but had to oblige. He re-ran the story once more through his mind before beginning. They gave him their full attention as he relayed his tale of passion, pain and a doomed love. When he'd finished Jess was quick to fill in what he had omitted and told them that it was their story. The story of how they first met and why they were together now!

"That was beautiful! No wonder you've decided to become a writer!" Amber told him.

"You should work that storyline into your book!" Andrew added.

"Maybe I can!" He replied keeping his answer short to move the conversation along.

They returned to the meal and Jess rekindled the holiday question and proposed that they added Rome or maybe Pompeii to compete with the lure of South America. Amber dismissed Rome as they'd been there but Pompeii sounded attractive. Sean and Andrew both drew on what they knew of Pompeii and its plaster casts of the bodies of fallen Romans revealing their final moments. Sean had several books on Pompeii and would bring them over the next day.

"Whilst we're on the subject why don't you get them after dinner!" Amber asked.

Sean agreed and after dinner helped Andrew clear the table ready for their sweet. Sean made his excuses to miss out on the sweet and use the time to dart home and get the books. In his absence Amber sent Andrew to have his sweet in the kitchen so she could talk frankly with Jess about her progress with Sean. Jess was suspicious of Ambers intrusive interest but was happy to tell her what an obedient lover he was and how they had connected on another level. Amber ached to question her for more accurate and detailed information but anticipated Jess's unfavourable reaction and left the subject, for then at least.

Sean dashed into the conservatory from the heavy rain. Molly was pleased to see him but he only had time to pat her on the head as he passed. He put four books on the dinner table and opened the fifth to the pages containing the plaster cast bodies and passed it to Jess. Amber rose from her chair and moved to peer over Jess's shoulder.

"That's macabre!" Amber said as she prevented Jess from turning the page. Andrew took a book entitled Villas of Pompeii for himself whilst Sean retired to the kitchen to make the teas.

"I want to go there!" Jess insisted. Amber agreed and suggested that instead of it being a holiday for the two of them that they all went together to which Jess wholeheartedly agreed. Andrew remained aloof and continued to stare into his book as if he'd not heard the suggestion. Amber forced an acknowledgement from him and he submitted in his perfected monotone that it was a very nice idea indeed. Sean brought the tea tray in and sugared his and Jess's teas.

"We've decided that we're all going to Pompeii as a foursome!" Jess announced to Sean's apparent surprise and full agreement.

Amber took another book from the table and called for Andrew to attend her in the lounge. Jess became so engrossed in the book containing the pictures of plaster casts that she neglected her tea. By the time she reached for it felt through the walls of the cup that it had gone cold. She ordered Sean out to make her another one and told him to bring it through to the lounge.

When he returned Amber was led on her sofa flicking through her book with Andrew sitting with her feet reading his and half heartedly rubbing her feet with one hand. Sean put Jess's tea down on the coffee table and whispered to her that he should spend some time with Molly in the conservatory. Jess agreed and returned her attention to the book.

Molly was glad of the company and sat half on the sofa and half on him having her tummy rubbed. Glad of the time to rest his tongue even from talking he rubbed Molly's tummy and chest for the longest time. The rain trickled down the glass reminding him of Jess's tears. Her insurmountable beauty and charisma had drawn him in, her kind and affectionate nature was apparent but deep inside her was the demon that would awaken on arousal. The demon was a part of her and he had no wish to purge her of it. It served her and it had a purpose to redress the balance in her soul. It was a wanton demon that ensured she achieved climax and ultimate release from her lust. He looked forward to his next meeting with it and wondered what the consequences might be if he were to tease and taunt it into a blind rage.

Jess popped her head in the room and told him she was ready to retire to bed. He slid himself out from under Molly and ruffled the hair on her head. They walked through the darkened house and said goodnight to Andrew who would always be the last to ascend the stairs after checking the doors and plumping the cushions.

They undressed for bed and Jess climbed in first. He watched her getting into bed and blessed his good fortune to be with her. He joined her in the bed and ran his hands down her sides to her thighs. She nuzzled up to him and stroked the side of his face. He kissed her forehead and willed her to send him down on her again but she stayed silent. With his growing erection he asked if he might go down to pleasure her but she was too contented as she was. She only wanted to cuddle up and drift into sleep. He wondered how he could possibly get to sleep wanting her so much and unable to have her. The ticking of the clock eventually helped his troubled mind to wander away from sex and run a scenario about what might have happened to the characters in his made up story after they were separated.

"Re-set the alarm for seven o'clock! I'll want you down on me in the morning for certain!" Jess told him sleepily.

CHAPTER SEVEN

He'd drifted in and out of sleep all night. Now as he checked the clock in the dim morning light he had just fifteen more minutes before it was due to rouse them. Staring at the clock face he picked it up and moved the minute hand forward to trip the alarm. It rang out its terrible din and he replaced on the table and muted it. Secure on its three little legs he flicked the duvet to one side and dived down between her legs and began his pleasures there. Jess opened up for him and flicked the duvet back over to shield herself from the cold. Her eyes not yet opened she smiled and held his head in her hands.

"Slower!" She said softly still not having opened her eyes.

Against his desire he reduced his pace and pressed hard and slow on her the way she liked it. Feeling her finger nails pricking his scalp he knew he could increase his speed and lengthen his stroke. Three quick taps on the head told him he'd either increased his speed too much or lengthened his stroke too long so he reduced both by a fraction. Her feet came to rest on his hips and Jess began to rise from the bed as he explored her torso with his fingertips. Occasionally he could hear her whispering above her heavy breathing but it was so faint that he couldn't make out any of the words. It was getting hot under the covers and he had to lift the quilt high above him to draw in the cool air and as the quilt sank; expel the stale hot air. He changed his position to lay flat with his legs below the knees sticking out the bottom of the bed. Now he could writhe with her and try something new. As he licked her clitoris he used the knuckle of one finger to rotate just inside her lips.

She gave a welcoming Mmmm sound and he knew he'd heightened her pleasure. His excitement grew and he had to cast his mind from the present so as not to finish before her. He cast his mind to his garden and sitting at night by the fishpond listening to the sounds of the croaking frogs and toads in the summer. He thought of how rich and black his compost from last year had turned out and how it had served his potatoes particularly well. If he took Jess to the coast one weekend he would enrich his current compost with seaweed. He continued to lap at her and wonder why his raspberry bushes hadn't taken off as he expected. Jess pressed her fingernails harder into his head and at last her cursing became audible.

"Use your fingers!" Serve your mistress! Pleasure me!" She whispered to him between breaths and flung the duvet to one side.

Sean put his fingers inside her, fucking her with them as she relinquished control to the demon inside her.

"Are you happy now? Happy to serve your mistress? Are you happy when I beat you? Eh? Eh?" Her voice grew louder and she slapped him in the side of the head. She slapped him again but this time she drew her hand back some distance and struck him hard and to the side of his face. Another hard slap went to him then she grabbed at his hair.

"You're my property! You belong to me!" She pressed him into her, building up to a climax. "You'll do what I say! Anything I say! Is that understood slave? YOU'RE MINE! I'LL BEAT YOU! I'LL . . . SHOW YOU . . . WHO I AM!" She pushed him away and rolled on top of him as he erupted clenching her buttocks tremendously tight in his hands. The duvet slid to the floor and she breathed in deep and slow. From where he was Sean could see the droplets of sweat that peppered her wonderfully taught and flawless brown skin. She remained over him releasing her breath on his face like a lioness on her prey.

"Did you cum that time too?" She asked still breathing heavily.

"Like a pyroclastic surge, yes!" He said still taking large gulps of cool air.

Jess collapsed onto the bed and stared up at the ceiling.

"You know, in my head just then I was the priestess and you were the temple slave! I was certain that once I had cum I would beat you with a belt or something. I really planned in my head to beat you! I wanted to hurt you . . . bad! Lucky for you I came when I did!"

"Yes, once you've cum you send the demon back down deep inside you! You become . . . you again! Refreshed and renewed!" He told her smiling and running his fingers lightly down her skin.

"But what if one day the demon didn't disappear? What if it stayed in control of me and I become the one trapped on the inside?"

"In that case they'd better watch out at the bank!" He told her and made her concern turn to laughter.

"I'm sorry I hit you!" She said looking at the side of his face for any tell tale marks.

"Three times, three times you struck me!" He said smiling widely at her. "It's all a part of my fantasy too now! I'm the one who made up the story remember! How you climax is simply brilliant to me! I love it! It's exciting!" He reached for the hand that struck him and kissed it. "Anyway its not you doing it, it's the demon inside."

"Don't say that anymore! It's too frightening!" Jess was serious and waited for his acknowledgement that he wouldn't mention the demon again.

Jess led him by the hand into the shower and handed him the big bar of amber soap. He lathered her from her neck to her stretched out arms. She closed her eyes and enjoyed the most sensual stroking of her skin that she'd ever known. He ran and rubbed the soap over her back and round to her stomach then squatted down and worked up a thick lather that he spread from abdomen to her feet. Jess felt energised and taking the showerhead in hand she washed the lather down her body. Sean applied his open mouth to drink the hot water from her hips and as she turned; from the small of her back too. Time was a factor and Jess had to get to work. Reluctantly she cut the jets of water and opened the door. Sean stepped out behind her and taking the purple bath towel he dabbed her dry. She dressed as he dried himself and stood watching her hide her magnificent body under her dark clothes.

They entered the kitchen hand in hand and Sean went to let Molly into the garden but Andrew had beaten him to it. He sat at the bar and thoroughly enjoyed his tea and toast. At the smallest break in the conversation he and Jess would just stare at each other. Smiling was no longer necessary between them; each of them knew they were smiling widely inside. Jess sent him back up to her room for a black hair band and on his speedy return she pulled her hair back into a ponytail and applied the band. Every contour of her face was displayed and ultimately perfect. Amber kissed Andrew goodbye and Jess; once she had squeezed her feet into her high heels reached up to kiss Sean on the lips. Again her minimal height and small proportions belied the extreme power she wielded effortlessly over him. He wanted to be with her everywhere and every second of every day. If he could he would go with her to work and secrete himself under her counter to stroke her legs and feet as she served customers and tried to retain her usual serious and deadpan expression. He watched her get into Amber's car and stared through the glass until the car was gone from view.

Jess opened the conversation for the short journey to work with her concerns about the violence she was unleashing on her kind and undeserving lover. Amber listened with interest as she described her thoughts of brutality towards him and her fears that she may soon push him too far and lose him. Amber bided her time and let Jess fill the silence with more and more detail. Finally she offered her experienced judgement.

"Jess, for the first time in your life you have obtained control over another human being to a far greater degree than any young, new lovers! You are experimenting with your powers and experimenting with his depth of feeling for you! You are like a tiny village that has just become the capital city of an enormous uncharted country. You're sending out your soldiers and spies to map out this new land and find its boundary's! When you find your borders and have mapped the lay of the land you will settle down well enough! I went through with Andrew exactly what you're going through now with Sean . . . I used to slap him for no reason! I remember I used to beat him and push him around goading him to retaliate or leave! He never retaliated and when I realised he wasn't going to leave I settled down safe in the knowledge he was there for me no matter what!" Amber pulled up outside the bank.

"Hmm Thanks for that!" Jess got out of the car and waved her off.

With the girls gone Andrew made two more mugs of tea and sat in with Sean and Molly. Andrew asked if he would like to accompany him on the mornings shopping trip and he agreed as long as he could get his head shaved first. Andrew agreed and suggested the use of Sean's car would take the misery out of the mundane trip in such dismal weather.

They called in to Sean's usual barbershop and after explaining what had happened he had his head shaved all over down to a number four. They walked around Sainsbury's with Sean pushing the trolley and Andrew loading. At the checkout they filled Andrew's two heavy-duty shopping bags and an extra two carrier bags. Andrew paid the seventy-six pounds and headed to M&S to pick up some of Amber's and Jess's favourite deserts.

Sean helped carry the shopping through to the kitchen and left Andrew to unpack.

"If you can spare me another hour tomorrow I'll show you how we . . . I get the washing done around here." Andrew told him as he began emptying the bags.

"I've always done my own washing, I have a good idea how to work a washing machine, as long as you separate the whites from the coloureds and keep the temperature no higher than forty it's fine." Sean told him.

"Ah, here it's all done by hand. No need of machines. All you need is a bar of soap, some bi-carb and a lot of elbow grease and time. It's . . . become a part of our society's rules I'm afraid. It's supposed to tap our energies and focus our minds as well as save money on energy bills." Andrew told him and stopped sorting the shopping to watch his reaction.

"Well maybe we can sneak it off to my house and do the washing there? It'll save on time." Sean suggested.

His reply drew a wide smile from Andrew who agreed. Sean called to Molly to join him and re-embarked for the journey to the farm nearest his stone quarry.

He drew up and pulled over onto the grass verge off the single-track road outside the almost derelict farmhouse. He knew Kenny the aged, flat-capped farmer as he'd twice called at his house to report a sheep caught by the fleece in a thicket and on another occasion to report a ram on its back in a ditch. He'd tried to roll the stricken animal to its feet but after ten minutes of trying he resolved to involve Kenny and some mechanisation. Kenny had told him on his first visit that there was no public right of way in those fields but appreciated his help and he could continue to walk Molly there as long as she didn't panic the sheep. On his second visit to the farm he'd returned with Kenny to the troubled ram and to his surprise Kenny simply produced his shotgun and blew its head clean off. He explained after the act that the sheep was in the final stages of pneumonia and wouldn't have lasted the night. On their way back to the farm Sean had obtained Kenny's permission to metal detect his land with a fifty-fifty split on any finds. After three very long afternoons detecting the sum total of his finds were two horseshoes and a length of chain probably from an old plough horse.

Kenny took his time answering the door and recognising Sean he expected more bad news and was pleased to hear that he was only interested in the stone rubble. He happily told him he could take it all. As if he was glad of somebody to talk to he told him that there had been bad blood between him and the unfortunate farmer who'd lost his farm to the bi-pass.

"He was a miserable tyrant of a man! It was Gods own doing that had the bi-pass put through his farm some thirty years ago now!" He went on to explain that he'd planted the copse in the rubble of the farmhouse when he'd acquired all the land up to the new road. His intention was to hide any reminders of his old rivals farm ever existing there so whatever Sean could gleam from the land he was welcome to. Sean thanked him and drove off to the site. Turning his land rover into the field he drove up to the copse and backed up as far as he could. He picked through the undergrowth to find the best of the stone. Around by the well he scraped the moss from some flagstones but they were too heavy to load unaided. He found some worked stone pieces, cleaned them off and loaded them into the car. More than pleased with his finds he whistled for Molly and drove back to Amber's house where he unloaded the stone on to the patio. Andrew watched the growing line of stone pieces with an impressed grin. Sean put his head just inside the door and told him he was going back for more of the same.

After unloading his second carload Andrew called him in for a coffee. Sean was covered in mud front and back and refused a seat choosing to drink his coffee standing up. In minutes he was off on his third outing stopping at the newsagents for two bars of chocolate, two meat Samosa's and a milky drink. Using some inspired ingenuity he managed to rope and pull a huge flagstone from the copse and haul it up on top some boulders to form a ramp. He returned to the copse and hauled out another flagstone onto the improvised ramp from where he could man handle it into the land rover. Using this method he managed to get three enormous flagstones into the back. With the suspension heavily weighed down he drove back and called for Andrew to help him unload them. He had to wait as Andrew donned his apron and rolled up his sleeves. Taking the stones great weight they shuffled their feet to the lawn and on a count of three let them drop. Andrew was deeply impressed by the acquisitions so far and expressed his fervent belief in the outcome of his project. The daylight was fading fast; Sean went to wash and change as Andrew made two cups of coffee. He had warmed to Sean and far from his initial, low first impression of him was now surprised at how quickly he'd come to value and appreciate his company. Sean flicked through the phone book and ordered the sand, gravel and cement to be delivered the next day. Andrew tapped his watch indicating that Jess was due home in minutes and Sean replaced the phone book on his way to shower and change. The white Corsa pulled up at the end of the drive and he opened the porch door early enough to enjoy the sound of her stiletto's on the tarmac drive. Jess stepped in and offered up a kiss and a smile.

"I actually like your hair like that!" She stood in front of him and waited. He closed the porch door and when he turned to face her again he saw that she was stood staring at him. He looked at her then to the door that he expected her to have moved through moments ago. Jess looked at him and tilted her head slightly to one side. Suddenly he knew what she wasn't telling him. He dropped to his knees and as she lifted each foot he pulled off her shoes and placed a kiss on each foot on the cool skin just above her toes.

"Well done! We've just discovered another daily ritual!" She told him.

He reached across for her slippers but she had already moved into the lounge and told him to bring them with him. Dropping heavily onto her sofa she lifted her legs to lie flat as he sat at her feet and began his soothing magic.

"I've looked forward to this all day! I hate those shoes but they are a necessary evil I'm afraid!" She told him.

"Why do you wear them if they hurt you?" He enquired already guessing at her reasons.

"Because they give me some much needed height! Even with them stupid shoes I'm the shortest in the bank!" She revealed but Sean's perplexed expression needed more explanation. " . . . If someone has to look down on you to talk, and see you looking up to them it's a psychological fact that they will see you as a child-like. Un-authoritive! They won't receive you as an equal and you're not credited with any air of authority. The same it true in reverse. Tall people are credited with a natural sense of authority especially in the banking world!" She explained.

"I see what you mean! Hence in the bank you maintain that very serious expression!" He submitted. "However you do actually carry authority without try-ing! You have a tremendous sense of presence! I don't see you as childlike because you're short and I do credit you with authority and you get that through your . . . natural charisma!" He spoke as he felt.

"Hmm, but don't forget, you view me most of the time from your knees!" Jess pointed out and continued. "No Sean, them shoes are a nessaccary evil I'm afraid. Nice try but no Goldfish!"

"Shouldn't that be banana?" He asked.

"Shut up!" She snapped back at him wanting some quiet.

"Or Coconut?" He continued; provoking her into taking a swipe at his defiant mouth with her free foot.

"Or cuddly toy!" He persisted but received only her silence as reply.

"If you found that you could exert power over me. Have me as your slave . . . would you?" She asked turning the conversation to a serious one.

"No! I wouldn't!" Sean found the question distasteful.

"Why not?" She pressed him.

"I honestly don't know. My idea for you is to make your life perfect, not con-trolled by anything outside your own wants and desires. I've been telling myself since I first saw you that I'd give anything . . . everything to know exactly who the person was behind those piercing eyes.

Jess let his answer pass into silence and bided her time.

"I love you Sean!" She told him watching closely for his reaction.

He stopped his rubbing of her foot and turned to face her. She looked seri-ously back at him and neither of them knew what was going to happen next.

"Of course you do! What's not to love?" He said smiling and returned to the massage.

Jess smiled to herself, closed her eyes and led her head back on the cushion.

Amber returned home said hello and went straight through to the kitchen. Jess and Sean followed her in for a drink and to find out what was for dinner. Andrew announced that it was to be chicken in a white wine sauce with new potato's and vegetables. They all sat at the bar and drank tea then Sean remembered the stone he wanted to show them. He summoned them all to the conservatory and they peered out at the arrangement of stones. Sean told Amber how much the materials and hire of the mixer cost and she was happy with it. He added that he'd only need the mixer for the foundations, as he'd mix the cement by hand when building the wall due to the slow process of matching the stones.

At dinner they discussed when would be the appropriate time for the Pompeii holiday and settled on the beginning of June. Sean didn't involve himself in that particular discussion; he was the only one of the four of them that was uniquely free. Amber and Jess had their work commitments and Andrew had time schedules for the submission of drawings.

After dinner Sean helped Andrew with the dishes as Jess waited for him in bed. He said goodnight to Amber who was watching the television with a magazine on her lap then vaulted up the stairs two at a time. Jess had one of his books on Pompeii and dropped it to the floor as he entered.

"I want you to do exactly what you did the last time!" She told him as he hurriedly disrobed.

"It'll be my pleasure!" He replied and entered the duvet from the foot of the bed. Her feet rested on his hips and her hands held his head but she said nothing. Her breathing became heavy and she writhed faster and rose higher from the bed still remaining silent. As she approached orgasm in aerie silence her fingernails just made their presence known to him for a few short seconds. She climaxed unexpectedly and in almost total silence but for a few gasps and groans. Sean led between her legs throbbing with his still growing lust for her but she became loose, relaxed and floppy, for now she was finished with him.

"Is that it? Did you actually reach orgasm?" He asked her disappointedly.

"Yes I did what's wrong?" She asked innocently.

"Well where was the passion? Where was the cussing; the verbal abuse? Where was the. . . ." He remembered he wasn't to mention the Demon. "Where was the beastie in you?"

"I have knowledge of the demon in me now and knowledge is power! I no longer have need or want of it!" She explained stroking his spiky head.

"Oh no!" He exclaimed in his best Scottish accent and cupped his hands to his mouth to shout into her vagina.

"Hello Beastie, Will you no come back? Beastie I have a wee juicy bone for you if you only come back!" Jess kicked and pushed him to the bottom of the bed trying hard not to laugh.

"I don't want the Beastie back! The Beastie frightens me I told you that this morning!"

"But the wee Beastie is a part of you! How do I get my jollies if there is no Beastie?" He asked.

"Come here and I'll show you!" She told him beckoning him up the bed.

He led next to her as her hand found his cock. He rolled onto his back and she knelt beside him and pulled at it. Bending lower she kissed it and took it in her mouth. Sean became serious and lost his terrible Scots accent.

"Jess I wasn't hinting . . . ! I can get my jollies in other ways you know that!" For the first time he felt as if he had coerced her and it didn't sit right with him.

Jess halted and told him firmly to shut up. Faced with her determination and knowing that she was performing something she desired he smiled and relaxed onto the bed. She soon became uncomfortable at her position and told him to stand. He stood at the edge of the bed and she sat in front him and placing a hand in the small of his back she drew him into her mouth again. She massaged his testicles with her fingers and drew him in deeper then closed her lips around him. Slowly she drew her head back repeating the operation gradually getting faster. Sean went to hold her head and drew his hands away before they made the forbidden contact. Instead he rested his hands on his head and let out a series of groans as his body twitched with a will of its own. Jess reached her top speed and his hands found work covering his eyes then his mouth then back to his head. They ran down his face and pulled on his earlobes anything to keep them busy and not imply domination of her by holding her head. His shoulders jolted with the ecstasy and finally he put his hands on her shoulders and pulled himself away as he erupted onto her neck and shoulder.

"Wow!" She exclaimed with a smile of discovery.

Sean picked up his shirt and wiped her down then they showered together taking it in turns to lather each other.

He dried her and she got into bed and watched him dry himself before he climbed in next to her.

"Getting back to the Beastie, I think it serves you well! I think that was probably your least of thrilling orgasms! It lacked the intensity of previous orgasms . . . didn't it?" He asked her looking into her eyes.

"Hmm spoken like a true slave with only his mistress's best interests at heart!" She said turning to stare at the ceiling. "True enough! It was a . . . lacklustre climax . . ."

"An anti-climax!" He quickly added.

"Well yes! Now you come to mention it! Maybe I did miss venting my . . . creativity . . . and for future reference it's not a Beastie it's the priestess that takes over me." Jess ran her fingertips up and down his arm as she spoke still staring at the ceiling.

"Then are you going to unleash her again?" He asked expectantly.

"Yes! Now I know I can summon her or banish her at will I could use her again!" Jess climbed on top of him and sat on his chest. "I think she heard us!" Jess said.

With a finger over his lips to prevent him breaking the silence she listened and moved her sloe eyes to the corners. "I think she's on her way right now!" She said as she began to rub herself against his chest. "Okay slave I believe she's just . . . under . . . my . . . skin!" Jess suddenly slapped him across the face.

"Damned impertinent slave! Your place is at my feet!" She slapped him again just as hard then rolled off him and unceremoniously pushed and slapped him down the bed.

"Make me cum!" She took her position on the bed and opened her legs to him.

Sean went straight down on her as her feet rested on his hips and her hands grabbed hold of his head.

"I suppose I've got you to thank for releasing me so soon!" She dug her heels into his sides like kicking a horse into motion. "Well . . . your only reason for being is to serve me!" Jess lowered a leg and slapped his face. She tried to grab hold of his hair but it was no longer long enough for her to get a hold. In her frustration she slapped him again and he increased his range and speed as he applied his tongue to her. "I want to hear from you who you think I am!" She told him but he just carried on licking at her. She slapped him again and repeated herself louder.

"I want you to tell me who you think I am!" She got his attention and he raised his head.

"You're my mistress . . . a priestess of Isis!" He said his piece and she pushed his head back down to her.

"Then don't think you can have this honour without consequence! When you've served me to my full satisfaction I will crush you under foot for knowing me! I know you love me and I'll beat you for it! Do you hear me? I WILL BEAT YOU FOR LOVING ME!"

Outside the bedroom Amber was listening at the door. Holding her hair back with one hand she pressed her ear to the crack of the door. The top stair creaked and Andrew drew up silently behind her. She broke from the door and whispered to him.

"I don't think I should worry about her anymore! She's certainly asserting her authority in there!"

She went back to listening and Andrew left her to it. Amber listened for every sound and clearly heard the slaps and most of what Jess was saying. She shifted her weight from one foot to the other as she listened until she heard Jess cursing him with a whole series of profanities and then silence. She walked quickly to her room and quietly closed the door behind her. Seeing Andrew in the bed she ordered him out to kneel at her feet and remove her slippers.

"I think it's time you showed me some reverence!" She told him as she put her foot on his back.

CHAPTER EIGHT

The next morning at breakfast Jess was at her most tactile. She had Sean move his stool directly next to hers and kept her knee in contact with his leg at all times. Their closeness wasn't lost to Amber and Andrew who exchanged knowing glances. All too soon for Jess it was time for work. Sean followed Jess to the porch door and kneeling at her feet removed her slippers and pushed her stilettos on each waiting foot. Jess kissed him at the door and half way to the car walked back to kiss him again.

Sean dressed for a days work on the wall and went to the garden to sort out the bricks and stone he would use for the foundations. Andrew shouted out of the conservatory door that a delivery lorry had arrived at the front and he went to oversee the delivery. One by one he carried the bags of cement over his shoulder to the dry of the brick shed. The one tonne bags of sand and gravel had to be craned over the hedge onto the gravel front courtyard. Sean took Molly with him to collect his wheelbarrow and trowel and wandered around the silent house collecting his thoughts and ideas as to what to do with it. As Jess had pointed out, whether he let it or sold it, it would have to be redecorated from top to bottom. There was no hurry to get anything done yet as he had a job to do in raising a monument to Jess.

With a few more bricks and boulders gleamed from his garden and rockery he drove back to Amber's and began a dry mix of sand and cement to line the bottom of the trench. Using the hosepipe he ran water into the trench and tipped in the dry mix.

Finally his first phase of the day was completed and he shouted up the stairs that he'd put the kettle on. Andrew appeared in the kitchen as Sean finished making the coffees. Andrew sliced through a French loaf and made some open sandwiches with cream cheese and tomato. They chatted for so long they had a second coffee turning the coffee break into a coffee hour. They were still chatting when the mixer arrived spurring Sean once more into action. He was enjoying every moment of the work and as a fine rain began to fall he hardly noticed it. Eager to get to the stages above ground level he worked on tirelessly through the rain. Ultimately as his clothes soaked up the fine rain droplet's he was forced to call a halt to his labours. Showered and changed he made himself a coffee and sat with Molly in the conservatory listening to the kitchen radio. His frustration that he wasn't outside working on the wall turned to sheer boredom. Andrew was holed up in his office so he decided to utilise his time and pay his parents a visit.

Sitting at his usual spot in the front room he was soon served with a cup of tea and a large slice of homemade coconut and cherry cake. His father was engrossed in his daytime property and antique programs but was drawn in as he told them about his new girlfriend. He was careful not to tell them that he was already living with her and planning to let his house out. His mother was happier for him and paid better attention to his spilling of love struck information about Jess, her job, her outstanding beauty and down to earth personality. Very quickly he ran dry of what he could tell them without activating their over cautious concern for what they would view as his recklessness in matters of the heart. Sean cut his visit short as the time was getting on for five o'clock and he needed to avoid the rush hour traffic and get back home.

At the end of the street he realised that he was at the tail end of the school run and he wasn't making very good headway. It took him twenty-five minutes to reach the main road to town where the cars were already backed up bumper to bumper. Half an hour passed and he'd only managed a third of his journey and was just edging towards the town center. The next two miles were even slower progress but eventually he made it into the old town finally pulling up at Jess's at five-forty five. Not overly concerned about his lateness he bowled into the kitchen from the conservatory and greeted Jess with a big smile and a kiss. To his surprise she remained passive and unmoved.

"Sorry I'm late! I popped round to see my folks and I forgot how bad the traffic is at this time of day!" He explained to a furious looking Jess who rose off her stool and pulled him by the collar through the house and up the stairs to the bedroom. Not knowing how seriously Jess had viewed his lateness he allowed her to lead him by the collar without either complaint or jest.

Once in the bedroom she let go of his collar and moved rapidly to sit at her dressing table. Sitting cross-legged on the floor in front of her Sean waited with his head bowed, staring at the space between her feet.

"Four things . . . Points I'd like clarified! Number one . . . who was it that said they wanted to be mine more than anything? Number two . . . who said that they would be here for me everyday when I finished work? Number three . . . who was told that if they wanted a kiss they would do the kissing? And number four . . . how long ago did they say these things?" She asked him like a schoolmistress to a pupil.

"Um. . . . Me! Me! You! And three days ago!" He bowed his head lower in a show of remorse.

"Correct on all counts! And what should I do with you who so quickly disappoints and disobeys?" She said relinquishing her smile as he looked up to her.

"Oh, beat him! Beat the unruly brigand with the big stick from the garden!" He told her determined to put a humorous almost pythonesque slant on the situation.

"Then go and get the big stick from Andrew!" She told him.

He went down to the conservatory to where he'd seen the stick earlier that day. He walked through the kitchen and glanced at Andrew with a wry smile and raised eyebrows as he passed.

"Here we are . . . one big stick from the gard-on to beat the slave with the hard-on!" He said as he ritually went down on one knee and held it out to her balanced across his open palms.

Jess stood up and swished it twice through the air in a figure of eight.

"Now then prick, shirt off and quick!" She said unconcerned to let him see her smile.

Sean tore his shirt open and the buttons pinged off and flew through the air to collide with and clatter off the wardrobe and chest of drawers. He pulled the shirt off and dropped it to the floor hoping that his feigned acceptance of a caning would outlast hers.

"Take hold of the bed and lower your head!" She instructed him.

He did as he was told moving more slowly as it began to sink in that she may actually go through with it. Jess swished the cane again.

"If you beat this prick will you not be sick?" He reminded her of the first time she'd beaten him and how it made her feel after it was done.

Jess waited but whether it was for a rhyme or the wavering of her willpower, he didn't know. As the seconds ticked by he sensed she might have lost her determination. Then another rhyme occurred to him.

"Who beats me now? High priestess or my sweet Jess,

I know not who or which,

But here I am a hard working man being beaten by my . . . bitch!" He trusted in her knowledge of his sense of humour and looked to smile at her. She smiled back and moved towards him placing the tip of the cane to his shoulder.

"Jess has learned to give what's earned or you can take your leave!

To serve your master you must get home faster and through the traffic must weave!" With that she took position beside him and glancing at the stripes she'd made on his back she wasted no more time.

THWAK! The cane cut through the air and struck across his buttocks. The surprise at her change of target choice made him reel forward across the bed and she waited for him to step back again before she continued. The first strike had stung even through his jeans and he gripped the posts tighter hoping not to receive a second blow.

THWAK! The second blow came to the back of his legs making him exclaim the pain of its sting in one sudden short outburst.

THWAK! The same area was hit again as the pain made him increase his grip on the bedposts.

THWAK! She lowered her aim still further and made his legs buckle and Sean to fall on his knees. He summoned the strength to re-assume his position and his eyes were watering as much as if he were crying uncontrollably. He braced himself for another blow but Jess threw the stick to the floor in his line of sight to let him know it was over.

"Well done! We both needed that clarification! You need to take your promises to me more seriously and treat me at all times with respect and not just when you feel like it! I'm serious about you Sean but I want far more than the norm! I want the Sean who wrote that card!" She told him and sat on the bed as he stiffly moved around the room to sort out another shirt.

They went down to the kitchen together where Andrew was finishing the dinner. He told them that Amber was on a late one and didn't know when she would be home.

Jess went into the dining room alone as Sean walking very gingerly and straight legged helped Andrew bring the plates in. Sitting carefully on the very edge of his chair he was in obvious pain and discomfort but Andrew said nothing. After the ice-cream dessert Andrew cleared the table and left them alone in the dining room. In the uneasy silence Sean slid from his chair and more comfortable on all fours he gave her the most sensuous massage yet. For the first time since they sat down to dinner he'd put a genuinely contented smile on her face and though he couldn't see it he new it was there. He permeated his massage with gentle, slow kisses showing his total love and acceptance of her as a contemplative silence and serene peace enveloped them from all four corners of the room.

Amber returned home and was met at the door by Andrew. Famished she made her way directly to the dining room to receive her dinner and took her position at the head of the table. Andrew dropped a pile of travel brochures on the table and left to re-heat her dinner. Amber slid a brochure to Jess at the opposite end of the table and they both began to browse through them.

"Where's Sean tonight?" Amber asked noticing his absence.

"He's here. Under the table." Jess answered not lifting her eyes from her reading.

Amber couldn't resist checking. She was ever more impressed at the depth in which they were both taking their roles beyond anything she expected of Andrew. Sean was more of a slave in a far shorter time than she had ever thought possible and put her brochure to one side.

Jess looked under the table and told Sean that they were retiring to the lounge and took another brochure with her. She settled on her sofa but Sean's beaten backside and legs denied him the comfort of sitting so he visited Molly in the conservatory. Sometime later he was called back into the lounge. He stood beside Jess on the sofa and waited to find out what Amber had to say.

"I'm going riding at the weekend and wondered if you and Sean would like to come too?" She addressed Jess and watched for her anticipated happy reaction.

She wasn't disappointed and in her excitement Jess smacked Sean on the backside and sent him into sudden and reeling agony. Amber looked puzzled at his seemingly over-reaction to such a mild slap.

"Have I missed something?" She enquired.

"Not really! I forgot that I've just given him a whipping there . . . for getting home late . . . amongst other things!" Jess told her and rubbed Sean's arm to show her renewed affection.

Sean was at a loss as to why Jess would be so excited to visit a farm but reasoned it away to her love of horses. Everyone apart from Sean was comfortably seated and he asked Jess if it was all right that he went to lie on the bed. Jess was obliging to his request and informed him that she would be joining him shortly.

Amber made the plans for the coming Saturday and stated that there would be an early start and as they were all going they would need to take both cars. Whilst she and Jess rode out Andrew could take Sean on a tour of the grounds and development site. Should Rebecca be available they would possibly pay her a visit and introduce Sean to her as Jess's 'long-term' boyfriend. On no account should they let it be known that Sean was only days into his initiation. Jess was on the edge of her seat and listened to Amber with growing excitement.

She entered the bedroom and saw Sean lying face down on the bed in just his boxers. She could see three of the four fresh marks she'd just inflicted on him and the three fading stripes on his back. Jess turned her eyes away. Her intention had been to make the punishment a less traumatic event but she now realised that she'd actually caused him far more pain and discomfort. He was fast asleep and she passed over him sliding her legs under the covers and turning to lie on her side to watch him sleeping.

CHAPTER NINE

The sound of keys clattering and a heavy metal mechanism sliding and clanging into position resonated out as the small blue door creaked open to the side of the huge metal clad gateway. Two men emerged from within the first of which was short, stocky and balding his short spiky, grey hair put him in his mid fifties. Dressed in jeans and a brown bomber jacket he waited for the next man to walk ahead of him. This man was tall, towering over the older man. Somewhere in his early to mid thirties he had a full head of light brown curly hair and glasses. As he walked he fumbled around in his jacket pocket for his keys and walked at a pace that made the older man hurry along in his wake. They walked through the predominantly empty car park with a nine-foot high fence and came to a halt at a dark blue Volvo estate. The short man waited as the tall man cleared the front passenger seat of his soft leather briefcase and broadsheet newspaper. He took a last look over his shoulder at his place of incarceration and sat in. They were in motion as soon as the engine started performing a fast U turn and accelerating to the manned barrier as Tom struggled to clip his seatbelt on. Travelling at speed along the motorway he stretched to the back seat for the newspaper and flicked its pages to the sports section. Paul became irritated and snapped at Tom to fold the damned thing and not have it obscure his view. Several times Tom commented on the sports news but Paul refused to be drawn into any sporting conversation and switched the radio on turning the volume up loud.

Driving into town Paul chose silence over the radio and finally broke his silence to point out the police station and other landmarks. He pulled into a one-way street and almost immediately down a narrow drive at the side of a large white house. He parked up in the gravel car park at the rear of the property in front a high wire mesh fence overgrown with brambles and ivy making it sag exhaustedly from its burdens. Paul opened the boot of the car and Tom pulled out two bin liners and a bulging holdall of clothes. Paul explained to him that he front door wasn't in use so they entered through the rear door beneath the zigzagging metal fire escape. They walked by a line of two fire extinguishers, a red bucket of sand and an encased fire blanket. Next there was an ancient payphone heavily graphitised and a table piled high with unopened letters and junk mail. They climbed the Victorian staircase to the third floor where Paul unlocked the door to the number six bed-sit and pointed out the toilet and shower room doors before entering. Inside the room was a single bed, portable television on a flimsy looking table, bed settee and a frayed armchair. The kitchen area was fitted functionally with a cooker, a fridge and a sink unit. The window was situated too high for Tom to see anything but the grey sky so he turned his attention to the cupboards and scrutinised the crockery and utensils therein. Paul sat on the arm of the sofa bed and pawed through some papers leaving the relevant sheets on the seat next to him.

Tom put his signature to the dotted lines and listened as Paul reiterated what was expected of him during his time in the house. He zipped up his briefcase and handed Tom two keys on a large blue, plastic fob with the house and room number marked on it in black felt-tip.

Alone in his room he put his clothes away and made a mental note of what he needed to buy. He left the house and walked into the town to draw out some money from a cash-point and visited every charity shop he came across. Equipped with a corkscrew, tin opener, tiny black, plastic battery operated alarm clock a chopping board and a small watercolour picture of four children playing on a beach he began his food shopping at the nearest supermarket.

With two full carrier bags of food and his blue charity shop bag he sought out the high street department stores and took every free magazine and catalogue with him. He arrived back at his door and stepped inside to put away his shopping and plug in the fridge that burbled and whirred into life. He made himself his first cup of coffee and with a packet of custard creams beside him he watched the television and stretched his short legs out.

Light faded to dark and Tom switched the single light on and made himself a meal returning to watch the television and eat his dinner from his lap. He opened a bottle of white wine and poured it into a mug almost filling it to the brim. Drinking the wine as if it was beer he soon finished the bottle and rolled his third cigarette using his empty tea mug as an ashtray. Turning the television off he sat on the bed with his free magazines and thumbed through each of them in turn until he became sleepy.

In the morning he woke up cold having only a single blanket and a thin throw to cover him. After a warming coffee and still in the clothes he'd slept in he made the short walk into the town center to acquire more essentials. He returned with a duvet and pillow amongst other things and found a folded sheet of A4 paper pushed under the door. It read that Paul had called and wanted him to make contact as soon as possible. Tom went to the payphone and called him at his office. As Paul spoke Tom's head lowered and keeping the phone to his ear he rubbed his forehead over and over again. He thanked Paul for the information and carefully put the receiver down. Instead of returning up the three flights of stairs he checked he had pocketed his wallet and made for the town again. He was in no hurry, he sauntered along, his eyes cast down to the ground unless he was about to cross a road, once over his eyes would lower their projection again and notice every crack in the paving stones, every patch of chewing gum and cigarette butt on route.

He returned home over an hour later with a carrier bag bulging and stretched dangerously close to breaking point with wine and beer. He kept the quarter size bottle of whiskey safe in his inside pocket. Once through the rear door he opened a can of beer and drank deeply from it. He traipsed up the stairs stopping on every landing to drink from his tin. Inside his room he drained his first tin and opened the wine; again pouring it into the mug and drank from it until empty. He repeated the sequence until the contents were consumed whereupon he opened another tin of beer. With the bag of booze beside him he sat in his chair and watched the television with the volume turned up blaringly loud. Another tin emptied he hurled it in the direction of the sink and opened another. Chain smoking and drinking heavily he stared into the television unable to concentrate on the programs but needing its company.

Venturing out to the landing he violently flung the door open making it impact with a bang on the wall before staggering through it. Standing over the toilet he chose to urinate on the floor either side of the bowl rather than into it. Back in his room he opened his preferred magazine and took it to flick through its pages on the bed.

A loud noise of a door being slammed stirred him and hunger ensured that he rose from the bed to feed. It had grown dark as he slept so he switched the light and the television on before preparing his sausage and egg sandwiches. He changed the channel when the local news came on and settled to watch an early evening quiz show. Some loud music started up thumping its repetitive bass through the floorboards from the room below. Tom simply turned the volume of the television up and sat back down to his coffee and cigarettes.

The music went on until nine-thirty when the slamming of a door announced an end to the vibrating floorboards allowing him to turn his blaring television down. Tom made his plans to return to work and find himself a job on the buildings as soon as possible. He'd noticed many development sites as they'd driven off the motorway and new it wouldn't be long before he was operating a J.C.B or dumper truck and bringing in good money.

The next morning he found an employment agency displaying several billboards asking for drivers and experienced heavy plant operatives. He completed the application form and after a short interview with a pretty young blonde woman he was told he could start the very next day at eight. Tom was delighted with the job offer and the hourly rate but his site was on the very outskirts of the town and not yet served by public transport. Walking to work wasn't an option he had to get himself some motorised transport and his bank balance wouldn't stretch to a car plus the insurance so he browsed through the local paper and arranged to see a moped for sale at the bargain price of £200. On viewing the vehicle he beat the seller down to £175 and had a helmet thrown in with the deal. The insurance cost ran up his total expenditure to £259 exactly and he rode his yellow moped around the town sporting his blue open face helmet with its flimsy plastic visor. Checking out his route to work he pulled onto the dual carriageway and hit his top speed of thirty-three miles per hour. Taking his contraption down the muddy works access roads he found his site and stopped to roll a cigarette. The site was huge with houses and apartment blocks in all stages of development. He finished his cigarette, pressed the engine start button and pulled back on the throttle to perform a U-turn on the wet muddy road. Unused to a life on two wheels he only managed to get half way through his turn when the front wheel slid out and sent him crashing to the ground. He checked himself over with no apparent injuries but that to his pride. Covered down one side in wet clay and mud he lifted the bike upright and checked it over. One wing mirror was cracked and his front left indicator was hanging on by its wires with its engine still running he re-embarked and pulled away heading for home.

Paul received his phone call just as he was leaving his office and jotted down on an envelope his place and hours of work along with his moped type and registration number. He thanked Tom for the information and replaced the receiver and exited the office throwing his keys in the air whistling a happy tune.

Tom went upstairs and opened a tin of beer before undressing and running his jeans under the tap to wash off the mud. He took his biggest saucepan and made himself a basic pasta in tomato sauce. With slices of cheese turned into the mix he put the saucepan on a magazine and ate it on his lap straight from the pan.

His first day at work went well, he got along with the site foreman exceedingly well and at break times joked along with his comrades, the conversation and banter flowing so well that he'd not managed to even open his tabloid newspaper. The natural inquisitiveness from his colleagues caused him to lie time and time again. Well prepared with a cover story why he, a west-countryman from a town with it's own extensive development program should take the trouble to up sticks and move a hundred miles he laid the blame squarely on a messy divorce. Using humour and clichés he dodged a great many searching questions. Dismissive of the blatantly more probing questions as if they were too painful to think on he soon had his inquisitors firmly on his side and feeling sorry for him.

CHAPTER TEN

Sean and Jess made their appearance in the kitchen shortly after six in the morning. Even the long hot shower hadn't fully revived him from his few hours' sleep and a succession of yawns dogged him into his second coffee. His eyes fully opened only when Jess returned to the kitchen dressed in her white jodhpurs and riding boots. The boots were dusty and greyed so she asked Sean to get a wet towel and give them a wipe-over. He performed his task keenly bringing back the almost reflective blackness to them in no time. Amber wouldn't be travelling at a land rovers pace and Jess, on her few visits to the farm had always slept through the journey so Andrew had thought ahead and prepared Sean a basic route map of the journey. On Amber's word breakfast was over and there was a flurry of activity and military-like urgency until they embarked for the journey. Pulling into the main street Amber accelerated into the distant grey early morning as if Sean in his land rover was stationary. Jess was too tired to show any great enthusiasm especially for the first leg of the journey and settled into her seat to look out the passenger side window and let her mind drift into an impatient slumber.

Driving east under a blanket of dense grey clouds towards a narrow band of blue sky the scenery took on the most English of forms. The countryside became equally divided between undulating green fields and woodlands. Bathed in the sudden brightness Jess lifted her head and rubbed her neck. They passed through the last village marked on the map and into more arable land of vast ploughed grey fields. Sean slowed as he passed the building site and turned off the old roman road onto a single-track country lane. After around half a mile of the high-hedged lane they turned off and entered the tree-lined avenue speeding to the brow of the hill. The view from the summit was illuminated by the golden morning sunshine and the clouds they'd driven under were just a narrow band of grey in the furthest distance. Paddocks and meadows surrounded the farm with two lines of off white gallops leading up to the ridge of the high chalk hill.

Sean pulled up next to Amber's Audi on the well kempt gravel car park. Walking behind Jess and carrying the holdall in one hand and holding Molly's lead in the other they marched by the red brick stables and into the high walled courtyard of the farm. It was the neatest, tidiest farm he had ever seen. From the finely raked car park to the inner courtyard of the farm there was nothing left discarded or abandoned. Even the grass that grew around the base of the posts and walls was trimmed to the uniform height of just a couple of inches. Sean followed Jess to the first outbuilding inside the courtyard; its slate roof ran down from the perimeter wall where it met a glass frontage. Four shallow steps led to a glass door and he followed her inside and unclipped Molly's lead. The building was a peculiar mix of old and new. Beyond the glass frontage were the rustic oak beams of the ceiling and red brick and grey stonewalls. The counter and display units were new and spotlessly clean, the tables and chairs were of aluminium and set in a sea of blue floor tiles. Jess chose a table by the door where they waited and watched through the glass at the activity in the farm units opposite. A tall thickly built man in his early twenties dressed in black trousers and a brilliant white shirt approached their table and asked if he could get them anything. Jess ordered two cappuccinos and he returned to the counter. The glass door opened and a troop of five women dressed in white jodhpurs and black jackets entered the cafeteria. Their loud conversations reduced in volume, slowed and even paused as they each took the time to observe Jess and Sean. Ranging in ages from around nineteen to the eldest, probably in her mid-thirties they took their trays of cakes and coffees to the next table but one from Jess and Sean. One of the women whistled for Molly to come over so she could make a fuss of her but Molly played ignorant and settled down beside Sean as the coffee arrived. He watched as two middle-aged men also dressed in black trousers and white shirts walked by the window one of which was pushing a wheelbarrow laden with gardening tools. Coming from the direction of the farmhouse Sean saw that Andrew, Amber and another woman were walking towards them. Amber and the mystery woman were both dressed in their in riding gear of black and white.

"Does everyone here wear black and white?" He asked Jess aware that he was the only person he'd seen not wearing black and white but in very conspicuous blue jeans and sweatshirt with a dark red 'V' neck jumper.

"No I don't think so! I know the men who work here do as a kind of uniformity thing and I suppose the riding gear's traditionally black and white too but I don't think it's a written law!" She told him.

"Well at least Molly's the right colours even if I'm not!" He remarked.

Andrew entered the café first and held the door for Amber and her friend. As they approached the table Sean followed by Jess courteously stood to receive them.

"Rebecca this is my little sister Jess and her man Sean!" Amber introduced them as Andrew fetched another chair for himself.

Rebecca was as pretty as she was tall and slender. Her light brown slightly wavy hair was pulled back and netted into a bun low enough for her to wear a riding helmet. A few flecks of grey hair added some years to her youthful complexion, which bore no signs of make-up of any kind. The noisy chatter from the table of five dramatically reduced in volume as Rebecca ordered three more coffees from the male attendant.

"It's always nice to meet new people. Amber has told me a lot about you both and you are very welcome." She said addressing them both but looking mostly to Jess.

"I believe that Andrew is going to show Sean around and we are going for a little ride!" She spoke directly to Jess then focussed on Sean as she listened to Jess's short reply.

As Andrew knocked back the last of his coffee he waited for a lull in the conversation and announced that he was ready to take Sean on his tour. Sean clipped Molly's lead on and looked across to Jess who offered him a gentle wave goodbye.

With the men absent Rebecca asked Jess to tell her more about her man. Jess knew what she wanted to hear and smiled knowing that she could supply the perfect report. With the one question Jess readily told her of the pride she had in him informing her in detail how he'd get tongue-tied and nervous attending her counter. His total obedience in all things including taking her wrath without so much as a look of protestation in his eyes. His artistic streak, love of nature and capabilities in everything with the exception of home decoration all spilled out as if she was a mother talking proudly about a son. She told her of the valentine card and the poem he'd written revealing his want of becoming her slave and ultimately of his response to Andrew's little test.

"I know he's still rough around the edges but that's just another part of him! His heart is where it should be and I've never been surer of anyone. I'm not wrong to trust in him!" She summarised.

Rebecca smiled and told her that she was most welcome into the fold and as Amber's sister she had high hopes for her rapid advance in the fledgling society. They left the café and headed for the stables as Rebecca told her that they would first take her to the almost completed village development then they would head along the Ridgeway returning to the farm via the lake.

"I envisage us getting back to basics with no need of heavy farm equipment! We already have a multitude of members working traditionally in the fields and grounds and soon we'll be starting on the health club!" She informed her.

Andrew led Sean around the courtyard showing him the work units some of which were hired out to small businesses all of which were connected in no small way to the society. There was a stained glass window maker next to a pottery and a veterinarian's office. Opposite the café was another large unit that made rustic garden furnishings. Andrew stopped to speak to the two workers in the next unit that welded old and new pieces of metal together into some weird and wonderful artistic shapes of futuristic, robotic looking creatures. Here were the first people to be found not wearing black and white but blue and brown boiler suits. Sean believed he recognised the man in brown by his peroxide blonde hair. The more he looked at him the more certain he became convinced that he was the biker from the pub who'd launched the attack on the seated man. They both stopped what they were doing and the one in blue lifted off her welding mask to reveal a hazel haired young woman with a band of freckles adorning her pale skinned face. She walked over to greet them and Sean saw that she had the most intense green eyes. She led them into the unit and up to the work in progress that Andrew had commissioned from her. It appeared to be of an angel in armour with one arm raised above its head as it flew looking down from the heavens. It set Sean's mind straight back to the fright he'd had on the early morning walk along the old railway track. It was exactly how he'd imagined God's avenging angel with only its sword missing. Andrew viewed it with an unguarded expression of sheer joy. He explored the lines of the figure with his hands and told them he looked forward to its completion. They stepped away from the sculpture leaving Sean still stood staring at it. They stopped at the entrance to the unit and all three stared back at Sean. Sean snapped out of his trancelike state and turned to rejoin them. As he and Andrew walked off Sean couldn't resist stopping and returning to ask the girl if the figure would be holding something.

"Yes. Yeah, she'll be wielding a flaming sword." She told him and smiling at the possible miss-interpretation of her words left it to him to find out how she'd meant it in good time. Her reply made a chill run through him and he turned to catch up with the waiting Andrew.

They left the courtyard through an iron gate in a small hidden archway and across an untidy lawn with bare patches of soil to a large grey ironclad warehouse. They entered through a small door in the corner and Andrew flicked the switches for light. It was a shooting gallery the cold stale air was thick with the smell of cordite. Paper targets of a silhouetted human figure hung on lines of wire all perforated with dozens of holes.

"This is the shooting range. There's a gun club here that shoots everything from air rifles to Kalashnikovs! We also do a lot of clay pigeon shooting and archery. Are you interested in guns?" He asked him.

"Yes I've always been interested in guns! I've had a fair few air rifles and pistols in my time!" Sean revealed.

"Ever kill anything?" He questioned him further.

"Unfortunately yes! As a boy I used to go out with friends and shoot rabbits, pheasants, birds anything that moved. I don't know how I could've been so cruel. . . . Dishing out death isn't fun and I think that by the time I was fourteen I'd stopped killing things and changed to tin targets." Sean told him.

Andrew remained silent so Sean asked him about his relationship with guns.

"I was in the army around the same time you were shooting your air rifles! I too don't hold with killing but there are times when its nessaccary! They say that guns make killing easier but I don't agree." Andrew turned around ready to leave and promised Sean a session on the range one day.

He took him beyond the rifle range and the huge hay barns to the allotments where several men were digging over the soil and another man tended a bonfire. These men weren't in black and white but none the less were all wearing the same brown trousers and grey fleeces. At the far edge of the allotments were eight white mobile homes set against a tree-lined hedgerow. Behind the farmhouse were three long greenhouses nestling on a green slope that ran down to a lake.

"That's probably Amber and Jess up there!" Andrew pointed out the silhouettes of three riders on the hilltop moving away from them.

They walked on through fields where a number of horses and ponies grazed then over a wide wooden bridge across the slow moving river. Molly descended the embankment only to find the river too deep to cross and lapped up some of its water before returning to cross by the dry option. They climbed to the top of the hill where Andrew pointed out the building site and told him that Rebecca had sold off some of her land for development, the nearest site was hers. She was building a walled off village around her site of what would be twenty-eight homes only available to society members. A further development was planned to make more residences in the vicinity of the farm itself but they would either be for leading members or the very well off. They walked along the ridge of the hill away from the farm to a spot where Andrew sat to take in the view.

"That's a nice sight! Not a road or a solitary building in sight! Just undulating fields and woods!" Sean noted aloud.

"Actually there's a manor house just the other side of the woods, you can just make out its chimneys. See?" Andrew pointed it out. "That's where Rebecca lives." Andrew paused then asked him. "So what do you think of our little place so far?"

"Well, it's idyllic, well kept and seems to be very relaxed and laid back. Its full of very beautiful people too I've noticed. . . . It's like Baywatch with jodhpurs!" Sean told him.

Andrew cringed at his comment and told him straight that he was glad that he'd made that comment now with only him to hear it.

"Sean! We do have a sense of humour but that's just the sort of comment that wouldn't go down at all well with Rebecca. Amber and Jess too for that matter. For God's sake don't make light of what you see here and if possible show Jess even more respect here than you do at home!" Andrew slapped him hard on the back and shuddered at the thought of Sean making that comment in Rebecca's company.

Soon the three riders appeared again in the distance. Andrew and Sean watched them approach until they could clearly see that it was certainly Amber and Jess. Andrew told Sean to stay close to him then suddenly turned and bolted along the ridge towards the farm.

"COME ON!" He shouted to Sean who remained standing watching him run and wondering why.

Sean turned back to see the riders galloping towards him. He guessed it was to be a race to get back to the farm before them and took to his heels some distance behind Andrew.

They ran at full pelt along the ridge then down the hill to the fields, the sound of horse's hooves pounding the hollow sounding chalk and rebel yells growing gradually louder. Sean began to catch up with Andrew as they hurtled down the hill until his legs could no longer keep up with his rate of descent. Head over heels Sean took a tumble seeing only grass then Molly then sky. Grass, Molly, sky over and over again until he managed to halt his fall and get to his feet and resume his run. Andrew heard the whooshing of Sean's approach in the long grass as he drew nearer. Laughing so hard that he had to bend double and only stagger onwards he allowed Sean to pass him.

"Run Forest! Run!" Andrew shouted through his debilitating laughter. One look over his shoulder told him that the riders were gaining on them fast and summoning all his reserve energies Andrew increased his speed and called out to Sean to bare right towards a gap in the hedgerow and another bridge over the river. With just one more field to go they ran towards the farm. The sound of the horse's hooves grew louder and louder like the rumbling of thunder. In seconds Andrew felt the cold leather tip of Ambers riding crop on his neck. He ceased his run and dropped to the ground exhausted. Rebecca and Jess rode by him still in pursuit of Sean. Andrew sat up to watch as Rebecca bore down on Sean until he sharply changed his direction and gained some crucial distance. Running towards the hedge hoping for another way through he thought he might make it until Jess increased her speed on the flat and sandwiched him between her and the dense hedgerow. She drew up next to him and leaning out of the saddle she touched her whip to his shoulder. Sean fell to the ground gasping for huge quantities of air and with a pained expression looked up at his mounted assailant smiling in her victory. Molly kept her distance from the horse but wouldn't leave her master to his fate without a fight that she hoped wouldn't come. Jess dismounted and walked slowly toward the recovering Sean tapping her whip to the open palm of her hand. Standing over him she struck out three glancing blows to his upper arms with her whip.

Sean called out an 'Ouch' to each blow then protected his upper arms with his hands as he began to laugh.

"Run from me will you? Make a bid. . . ." She struck him again " . . . to be free of me?" Jess put a foot on his heaving chest and forced him to lie flat. "I think we've just proved that to run from me is futile. You're my property and I will beat out of you your need of anything other than me! Is that understood?" She said looking down on him with a contemptuous sneer and a look of disgust.

"I'm yours . . . I know. . . . Why I ran . . . I don't know, I have no desire . . . to be free of you." He submitted forming his words between deep breaths.

"The fact that you can even contemplate the words 'being free of me' tells me that you still have a very long way to go before you become what it is I require." She argued. "You are no more than furniture to me and now you shall be my mounting block." She told him and removed her foot from his chest. Keeping the tip of her whip to his chin she allowed him to cautiously rise to his knees.

"Have I your word you shall not run again?" She demanded to hear.

"No, I shall never run . . . from you again!" He submitted.

"Kneel here!" She told him pointing to the ground beside her horse.

Sean shuffled over to the horse and crouched down as she balanced carefree on his back to remount. Rebecca and Amber ambled closer and watched the unfolding scene with captivated interest.

"Your sister is a natural! I think we should be learning from her!" She commented impressed beyond her words.

"It's fifty-fifty with them two, they compliment each other almost too well!" Amber replied and kicked her horse into an about turn.

The riders went on to the stables leaving the men to make their way back in their own time. Andrew waited for Sean to reach him and they walked back to the café as Molly took the opportunity to investigate the last remaining thicket. They reached the secret entrance to the courtyard when Andrew suddenly stepped back and held his arm out guiding Sean aside allowing two young women and an older man to pass through first. The women were dressed in what looked to be Israeli army uniform, dark green combat jackets and trousers and eighteen holed soft black leather boots. They each carried a heavy-duty medium brown holdall undoubtedly containing some weighty and formidable firearms. Their male escort wore the regulation black trousers and white shirt but also wore a grey felt fleece with a zip front. Sean watched as the man ran in front of the women to open the door of the shooting gallery and stand by as they entered first. Sean turned to catch up with Andrew who had met with the girls outside the café. As he joined them two more women in riding attire slipped by them and entered the café. Rebecca asked Sean his thoughts on the farm. He glanced at Andrew and gave him a wry smile.

"It's a wonderful place! It's beautiful, inspiring . . . a very nice place to be!" He commented.

"I'm happy that you like it, you'll be a welcome addition to our number I'm sure! Now lets have a drink and a bite to eat shall we?" She motioned Andrew to lead the way inside. They settled down to a table and unloaded their trays passing them to the ever-attentive Andrew who returned them to the edge of the counter. Rebecca poured the tea and opened the conversation.

"We are desperate for people of your calibre to be here and help out. If you can offer any form of intensive labour I can supply you with excellent accommodation here at the farm!" Rebecca looked at Jess expecting her answer to be obliging.

"I'd love to be here with Sean and help out but we can't currently afford the time! I have my work and Sean has a project ongoing in our garden AND he's writing his first novel! We can spend weekends here and Sean can work wherever you think he's most needed but beyond that . . . for now at least, we can't live here no matter how much I'd love to!" Jess explained.

Rebecca acknowledged Jess's commitments but was adamant she would get them more involved.

"Whatever you earn at the bank I will match it and throw in your accommodation for free. Maybe Sean's project in the garden could be done at the weekends and you could spend your weekdays here? Amber's due to move in to the farmhouse soon anyway. She's going to take over the running of the farm, allowing me to concentrate on other matters. Its all systems go and I'd like you on board and here to support Amber and myself in the running of things!" Rebecca realised too late that she'd divulged a little too much information. "Maybe we should continue this conversation privately in the house!" She added.

Entering the house through the porch door they were in the large kitchen with its ancient and worn flagstone floor, hugely long rustic dining table of dark oak and gleaming black auger. Rebecca led them into the first reception room where they sat and waited for Rebecca to resume her persuasion of Jess to make the leap of faith.

"My head is full of ideas that I want desperately to implement! I have several new projects on the go and all connected to the same goal but I need people I like and trust to make my ideas a reality whilst I move on to the next big thing! Amber is primed to take on the mantle of running the farm whilst holding down her job in the police force! Maybe I've put you on the spot and should have let Amber talk to you about this first but I asked her to keep quiet about the new arrangements until I was certain that this was the direction to take. Anyway here we are and if you prefer I am quite willing to call my lawyer and have him draught the nessaccary contracts now . . . if you like?"

Jess declined Rebecca's offer of calling her lawyer and Rebecca decided to leave them alone to discuss her proposal amongst themselves informing them that she'd be back in an hour or so.

Andrew moved over to the fireplace to poke and probe the fire back to life.

"There really is no one else to take it on and it's something I really believe in so I told her I'd do it. After all it was Rebecca and myself that started this monster. It would help me out tremendously if you could be here for me and don't forget . . . you won't be losing out financially. If anything you'll be even better off!" Amber went to look out of the window at the paddocks. "Come on I'll show you where you could be living!"

Jess followed her out of the room and called for Sean to attend also. They walked through the kitchen as Amber opened a wooden door revealing a secret staircase. Up the creaking stairs there was a small landing with three doors. The first door led to a bathroom and toilet, the second to an empty room with two small leaded windows, the third to a spacious elongated bedroom with a small window in each of the three walls.

"We'll be sharing the kitchen of course and you'll have the run of the rest of the house too but this will be your private quarters!" Amber told her.

The idea began to work on Jess as she rubbed Sean's arm and showed him a smiling, happy face.

"What do you think Sean?" She asked.

"I'm happy to be anywhere with you and this certainly is a beautiful place to live!" He replied.

"Since we launched the website we've grown at an unprecedented rate and we're now in the position where we have to apply the brakes, there's just too much to do. The money is rolling in and people are chomping at the bit to get involved. As soon as we can we are going to do an open day and that's going to take an awful lot of organisation and preparation so . . . can I rely on you both to muck in and help out?"

Jess agreed and Amber led them to the office room underneath their living quarters calling out to Andrew to join them on the way. He walked in behind them and stood behind Amber at the computer. She summoned up the website and let Jess sit down to read it with Sean reading over her shoulder. Under the heading of Feminine Rights, The Cult of the Her was a colour picture of a suited woman sitting on a throne-like chair resting her bare feet on a man led on the ground. Jess pressed print and waited.

Sitting at the kitchen table with Andrew preparing a pot of tea Jess read through the sheets passing each in turn to Sean. Amber remained silent allowing them to concentrate on the material in hand. Finally Jess handed Sean the fourth sheet and turned straight faced to Amber.

"It's terrible! Hotch-potch! It comes across as some strange mix of an introduction agency for bored rich women to meet submissive males and a fetishist's dirty weekend at a health farm! The whole thing comes across as some tacky effort to obtain money from the sad the lonely and the desperate!" Jess told her dismissively, almost angrily.

"I completely agree! It certainly needs work but that said it has opened the floodgates and we simply can't cope with the response its provoked. It's all the work of Tracy who you'll probably meet later on. Anyway at this level the farm serves two main purposes. One, it's a huge source of income, we are asking an annual membership fee of fourteen hundred pounds for women and two thousand four hundred for men. And two, there is something to be learned from every man that has the desire to serve and every woman with the need to dominate!" Amber went on to explain. "There's four of us on the board, Tracy and Poy being the two you haven't met yet. We have a small army of members who we found through Tracy mostly and we need to get the accommodation sorted and the rule book written ready to start admitting new members."

"How many hopefuls have you?" Jess asked.

"It's over six hundred and the website has only been running for six weeks!" She replied.

"That's . . . over a million pounds per annum! No wonder Rebecca can afford to match my wage!" Jess thought for a moment. "Okay we're here to help! I have just one question . . . if I didn't have Sean would you still want me so much involved?" Jess submitted.

"Yes, I need you! You're going to be of vital importance helping me, if not running the farm yourself. "Tracy and Poy are great but they have their limitations!" Amber insisted.

Andrew shook Sean's hand and welcomed him aboard as Rebecca returned having gone home to change into jeans and a thick white pullover. Amber wasted no time and gladly announced that Jess was fully on board.

"Oh that's great! That is good news! You can move in whenever is convenient to you, the sooner the better! Now we should meet some of the crew?" She said and produced her mobile. She made two calls summoning the recipients to the house a.s.a.p. They followed her into the second and grandest reception room where Rebecca commented that from now on Sean should wear the black and white of the farm.

"It's not just a uniform! It's a state of mind! She insisted.

The door opened and there appeared a very petite Chinese woman dressed from head to toe in black. She addressed someone stood behind her and entered the room alone. Rebecca introduced her as Poy, her sergeant in charge of security at the farm. She walked confidently across the room to Jess and shook her hand. She glanced at Sean who'd left it a little late to stand and instead turned directly to shake the hand of Amber. Andrew signalled Sean to come with him to the kitchen and joined the man that had arrived with Poy. He was a short young man barely in his twenties with short curly brown hair. Andrew greeted him affectionately and only received a short-lived, forced smile for his efforts at making him welcome. He introduced him to Sean as Robert who limply shook his hand and resumed his excluding, folded arm stance leaning back on the wooden drawer unit staring blankly down at the floor.

Sean had no time for him and closely followed by Molly he wandered out into the courtyard. Moments later he was joined by Andrew who sauntered out to join him. He knew that Sean had taken an instant dislike for Robert and wanted to divulge some nessacary information to him.

"She beats him Sean! She used him last night as a demonstration dummy in her martial arts classes and he's suffering from a bad case of Karate!" He explained and defused Sean's distaste.

A cyclist drew up to them on a mud splattered mountain bike and dismounted leaning her bike under the kitchen window. Panting heavily she bent double and held her shins like an exhausted Olympic runner. She wore dark glasses, an all in one black and blue lycra suit and matching helmet. She appeared to be in her mid twenties with long light brown hair tied back and trailing halfway down her back. She said a quick Hi to Andrew as she passed and disappeared inside. Sean watched through the window as she called Robert to attend her and remove her muddy trainers before she entered the lounges. Sean didn't have to ask who she was before Andrew told him that she was the one who'd designed the website. She was Tracy and besides earning herself the label of nymphomaniac she had a reputation for being quick tempered and as a hyperactive extravert. She had a partner called Roger but liked to entertain the clientele and was the reason why so many of them had joined up already. She like Poy lived in a mobile home at the farm and was the third female founding member of the society. She had introduced Poy as the fourth member and was the driving force in bringing the society forward at breakneck speed with her incredible energy and enthusiasm.

Together they rejoined Robert in the kitchen who was now slumped at the table his head buried in his arms. Andrew had a text message and on opening it, it simply read . . . Tea! He primed the stainless steel tea-pot and busied himself finding the best cups and saucers. The clattering of the crockery brought Roberts head up from hiding in the hope of a libation. Sean waited for Andrew to disappear into the lounge with the tea before refilling the kettle and prepping three mugs for coffee.

The light faded as they waited and Andrew experimented with the array of light switches to get the required level of illumination. Before he got back to his seat Amber and Jess entered and were finally ready to go home. Andrew returned to the main lounge and retrieved the tea tray leaving it on the table in front of Robert. A couple of slaps on the shoulder told him that it was for him to complete the clearing up. They filed out led by Amber and Jess holding her riding boots handed them to Sean then with her hands around his neck jumped onto his back to be carried to the car.

Amber revved her car and turning in a wide arc sped through the car park throwing up a hail of gravel behind her and motoring down the avenue.

Jess was eager to lay down the plans to move in to the farm. She'd give her notice at the bank on the Monday morning and make a list of things they needed to buy. Sean said that he'd see about letting his house out through an agency the same day. He'd take most of the furniture to the tip and give the entire house a coat of magnolia. Whilst Jess worked her notice he would split his time between completing Amber's wall and redecorating his house.

Nearer home it had been raining. The roads were drying out but tell tale puddles said that they had missed some heavy downpours. Andrew opened the door as Jess walked in just her socks leaving Sean to bring the holdall and her boots back inside.

Entering the lounge Amber came in from the kitchen carrying a bottle of Champaign. With Andrew at her side holding a tray of glasses she popped the cork and directed the fast flowing foam to the glasses.

"To Jess and Sean! To welcome them to the farm and THE CULT OF THE HER!" Amber announced.

Jess pulled a pained expression. "That name has to be re-thought!" She said before accepting the toast.

"Oh I don't think Rebecca will be willing to change that. It stems from something she believes to be a fundamental truth about what we believe. Scholars believe that the first God to be worshipped on earth was Female. She was named Ur and she's been in the human psyche ever since. We unknowingly retain links with Ur to this day and from her name we derived the words Earth, Mother, Sister, Daughter, Girl and, of course Her. It was in these islands at the edge of the ancient world that her name survived, hidden in the English language! The chanting of her name causes the required vibration to bring this world into harmony with the other dimensions. So you see that in the time of Ur women were revered and highly respected. Only when man turned his back on nature in favour of his own corrupt purposes did Ur lose favour. Farming began and rather than living in harmony with nature man exploited it and found other good things to exploit too! He became greedy and selfish and wanted more and more until everything could be owned, a trait that he is still performing to this day!" Amber recited with conviction.

"Why did Ur's name only live on in the English language if she was a universal Goddess?" Jess enquired deeply taken with Amber's story.

"I asked that question! Think about it! England was at the edge of the known world! The knowledge of Ur travelled here and here was her last stand as the greed of mankind spread with its new ideas and discoveries! Around the time of the building of Stonehenge her fall from favour began and she was usurped by male

96

Gods of greed and don't forget that was over a thousand years before the pyramids!" Amber explained.

"That's exactly what should be on the website instead of all that . . . Tosh!" Jess told her.

"That's exactly what Rebecca and Tracy are researching now and in time it probably will be!" Amber told her.

Jess had her glass refilled and sat on her sofa thinking deeply about what she'd just heard. She asked Sean to rub her feet and gripping from the tip of her toes he slowly pulled her long white socks free. He pressed his thumbs hard from her instep to the sides of her foot to counteract the constricting effects of her tight riding boots and pulled on each toe individually just the way he knew she liked.

The doorbell rang and Andrew saw to the delivery and carried the two brown bags through to the kitchen. Jess was blissed out and quite content to have her massage take precedence over her hunger. Time passed and eventually Amber sternly called them to the table. Jess begrudgingly pulled her foot from Sean's lap and called for her slippers. Taking her place at the breakfast bar she suggested to Sean that he took his meal with him and resumed the phenomenal massage. Sean obliged her and took his plate to sink beneath the table. Placing his plate beside him he sat cross-legged and resumed his work albeit with one hand.

"We certainly have got things to learn from you! You take the Master, slave thing to new levels without putting any thought to it! As for you Sean, I'm sorry I ever doubted you." Amber spoke louder when addressing Sean as if he were underground rather than just under the table.

"Master? What makes you call me his master?" Jess asked.

"I don't think that the word mistress conjures up the sense of power you have over him! You master him pure and simple!" Amber explained.

"Hmm, I like that! Did you hear that boy? From now on you will refer to me as Master!" Jess too raised her voice to speak to him though he was no further away than Amber.

"YES MASTER!" He replied loudly in a subtle mockery of how they spoke to him just under the table.

Jess looked under the table and responded to his jocular disrespect by putting her foot squarely in the middle of his curry. She stifled a laugh as she felt the warmth envelope her foot. The food splayed out towards the edge of the plate and rose up between her toes until she raised it up and waited. She didn't have to wait long before Sean began to consume the curry cleanly and keenly from her foot.

Remembering his naan bread he stretched one hand to search the table in the vicinity of where he'd left it. Jess moved the bread out of his reach as they all watched his searching hand pat the empty table. A volley of laughter rang out as he put his fingers to his thumb and made his hand out to be a disgruntled Emu. They all found his antics amusing with Amber and Jess's laughter ringing out loudest verging on the hysterical. Amber ripped a piece of her bread off and pressed it into the beak of the hungry hand and it immediately disappeared.

As soon as the laughter died down Jess again placed her foot in his plate and leant back to watch as he licked it off. Amber noticed a slight peculiarity in Jess's facial expressions and looked under the table. Andrew too was drawn to see what had taken their interest. It was too late to do anything about it by the time Jess looked up to see the top of Amber's and Andrew's heads as they voyeuristically watched Sean taking his dinner from her foot. Jess cleared her throat to gain their attention and obtain some privacy.

"You pair are truly beginning to worry me! Where on earth does it come from?" Amber asked her no longer able to concentrate on her meal.

"It comes from him . . . Sean will do whatever I want. The way I see it . . . I am as much his as he is mine. We're like two sides of the same coin!" Jess told her whilst stealthily attempting to find Sean's plate with her other foot.

The knowledge that his under the table antics had been observed made Sean cringe and curse the fact that they'd not had the foresight to take their dinner in the dining room. Keeping one step ahead of her Sean slid his plate to safety at every attempt of her searching foot. After several unsuccessful attempts Jess kicked out at him and caught him square in the side. He'd toyed with her long enough. Taking hold of her ankle he guided her foot down onto his plate.

CHAPTER ELEVEN

Jess had the entire Sunday planned out by Saturday night. Sex followed by breakfast in bed as usual followed by more sex of the unusual followed by a hot shower. A trip to a car boot sale would have her home in time to go jogging with Amber whilst Sean worked in the garden. After another home delivered curry they'd settle down and watch a film of her choosing and retire to bed early for an oily all over body massage then sex, shower and sleep.

As if by magic Sean woke three minutes before the alarm was due to sound. Breakfast was over an hour away and the house was in total quiet. He slipped under the duvet and began his pleasing of her in the most leisurely, slow motion and silent session they'd experienced so far. Whether it was the fact that it was morning and the house was still sleeping or whether it was their subconscious preserving their energies for the day ahead? They enjoyed every heightened sensation with the total absence of sound.

He was drying off from his shower when Andrew knocked the door and on Jess's word entered and deposited the tray at the bottom of the bed. As they ate Sean explained that he would rush ahead with the wall but forgo the original design in favour of a far less complicated structure. Jess agreed, herself having lost all enthusiasm for obtaining a fine garden that she would no longer be around to appreciate. Doubts about leaving her job niggled away at her conscience and fear of the longevity of the new venture made her experience both guilt and fear. She articulated her thoughts to Sean who laid her fears to rest having experienced a great many job changes in his life. He allayed all her fears and rekindled her excitement of the new venture by pointing out the reasons why they'd said yes in the first place.

"We're moving to somewhere with beautiful views, clean air, real dark, real quiet, birdsong instead of the drone of traffic and the leisure time to enjoy it all. I can't think of a better place to sit and write my book looking out at green fields and rolling hills!" He told her.

He sat on the edge of the bed and watched as for the first time she revealed a pair of faded blue jeans and pulled them over her hips. No bra required she pulled a black T-shirt over her head and topped it with a black polo necked jumper. She tossed a pair of dark blue socks across the room at him that landed accurately on his lap. Sean unpaired them as he moved across the room to the dressing table chair where he knelt to apply them.

Amber was on her mobile talking to Rebecca when Jess asked again if anyone else fancied going with them but both had plans of their own. The forecast was for more rain so Jess took an umbrella and cleared it with Andrew that Sean could borrow his.

They pulled off the farm access road into the hay-strewn field. The sky was two-tone grey but so far the rain had held off and there was a fair number of people milling around the multitude of vans and paste-tables. Jess put her arm in his and they walked past the first stall selling baby clothes, toys and children's books. At the second stall Jess released her hold on his arm and wandered on ahead as he scrutinised the display of tools old and new, big and small. He caught up with Jess at a stall displaying a menagerie of items from horse brasses, wall plaques and crockery to Elvis Presley mirrors and scenic puzzles. Jess picked up a riding crop, it had lost its wrist loop and the leather loop at the tip was worn through to just a single flap of torn leather. Sean commented that she should buy a new one for the farm and not be seen with such a tatty whip. Jess took hold of his jacket and led him a couple of steps back from the stall and the largely looming lady seller.

"It's not for riding, it's for you silly!" She told him in a hushed tone. "Buy it for us!" She insisted.

He bought the whip for a pound and the seller dropped it in a carrier bag for him. He offered the bag out to Jess only for her to refuse to take it.

"You can present it to me later. Ritually! The way you did with the cane in the bedroom. We'll have our own very private and highly disturbing ceremony okay?" She said developing a wicked smile. "I'm going to give you a crash course in what life as my slave really means!" She added turning to face him, searching his eyes for signs of compliance then realised her statement had been overheard by at least six others. Nearest her was an old couple that blatantly looked upon her with suspicion as others viewed her stealthily with widening smiles as they turned their heads away to hide their uninvited involvement. Her sudden embarrassment led her to desert the stall and pull the passive Sean by the arm along with her.

"Please won't somebody do something?" Sean regained their attention. "She beats me terribly you know!" he called out feigning attempts to break free as she led him away.

Jess laughed as she grappled with him; pushing and pulling him further from the stall and it's audience but only adding to their number. "For God's sake come on!" She said losing the ability to say more due to another eruption of embarrassed laughter. Her laughter grew when she saw the mock terrified, pleading and pitiful expression he donned for the onlookers. Determined to have him comply she

100

snatched the bag from his hand and unsheathed the whip raising it out to her side and threatening to make a strike at his legs. He backed away in the direction she wanted him to go and like a lion tamer she edged forward wavering the whip ready to strike if he made a move in the wrong direction. Suddenly he broke away, running across the middle of the field and through the stalls on the opposite end. Jess watched, her mouth open in disbelief as he scaled the fence continuing his run through the neighbouring field of sheep, scattering them like water on a patch of oil. Cautiously glancing over in the direction of the first stalls she saw that a number of people were laughing and watching his diminishing figure continue its bid for freedom. Embarrassed and wondering how he could quite literally take the joke so far she bagged the whip and turned back to resume her perusals at the previously bi-passed stalls. Feeling a hand on her shoulder she turned to see the old man.

"Don't worry! I've got a feeling he'll be back, especially to a girl as pretty as you!" Jess acknowledged him with a forced, simple smile and moved along to the next stall.

Sean made his way back to the access road and returned to the sale field. Stealthily he sneaked back up to Jess and put his arm around her waist as if nothing had happened. Jess squeezed his arm and pulled him close.

"You've just earned yourself your very first, very real taste of excalibre!" She whispered in his ear

"Beat me if you want! I live only to serve you my sweet lady!" He replied softly in her ear.

"You've just earned yourself another three lashes right there! I told you only yesterday that you will refer to me as...Master!" She returned the whisper.

"Sweet master, I am sorry for my short, imperfect memory and look forward to said punishment to redeem myself in your eyes!" He whispered back.

"Then you shall have a fun filled evening indeed! An evening of corporal punishment awaits you until you grovel at my feet like the dog you are!" She told him rapidly losing the will to whisper and finding the need to bite his neck.

"The evening seems so far from now! Maybe it would be prudent to return home directly?" He whispered back in her ear then kissing her cheek and jaw-line.

"Yes! Yes we should get this whole unfortunate business over with as soon as possible." She told him as her passion grew and her wandering hand pressed against the bulge in his jeans. The crime of kissing her uninvited passed by unnoticed by her and she pulled his head down to kiss him passionately on the mouth as a distant, frail voice called out from the meandering crowd. "I TOLD YOU!"

Sean drove home fast, making the most of every gear and leaving it later to brake than ever before. Jess hurriedly opened the front door and they burst inside where Sean pulled her black ankle boots and socks from her feet and tossed them into the porch. With Jess leading the way they ran up the stairs and Sean closed the door behind him. Jess turned to face him pulling the whip from the bag and striking out at him across his shoulder. She ordered him down to kneel and went to the window to collect her thoughts on the events of her choosing to follow.

"Running away at this stage is unforgivable . . . it could warrant your death. The fact that you returned of your own free will is no defence against committing the crime in the first place!" She told him and suddenly turned to unleash a lightning volley of lashes that forced him to curl up into a protective ball.

"You swore to me that you'd not run again! That you had no desire to be free of me! In every joke there is a glimmer of truth and I shall beat it out of you! I want to see you grovel, licking my feet as if your very life depended on it! You WILL show me the proper respect!" She said and stepped closer as he clasped his hands around her ankles and began to lick speedily at her feet.

Three more blows rained down on him in quick succession making him clamp his hands tighter on her ankles and increase his rate of licks and open mouthed kisses.

"Sometimes I think you actually forget you're my property . . . so now we're about to embark on a strict learning curve!" Jess moved to his side and pulled his sweatshirt up and over his head to assess the recent damage caused. As she suspected by his ability to bare the whip in relative silence there were only faint new marks, his sweat-shirt had afforded him a good deal of protection. Her conscience clear to pursue his total subjugation she lashed the whip down on him repeatedly from one side to the other. In the relentless onslaught of blows he tried to remain silent choosing instead to lie flat at her feet and force her to bend to effectively reach him.

Jess ceased the beating and moved to sit at her chair leaving him in the middle of the floor. "GET OVER HERE NOW!" She bellowed at him and watched as he slowly raised himself up and crawled on all fours to her chair. Cradling her foot in his hands he licked it lovingly, fearfully and fast.

"This is exactly what it is to be mine!" Jess watched mesmerised as he licked each foot in turn and how her foot would sway with every application of his tongue. The occasional touching of the whip to his shoulder increased his ardour and gave her the knowledge and reassurance of the immense power she had over him. Finally she'd seen enough and disrobed to have him pleasure her on the bed. The desire to persist in her domination of him never left her and the whip never left her hand. She occasionally brought it down on his now naked back but not with enough force to leave more than faint pink marks. With her passion enflamed at the highest peak in her life she pulled him by the ears up the bed and told him she needed more from him. As she opened her legs wider he entered her and she pulled his head down to bite his chin. Her breathing became heavy and deep and as he looked into her eyes he saw a wildness that he'd never seen before. Even when she was the priestess her eyes hadn't achieved that degree of dilation. The muscles in her face contorted and changed her appearance entirely. She was hungry for more, angry at her need and impatient to achieve total knowledge of what they'd both become. She hated the role-playing they'd embarked upon and craved the realism of the master and slave relationship of another time. She wanted to hurt him more deeply than he could take both physically and emotionally. She needed to break him, break his spirit and regret it at the point of no return.

Jess writhed higher glistening in sweat and with hate in her eyes as she took his length with a deep intake of breath.

"I'll kill you one day! I'll crush you beneath my feet!" She snarled baring her teeth to him and forced her fingers, almost her whole hand into his mouth. She slapped him to confirm he was hers and rolled him onto his back at the very edge of the bed. Putting her hand over his mouth denying him breath she dug her fingernails into his cheeks and drew them down to his lips. Wild, dominant and dangerous she put her hand to cut off both his airways and moved her hips in a circular motion occasionally thrusting at him. Allowing him to breath only when she raised her hand to slap him she alternated between the two acts at will forcing him to need and welcome every slap. Digging her fingernails into his neck she came to orgasm as the tension and violence in her body was thrown out of existence by the sudden impact of sheer ecstasy. She lowered herself limply to lie on him resting her head on his shoulder and gasping for air. Sean was so near completion that he had no choice but to take the initiative and continue for a few more, vital seconds. With his hands on the small of her back he denied her the room to pull herself from him and held her fast until he obtained his eventual release. Jess laughed at his facial expressions of desperation and how it changed to blissful enlightenment and near death exhaustion.

They led facing each other motionless but for their deep breathing until she told him to open the window and find something with which to fan her.

There was ten minutes of the morning left to them and Jess needed a second shower. She ordered Sean from her so she could recoup her energy and prepare for going out jogging with Amber.

From cementing in the very first stone of the day he lost himself in the joys of doing something constructive, something permanent that could well be there hundreds of years after he was gone from the world. The time spent on the wall proved to be the perfect therapy where he could empty his mind and concentrate on his weird and wonderful love life and the move to the farm. Jess was his world and nothing else mattered but her. The greatest thought ever occurred to him from nowhere. Suddenly he found himself contemplating selling his house and making a present of everything he'd acquired in this world. Every penny he'd ever earned could be reduced to a single strip of paper and presented to her in another handmade card of red and gold. It would demonstrate his total commitment to her beyond anything else in his power to give. The thought took root and he could find no reason not to go through with it. It would be his finest gesture and the words in the card would simply say, 'All That I Am Is Yours!' He became eager to know the experience of giving everything and owning nothing with the exception of his bike and car. Naturally he would keep back a couple of thousand to pay for the running of the vehicles and a couple of thousand so he could buy her the occasional present. Another couple of thousand would be needed so he didn't have to ask her for money to buy Molly food or pay vet's bills, but that would still leave the single piece of paper bearing something in the region of a hundred plus thousand pounds. Maybe he would give it to her in dollars as the sound of two hundred thousand dollars had more of the wow factor.

He realised that his greatest ever idea was born of his mainstay fantasy of paying into her bank a huge cheque from the publishers. That remained a strong possibility. Living an idyllic life at the farm would enable him to press on with his book and if need be write a sequel.

He was running out of building stone and resolved to clean out the mixer and take Molly to get more stone from the copse. The whole trip took a couple of hours and all he could think about as he unloaded the car was a glorious cup of tea and a hunger busting egg mayonnaise sandwich.

The rest of the household were in the kitchen and he had no choice but to head upstairs to shower and change before he could join them. Returning to the kitchen to feed and slake his thirst he was immediately summoned by Jess to rub her pounded feet. She made no attempt at changing position so he slipped under the table and removed her white sports socks without a mention of his dehydration and terrible hunger.

The conversation above table was relaxed and sporadic and Sean's stomach began to make its protestations known with deep, long growls. His position under the table prevented his tummy rumbles from being heard by those above so he hit on the idea of replicating the sounds artificially, more audibly and at the most opportune times. After several attempts he finally gained Jess's attention.

"Is that noise coming from you?" She inquired.

"Sorry yes . . . it's my tummy rumbling!" He replied.

"Oh the poor sod! He hasn't had anything since breakfast! Amber interceded.

Jess opened the biscuit tin and cast a single digestive to the floor. Sean picked it up and though his mouth was as dry as the biscuit he bit into it continuing the massage single-handed. Amber looked on with deepening concern and subsequent disapproval. The room fell into silence broken for a moment by a lengthy, genuine stomach growl. He noted Amber's legs move over to stand close-by Jess. Together Amber and Jess departed the kitchen.

Jess closed the dining room door behind her and the moment it clicked shut Amber began.

"I don't know who you are anymore! I don't know how you can treat him like that. I don't know how you can think that's at all acceptable to drop a solitary biscuit to the floor and deny him sustenance. How on Earth Sean can take it I just do not know! The last thing I want is another Poy on my hands and that's the way you seem to be going Lady!" Amber went on. "Having Sean as your slave should be a loving thing! He's devoted to you and you're treating him worse by the day! That display of . . . contempt was little short of atrocious and I'm disgusted and sickened by it! So please tell me what's going through your head because I need to know!" She told her sternly, pacing on the opposite side of the table.

"How I treat Sean is my affair! Trust me to know him better than you I know what he expects of me and I know what to expect of him! Is he complaining? Is he unhappy? No! So don't get on your high horse and think you need to teach me about morals!" Jess rattled off her defence angry at Amber's interference.

"You're wrong! He's hungry and you drop a biscuit to the floor, how do you think that made him feel?" Amber asked raising her voice.

"Less hungry!" Jess replied smiling.

Amber took the humour in her reply and let it be the key in defusing the immediate tension.

"Just treat him better will you? Give him some dignity or you'll lose him! That's all I'm saying, the rest is up to you!" Amber advised her sympathetically knowing that Jess was more likely to respond to that tone.

Sean was at the business end of the kitchen with Andrew devouring one of Andrew's famous salad sandwiches when they returned. As Jess took her seat at the table Sean approached her to re-enter his underworld but she prevented him and told him to first finish his sandwich. He emptied his plate and drank the remainder of his tea by which time Amber was jangling her keys and ready to take Jess to get the evenings film.

Andrew knew what he wanted to say but didn't know how to phrase it and in the lengthening silence decided that the best approach was to be direct.

"Sean, If you ever need to talk I hope you know that both Amber and myself are here to listen. You can share anything with us. You make Jess very happy there's no question about that! It's just that . . . I don't want to get up one morning and find Jess in tears and you gone because she's pushed you too far!" Andrew told him.

"I'm fine with it! I admit I have to blot out my embarrassment at times but I'm here for her! I'd crawl over hot coals and broken glass to be with her! To tell you the truth, I think that we're growing together in a way that only all this S and M business can make possible!" He explained and laid Andrew's initial fears to rest but raised concerns of his on-going light-hearted approach to the realism of the society. Andrew became more baffled at his ability to perform such base acts for Jess and still not grasp the seriousness of the world he was entering.

Jess opened up to Amber on the drive home, seeking her advice on what she was experiencing with Sean.

"The more I try to understand what I want from him the more questions arise. New thoughts and ideas are coming to me all the time! Things I want us to experience and act out. Sean's fantastic! He goes along with everything I want whole-heartedly. I just haven't found our boundaries yet and to be honest I don't think we have any! He'll do anything for me, which leaves me searching for the next big thing! We really do seem to communicate on another level. I'm feeling as if I'm in a dark room and no matter how far I walk I can't find the walls!" She told her.

"And what about having him eat his dinner off your foot, isn't that finding your borders? Pushing the limits?" Amber asked.

"That's just funning around! God! That's nothing compared to where we've been. " She answered.

"That didn't upset me! It was the biscuit incident that . . . well . . . frightened me! Amber replied as they pulled back up onto the drive.

"I'm going to test him constantly until my curiosity is satisfied!" Jess told her defiantly.

"Okay! Take him to the edge! Risk losing him! However it's my duty to tell you to slow down! You won't find another like him in a hundred years and that Jess is a fact I'm certain of!" Amber told her, hoping to scare her into a life of more domestic bliss.

All the way through the film Sean's mind was on bedtime. He tried to get into it but his mind kept tripping back to the joys he would bestow on his lover at the films end. When Jess ran her fingertips down the side of his face he held her hand to his lips hoping to ignite something in her that would lead directly to the bedroom. It didn't work she watched the film to the bitter, happy end.

Finally he was ascending the stairs behind her, his belly full of another fine curry and his mind and body rested sufficiently to perform anything she desired into the early hours. Jess climbed into bed first and he slid in beside her under her waiting arm. She set her hand on his cock then with one finger gently let it roam over his entirely sensitive area. As he grew in size she expelled the duvet to the bottom of the bed and went down on him.

"I'm curious to see it all happen!" She told him as she applied her hand to his cock and watched as she pulled at it faster and faster. Sean pressed the palms of his hands into his eye sockets and his legs writhed and toes curled until finally he erupted.

They showered together and Jess had him stand facing the shower wall to marvel in the growing collection of marks she'd made upon his body.

Out of the shower Sean was dabbing her dry when she found the need to have him kneel before her. She ordered him to keep his eyes fixed on hers and held him in her gaze. With no discernable expression on her face she slapped his face and waited for him to remake eye contact. Again she slapped him and hard across the face. With no hint of a smile or a scowl she stared deep into him again and slapped him once more.

"Tomorrow I think I'll blacken your eye. I want you to find me something that will do the job with a single blow." She told him coldly before ruffling his hair and retiring to bed.

"Be ready to do me in the morning . . . nice and slow so set the alarm for ten past six!" She told him and snuggled up to him content to talk about the forthcoming move and how they might decorate the annexe. Jess drifted off to sleep and freed Sean to wonder about her cold-blooded statement of intent for the next day. Maybe he would have to have a talk to Andrew and ultimately Amber about his treatment. The thought of going behind Jess's back ruled out that particular option at least for the time being. It was possible that Jess was testing him by deliberately acting like a schizophrenic but then again it was equally possible that she was a schizophrenic. The best course of action was to wait and see. The next day he would find her a hefty implement to blacken his eye and if she were to use it he would take the blow but then seek counsel from Amber as to how to curb Jess's violent streak. On the hand the only time since knowing her that he'd actually questioned her intentions and motives was just minutes ago. One solitary statement from her had put his mind in turmoil and maybe that was the intention. He wished he knew more of her past even her recent past might shed some light on her . . . state of mind, her grip on reality. Maybe it was his eagerness to submit to her whims that was entirely to blame. He was forcing her to take each and every step down a spiral staircase that would only bottom out when he reached his limit. Had he reached his limit? No! He too wanted to see where they could go with the slave and master thing and exactly who they would be when they got there. His lucid dream of the Chinese dragon and the Ninja's came back to him and in particular the words of the woman who told him to wear her chains with pride and he would be rewarded with a love sublime.

CHAPTER TWELVE

Jess had Sean drive her to antique shops near and far until she'd acquired every-thing she wanted for their new home. They repainted the magnolia walls a rich red, the skirting boards and windowsills black. She gave the annexe an entirely new identity creating a sense of luxury and by omitting anything contemporary she'd turned the clock back a hundred and fifty years. There were still things to buy such as pictures and plants but for now she'd ceased her spending spree. It was to be their first night in the annexe opening a new exciting chapter in their lives. On the kitchen table he'd left the bronze statue of a galloping horse she'd fallen in love with but declined to buy because of its price tag. As she entered he watched her gasp at first sight of it. After lovingly running her hands over it she walked into his arms hugging him tight and swaying.

"I've watched you spending your money and I've never bought you as much as a bunch of flowers so here's my first ever present to you!" He said swaying with her.

Jess cradled the heavy statue in her arms and sliding it from the table carried it up the stairs for pride of place on the empty, dark oak barley twist table. Viewing it repeatedly from the red and beige striped sofa she gradually drew herself back into her book and called for tea to be brought up.

Sean answered a knock at the door to find Rebecca with an unknown man standing at her side bearing a bouquet of flowers. Even from behind the flowers Sean could see he was a powerfully built individual, his short, mouse brown hair and much lined face implied he was a man who had experienced a lot in life. He truly did look like a man who had swam with sharks and spear-gunned them. Dressed in black trousers, close-knit black pullover and sports jacket he cut a dash-ing figure. Sean led them in and called up the stairs to Jess.

"I know you must be busy but I thought I'd just welcome you to the farm and give you these!" The man still at her side stepped forward and handed Jess the bouquet with a polite, gentlemanly bow.

Jess thanked her and looked around in vain for a vase. Rebecca told her that she'd find one in the far cupboard and Sean went to fetch it. After introducing them to Richard she invited them up to the manor for elevenses the next day then she made her excuses to leave them to settle in and departed.

As the day began to darken and the sun touched the hilltop they exited the farm for a romantic evening walk and to experience evensong. Not sure whether it was at all nessaccary Sean locked the door behind them and pocketed the over-sized brass key. Arm in arm they walked up the hill with Molly darting in and out of the hawthorn giving chase to rabbits and flushing out pheasants. To the accompaniment of what Sean claimed to be a song thrush with the occasional burst from a skylark they watched the blue sky blending with the orange sunset. A cold wind they'd not prepared for whipped up and drove them to make their way down the hill and from there slowly home.

Sean checked the slow cooker and a waft of the sweet smelling stew rose to the air making his mouth water. Jess was genuinely impressed by his stew and her fears of missing Andrew's culinary delights melted away. As promised Jess made the sweet and with one tiny saucepan on the auger she first produced a plate of sliced bananas coated in honey and sprinkled with crushed walnuts. Its accompaniment was a simple plate of walnuts covered in a sticky sweet brown dressing she called jaggery goor. Simple and brilliant and though they were full they relentlessly stabbed and scooped at the dessert until the plates were empty.

"Of course this food isn't only energising it's a potent aphrodisiac too!" Jess told him stroking his leg with her foot under the table.

Averse to being alone anywhere in the darkened farmhouse Jess waited for Sean to finish clearing the dinner table before having him lead the way to the bedroom. He immediately noticed that excalibre was close to hand and had pride of place on the bedside cabinet but his thoughts of unconfined and undisturbed romps in a king size bed still drew a smile.

"Don't worry about excalibre! There'll be few enough beatings for you here! He's just here as a . . . memento, a reminder of what has passed between us! " She told him, putting her arms around his neck and initiating the kiss.

For the first time in what seemed to be an eternity they made honest love. Jess was, as ever, in control but spoke in whispers to where she wanted him. She lightly stroked his scarred back and lined arms with her fingertips. Kissing his shoulders and lips when he entered her he seemingly effortlessly brought her to orgasm. He continued to lap against her methodically and slow. He believed he could control his lust indefinitely and found it impossible to conjure the will to be finished. Keeping at his steady pace only thrusting at her when she approached her second orgasm he worked up an all over sweat. Jess closed her eyes and bit her lip. Despite the noise of the creaking bed and the knocking of the headrest against the wall she saw herself on a four-poster bed being pleasured by her champion sworn to serve and protect her with his life. Jess came again and this time his thrusts kept

109

on coming faster and faster, she cupped his face in her hands and shared his breath kissing him into fulfilment.

The only light entering the room came from the nearly full and distant moon that shone so bright that it appeared more like a searchlight. Not a touch of the whip, not a single slap, not a bite or so much as a solitary curse word. Sean felt that maybe they had at last opened the door at the end of a long corridor marked 'Pure Sex.' Maybe love was the fifth and vastly most abundant element of all and he had earned a titans share of it. Seeing Jess in the magically bright moonlight he chose this sight as the picture he'd most like to keep with him forever. She looked radiant, she was a vision of absolute perfection, the angles of her face and the contours of her body down to her feet were illuminated by the moonlight and she was divine. She was only now to be worshipped and no longer feared. He didn't know how long he'd been watching her but it wasn't long enough. He could've gone on all night just staring at the magical moonlight on her form but for her partial awakening to pull the duvet over herself and disappear from view.

Neither of them had set an alarm and as Sean had spent hours watching her sleeping Jess awakened first and shook him rigorously. In the comfort of the new bed and its sumptuous mattress they had slept until almost ten o'clock. With no time to waste they showered together in the cold bathroom and quickly dressed for their visit to the manor. They didn't know how long it would take them to walk there so Sean hazarded a conservative estimate of twenty minutes. Jess dried her hair as Sean made coffee and toast consuming his before she made her entrance in the kitchen. He pushed her boots on her feet and zipped them as she took her first bite of toast. More concerned with punctuality then Jess appeared to be he found himself standing at the door holding open her coat to hurry her along. Jess took her toast with her and held it in her mouth as she slipped her arms in the waiting coat. Coaxing Molly back into the kitchen Sean hurried along behind Jess and locked the door.

Richard opened the door and formally greeted them showing them through the huge white entrance hall to the lounge. He pulled on a rope-bell and told them to make themselves at home whilst he went to see if Rebecca was ready. There was an eclectic array of seats in the drawing room and paintings from the late eighteenth century to the mid twentieth adorned the walls. There were paintings of military men in decorated red tunics and of ladies in fine dresses all undoubtedly former residents of the house. A single landscape painting hung on the far wall and was of the manor house as seen from the hilltop. Large Chinese vases big enough for Sean to fit inside lined the wall opposite the tall windows. Jess sat on a two-seated sofa nearest the large marble and gold leaf coffee table. Rebecca and Richard entered the room and Sean attended Jess's side. Rebecca's warm welcome and informality quickly put them at their ease and as they were all seated an African maid wheeled in a trolley of tea, biscuits, sandwiches and cake. She stayed to pour the tea and transfer the food and plates to the table then left without a single word. Rebecca enquired if they were happy at the farm to which Jess put her at her ease admittedly adding that she felt it a bit spooked at night.

"Everyone who stays there says that but don't worry nothing has ever been seen . . . inside the house anyway!" She told her.

"Well what has been seen and where so I can avoid the area!" Jess asked seriously.

"All the reported sightings have been of a groom who we believe was kicked by a horse. Don't worry my dear he's only ever been seen in the stables!" She told her touching her heart at the mention of him.

"And there were the skeletal bodies of the farmers wife and her lover they found when they dug the foundations for the annexe don't forget!" Richard added, winking at Rebecca.

Jess looked horrified at him then at Sean.

"Don't listen to him Jessica, he has a warped sense of humour and I assure you he's lying!" Rebecca told her immediately. "I don't know how he thinks he's at all funny! I think it stems from his service days in the navy!" She said and eyed him with a pseudo contemptuous look.

"Royal Marines then three years with the S.B.S . . . Special Boat Service!" He corrected her.

Rebecca asked Sean if he'd been in any of the services and feeling like a mosquito lava in a pond of big fish he knew the truth of his life would not serve him well in the present company.

"No unfortunately not. My father was in the army attached to the Ghurka rifles in Malaya but sadly died two years before I was born! My uncle was a career army man and highly decorated for actions all over the world! You name a race . . . he's killed 'em! He told them subtly changing his voice to speak the Queen's English and unable to stop his smile growing to give away proportions.

Rebecca emitted a short, controlled chuckle as Richard scrutinised him with disapproval and a hint of menace. Sean thought to himself how accurate his first assessment of him was and that here indeed was a man who had swam with sharks and that somewhere in the world there was a pod of dolphins missing their leader.

As Rebecca drew the conversation to Jess, Richard offered to take Sean away and show him more of the house and grounds and maybe have a game of snooker. Rebecca waved them on regally and Jess added her permission with a gentle, farewell wave.

"I will be coming back . . . won't I . . . Rich?" Sean asked as they left the room. Richard at last laughed, a short laugh but a real one, and offered his arm out allowing Sean to exit first.

"It's Richard not Rich!" He pointed out as they entered the hall.

After viewing just the library, leather clad study and walled kitchen garden they entered the games room. Four huge glass cabinets filled with trophies of war, sports trophies and memorabilia of the men who'd won them lined two of the walls. At the far end of the room was the billiard table bathed in sunlight and Richard racked the balls. Never happier than when he was talking about himself he spoke in detail about everything he'd done since leaving the forces to his current role as a Private investigator. Sean formed the opinion that he'd been starved of male company for too long and through his role as a private investigator; led him to spend too much time alone. Out-lived and out-played Sean questioned him on life as a P.I. Richard admitted that it was fifty percent stalking cheating spouses and fifty percent Insurance fraud investigations and ninety-nine percent sheer boredom. He'd met with Rebecca through his role as a P.I, hired by her to obtain evidence on her former husband. He'd fallen for her from day one but to this day she'd kept him at a distance. They had, had their special moments but her acute suspicion and mistrust of men meant that time and not deeds would be the deciding factor for them. Business was booming and he'd recently been working for thirty-eight days and nights straight through. He'd had to delay and refuse jobs to spend this precious time with Rebecca only to find that she was busier than ever with her latest ventures occupying almost all her time.

"She must've spent a year living at the farmhouse just riding once every day. I'm not sure to this day whether she was depressed or just missing the manor! Now, since she's started this society thing she's everywhere but home! He went on to explain. "She's busy eighteen, sometimes twenty hours a day and never still long enough for even me to track her down half the time!"

"That's where my Jess comes into it and soon her sister Amber too will be here lightening Rebecca's workload!" Sean tried to give him heart for the near future.

"Yes that's all well and good but then Rebecca plans to be jetting around the world obtaining properties in North America, South America, India and God knows where else! The farm and the society thing might be a real money-spinner but before it's fully off the ground, she's embarking on the next project! I just wish she'd slow down and see one thing through at a time!" He explained drearily. The game drew to its inevitable end and saw Sean annihilated.

"Rack 'em up Rick!" Sean said as if he'd won the match.

"It's Richard . . . for fuck sake! Anyway loser sets them up and winner goes to the ladies room and gets cake!" He told him determined to be a good host.

Again Sean was slaughtered on the snooker table and was setting up for another match when the maid opened the door. She leant in to tell them that Miss Jessica was waiting for Sean in the hall. Richard suggested that he returned when Rebecca was away and that they could have more games and maybe a bit of a session. Sean agreed but told him that he didn't know what work he would be doing at the farm and what free time that Jess would allow him.

"Leave it to me! I'll sort you out some bullshit jobs I need help with here and maybe we can even get down the pub!" Richard told him.

"No I can't deceive Jess like that! It's got to be legitimate or nothing I'm afraid Ralph!" Sean told him with a growing suspicion that he might be being set up for a test of honesty.

Walking back to the farm Jess relayed to him everything that she and Rebecca had discussed and agreed.

"Rebecca is leaving it me and Tracy to coordinate everything to do with the farm! The refurbishments, new builds and admin will be left to us! We're only to contact Rebecca with any queries through Amber! Amber is the managing director from today and our first point of contact regarding problems and finance! It's going to be a real challenge and we'll be learning on the job but there's cash incentive should we meet the deadline!" Jess told him bubbling over with excitement at her position of power and responsibility. "Rebecca has such faith in us that it makes me want to do my very best for her."

Tracy called at the farm late that afternoon and swung the bag from her shoulder and unzipped it to reveal her laptop. She handed it to Sean who placed it on the kitchen table as Jess went to greet her and shake her hand. Together she and Jess sat at the dining table in the main lounge and set to work. Sean brought them a mug of tea each as they mixed work with chat and getting to know one another. Jess soon began the task of creating a standard reply letter for the mountain of online applicants whilst Tracy worked on updating the website. They ate and drank wine and they worked through the evening into the night with Sean sitting with them and helping out both Tracy and Jess with his input. Eventually as they tired Tracy closed her laptop and asked if she could sleep on the sofa as she hadn't the will or the energy to make the short journey home to her caravan.

Jess was tired and tipsy but not prepared to let their first night pass them by without the having of sex. She hadn't the energy to arouse her passions so had Sean pleasure her the way he did best and smilingly drifted into sleep.

Sean responded to the alarm set just for him and prepared breakfast for three. Jess was next to enter the kitchen dressed in just her mauve bathrobe and looking fantastic if still a little groggy. Tracy responding to the smell of coffee and toast came through; her hair loose and bedraggled. She cleared it with Jess that she could use her bathroom and her shampoo before disappearing upstairs to shower. Sean fetched her a clean towel and left it hanging over the open bathroom door. Ten minutes later she re-emerged with the towel wrapped high around her head and only wearing a white T-shirt that was just long enough to hide whether or not she was wearing any knickers. As requested Sean made her some scrambled egg to have with her toast and made another mug of coffee for each of them before the day was to start in earnest.

Taking Molly along for the walk he walked through the paddocks and hayfields to where the property ran along the old roman road and located two major areas of the stonewall which were in dire need of repair. He reported back to Jess and claimed the job as his own. It was just the sort of work he loved. Although the road was at times busy he was in the countryside and working at his own pace meticulously rebuilding the dry stonewall to last another hundred years.

He didn't return to the farmhouse until darkness fell and Jess was eager for him to start preparing the dinner.

"Do you realise that there's between twenty and thirty positive responses to our website every day! Around sixty percent are men!" Jess informed Sean as he lit a fire in the auger. Tracy removed her head from her hands and looked decidedly worried.

"The major problem we have is getting enough accommodation ready. The single ladies and couples will have to have some tastefully furnished, spacious apartments in the courtyard and grounds. That'll be our top priority! I suggest that we split our time . . . in the day we organise the renovation and conversion projects and in the evenings we go on-line and do the admin side of things. I don't know that we can do this in the time we've got!" Tracy pointed out holding her head in her hands.

"Easy . . . not a problem! You start a monthly newsletter to keep them interested and feeling involved! As for the male members they can have the most basic quarters imaginable. Turn one of the barns into a slave dormitory where they can all feed off each other's misery and be all the happier for it. The people in the unit that makes garden furniture can nock up some basic beds. You can buy army surplus mattresses and blankets! Make them believe that this place is purpose built and organised even if it isn't!" Move some of the people in the other units to the old hay barn and convert the empty units into apartments. Sean rattled off his answer to their problem whilst milling around the kitchen and having half his mind on preparing the dinner.

Tracy looked astounded as did Jess. "Where did you get all that from so quick off the mark?" Tracy asked him.

"I was a production manager for years! I know how to organise people! Think of your members as a production line and work towards the goal of having them leave here fit, relaxed and happy. They want to experience a world they have only dreamt about and seen on your website. When I was first told about this place I imagined it as a country within a country and that's what they'll be wanting to find and experience." He told them giving them his full attention.

"Perfect! A country within a country! Bloody well done that man!" Tracy said excitedly and moved across the room to hug him. "Jess! We have to keep him close at hand and we'll get through this no problem!" She said, freeing the passive Sean to continue with dinner.

"Of course if you have bunk-beds in the dormitory you can fit twice the number in." Sean continued his brainstorming to the hush of Jess and Tracy. "I was impressed by the ladies in Israeli army uniform! I thought that was a nice touch!" He pointed out.

"Oh those. They're our resident lesbians. They do their own thing and have very little to do with the rest of us." Tracy told him and gathered some papers from the table. "I'm off to see Rebecca and get her approval for the dormitory and apartments. " She said as she gathered some papers from the table and hurried out the door.

Sean continued with the dinner of frozen fish in breadcrumbs with emergency frozen crinkle cut chips and peas. Jess called him to her and pulled him down to kiss him on the forehead then phoned Amber to tell her of Sean's ideas.

Tracy returned to the farm but not for another two hours. She had with her two bottles of wine courtesy of a very appreciative Rebecca. Sean produced her still warm but considerably dried up meal to her grateful thanks and a lingering stare. As she ate she relayed Rebecca's total confidence in them to implement their ideas from now on.

They retired to the main lounge and opened the wine. Sitting around the inglenook fireplace they drank wine and chatted whilst listening to a compilation of love songs. Sean and Tracy drank at twice Jess's pace and the two bottles were quickly emptied. Tracy asked Sean to get another bottle from the wine store and had to give him directions to get there. Entering the long, narrow room he saw it was stacked to the ceiling with wine and where the vacuum cleaner and ironing board were hidden away. Soon they'd reached the silly stage in their drunkenness and were laughing uncontrollably, as each suggestion as to what to do with the unclaimed slaves got more and more outrageous. They peaked out at Tracy's suggestion of tying them together by the bollocks and turning a hose on them in the courtyard. She fought hard to get the words out through her laughter to describe how they'd all be trying to run in different directions and causing each other more and more indescribable pain. Their laughter gradually eased and the draining of the third bottle marked the end of the session. Jess provoked a final bout of mocking laughter as she swaggered across the room on her way to bed.

Sean needed no instructions as to what to do and gladly performed acts of love and exactly as in the previous night he slept curled up at her midriff with her in his arms, his forehead pressing on her abdomen.

He didn't know how long he'd been asleep. All he knew was that it was still dark and he'd heard a tremendous noise from down below coming either from the kitchen or the office. He shot out of bed and looked around for something to arm himself with. He had no time to search so he took excalibre from the bedside cabinet and descended the stairs bursting into the bright kitchen ready to strike. Molly was content in her chair and behind the open cupboard door Tracy was restacking the saucepans dressed in only her T-shirt.

"I was trying to find a little saucepan to warm some milk!" She explained in a hushed tone and staring directly into his eyes.

"The fire in the auger's out by now! You'll have to use the microwave!" He told her equally as quiet.

"Oh of course! I'm sorry to have woken you but still . . . I'm glad to see you came prepared!" She stepped up to him and keeping eye contact plucked the whip from his hand.

Sean backed off and as he turned to go Tracy grabbed his arm and pulled him back. He responded angrily and told her that he was going back to bed.

"No you're not! You can tell me about these marks all over your body first!" She insisted.

Sean stepped back just inside the kitchen and explained quickly and quietly that they were from the past, another time and another place. Tracy wasn't convinced and pointed out that many of them looked deep and very new.

"Its my thing okay!" He told her dismissively.

"It might be your thing but I wouldn't mind betting it's more hers!" She gripped his arm tighter and moved her eyes slowly over him, viewing his multiple bruises and stripes.

"It's a private and very personal thing! Nothing about me involves you! Please can you just drop it and drink your milk?" His words were angry but spoken quietly culminating in a more pleading tone.

" . . . Look! I've just met you and you've impressed me no end! Let me just suck your cock and we'll say no more about it?" She suggested again unashamedly holding his gaze and reaching slowly out for her fingers to touch him through his boxers. Sean wrenched his arm free and backed away. Ascending the stairs she rushed up behind him and caught firm hold of his shorts. He desperately grabbed hold of them to prevent their removal but Tracy fought back with determination and with a final yank had them down to his ankles. He regained a hold on them with both hands and with the noise of the on-going struggle he froze to the spot invoking a return to silence. Tracy ceased her onslaught and they became locked in a stalemate. As neither was giving way Tracy offered her terms.

"We can either make a big noise now and have Jess find us here . . . or you can let me suck your cock this once and she need never know. Its up to you!" She whispered and moved invisibly forward with her eyes fixed on his. She moved ever-forward opening her mouth to envelope his semi-erection and felt the tension in his muscles ebb away. She released her grip on his pants and took his growing cock deep into her mouth. Sean waited until she drew her head back along his length then pushed her backward and scaled the last few remaining steps to the top of the stairs. Keeping his pants looped over one foot he darted to freedom and the dark, quiet bedroom.

His heart was pounding and he was relieved, angry and frightened then realised that he'd left excalibre on the kitchen table. Reasoning that after her defeat Tracy would've gone back to the sofa he quietly, painfully slowly descended the stairs. The kitchen was in total darkness and he couldn't locate the whip with his searching hands so had to cross the kitchen to the light switches. Flicking the main central light on he jumped out of his skin as something touched his leg. He distanced himself as quickly as he could and turned to see Tracy crouching by the light switches with excalibre balanced across her lap. She rose like a cobra and Sean ran to the opposite side of the table.

"Does she let you cum in her mouth? I will!" She said as she stalked him round the table.

"Where's your respect for Jess eh?" He asked her keeping at the opposite end of the table.

"Oh I respect her! That's why we're doing this now . . . as she sleeps! I want to suck your cock and I won't take no for an answer!" She was gradually raising her voice, blackmailing him into submission with volume.

"Okay if you really must, let's wait until morning and ask her! If she says yes, and she might, then it'll be fun and frequent!" He reasoned.

"I want it now, not later or tomorrow! I want . . . your cock . . . now!" She said, her breathing getting heavy and eyes getting wider and wilder.

"Keep the fucking thing and when she notices it missing I'll tell her everything!" He told her finally as he backed away to the staircase.

"She'll be wanting to weald it will she?" She asked sarcastically.

"If she sees it's not where it should be . . . YES!" He told her realising that her sympathy might bring about a quicker end to her lust.

"Here!" She called out to him. "Have the fucking thing but know this . . . I will have you!" She slid the whip fast across the table and turned her back on him.

CHAPTER THIRTEEN

Sean worked hard and long hours on the conversion of the units into self-contained apartments, dormitory and clubhouse. Jess refused to have him wear the regulation black and white. She explained to Amber that it wasn't just that she found it painfully drab but that he was working a lot with contracted plumbers and electricians and wanted him to dress according to the demands of his duties.

Andrew had afforded a few hours each day to help Sean plan and execute the conversions and at times made himself indispensable. Occasionally Amber allowed him to stop over and after a long days work he and Sean would continue their labours late into the night and have a drink as they worked. On two such occasions they, along with Raymond and Keith got thoroughly hammered making a memorable, fun time of it.

Ray and Keith were the first of eight weekenders to join the society, introduced by Tracy and sworn to secrecy by her as to how they'd actually met. Everyone had their own theories as to how Tracy had met with them and most theories drew on the same conclusion that she was or had been advertising her services as a dominatrix and they were her paying clients. Several times Sean had seen Tracy march one or other of them off their duties at the farm and disappear with them for anything up to an hour. She'd kept her distance from Sean since the kitchen incident but she would still give him a knowing wink when they passed and occasionally stand and watch him working.

The slave quarters were the first conversion to reach completion and even Poy who'd never had time for Sean, patted him on the back when she went to see the finished article. Jess took bookings from all of Tracy's crew eager to be the first to spend an entire week or weekend at the farm. This was great news for Sean who'd have a plethora of help to complete the apartments and clubhouse. Everything was happening ahead of time and with Sean's excess of aid he was able to begin unscheduled work demolishing the already derelict barns and clearing the site

117

ready for the Health club. Becky and Dan the welders were of great assistance in cutting the huge girders into manageable sizes and Jess arranged the sale of the scrap metal to a local merchant. Dan was constantly at Becky's side and not in keeping with the violent biker from the pub he seemed to have a gentle and aloof personality.

Andrew had an old friend come to do the surveying so they could get to work on the health club foundations five weeks ahead of schedule. The council had accepted his blueprints for the building and he was over-keen to see it rise from the ground. The health club had been his labour of love where he'd poured his creativity over his love of history and summoned into being a beautiful piece of powerful architecture.

As everything was going so well and considerably under-budget Amber suggested a party for all the second level members. It would be the first time that they were all under one roof and would be a great team building exercise. Rebecca was in Washington so wouldn't be attending but she had insisted that they used the manor house and asked her to extend her congratulations, thanks and regret that she was unable to be with them.

On the Saturday morning Amber and Andrew arrived and announced that for all level two members today was an impromptu holiday. Apart from overseeing the paying members they were to take the day off and ready themselves for the party. Tracy attended to the weekend slaves and had them all paraded in the courtyard before marching them off with Poy to clear the fields of horseshit, dig up thistles and cut back brambles. Jess arranged a ride with the lesbians and left Sean to help Andrew with the canopies. She was the only person to have made close contact with them and found them to be highly entertaining only resorting to use their telepathy when they were in a strangers company. Jess phoned him from the canteen and told him to come. Sean put his shoes on and ran from the farmhouse across the courtyard to the canteen arriving within seconds of her call. He could see through the glass that she was still with the Israeli women, all three of them looking very relaxed lent back in their chairs and watching his approach. He attended their table and stood attentively at her side as she waved him down with her finger to kneel at her side.

"This is my Sean! He's the one responsible for ruining the peace and quiet of the farm!" Jess told them with her hand lifting his chin. He's mine! Entirely mine and I'm very proud of him!" Jess ruffled his hair as the two women smiled at his treatment. "Sean!" Jess addressed him at last. "I promised T.C and Sara that you'd clean our boots so go and get what you need and get back here a.s.a.p!" Jess commanded him as if explaining what she wanted from a naughty child.

Sean knew his consternation and displeasure showed on his face but it was only visible to the company Jess kept.

"Yes, certainly!" He said through gritted teeth and lowering his gaze to the ground.

His desire to saunter back to the farm was over-ridden by the knowledge that if he did there'd be a banging on the glass and an angry gesture from Jess as well as experiencing her displeasure on his return. It was the request of making himself useful to strangers that didn't sit right with him. Jess was blatantly showing off and who was he to dampen her enjoyment of having him. His final thought on the matter lightened his mood and he returned to the canteen ready and showing his willingness to carry out his task.

Wetting a rag under the tap behind the counter he attended the riders who had moved to sit in the alcove and make the best use of its sofa and chairs. Kneeling before Jess he applied the wet cloth to remove the chalky dust then done the same to T.C's and Sara's. Returning to Jess he knelt and pulled her boot onto his lap. With a liberal amount of polish on his brush he buffed it on to within a centimeter of the top. As normal the lesbian's conversation dried up in a strangers company and Jess too was content to watch him work in silence.

Richard entered the canteen and ordered a strong black coffee. Jess tapped Sean on the shoulder and asked him in a whisper what his name was again.

"It's . . . Raymond!" He whispered up to her.

Coffee in hand Richard approached them.

"Hello again Jess, Ladies, Sean." He said as he sat at the nearest table.

"Hi yuh Raymond!" Jess replied with a welcome smile.

Sean with his head held low sniggered then a belt of a stifled laughter burst from his chest and vibrated his tightly closed lips. He clenched his teeth together tight and squeezed his eyes closed to quosh his impending laughter.

Richard didn't correct her, he didn't want to engage them and invade their private domination of Sean. It was Sean he'd been looking for and expected to find him milling around the conversions. Instead he found him grovelling around on the floor, cleaning boots. He made his one and only comment that Sean was doing a good job and would've gone down well in the Household Cavalry then he departed.

"I'll see you tonight Raymondo!" Sean called out reading the correct interpretation of Richard's statement.

With their boots restored to a brilliant, reflective black sheen and an ache in his right arm he hadn't had since he was sixteen he gathered his things and stood ready to depart.

"Thanks Jess that's very good of you!" T.C was moved to say.

"You're very welcome!" Jess replied and told Sean that he should return home and she would be along shortly.

Sean waited for Jess's return in the kitchen but as time drew on he retired to the small sitting room to kill time watching television. Almost three hours later Jess walked in and sat down on the sofa next to him. He pulled off her boots and gave each foot a quick rub as he waited for her to explain not just her lateness but why she'd found it acceptable to waste their day off together with the two most aloof people on the planet. Jess offered no reasons or apologies, she simply set him back down to give her feet a licking and stared blankly at the television.

"They're really funny when you get to know them! T.C's definitely the boss in that relationship! She's very sensitive . . . maybe a bit paranoid but pleasant and dead interesting!" Jess eventually spoke up.

Sean showed no signs of taking any interest and kept at his act of love.

"Tonight's going to be fun! I really wish I could've invited them but they probably wouldn't have come anyway! They're deeply suspicious of everyone! They pay their membership, which they refer to as rent and get on doing their own thing in their own time!" Jess went on believing Sean to be paying attention. "Apparently they've an arrangement with Amber that they stay here indefinitely for the flat rate fee! I'm going to have to ask Amber why that is, not that I mind, they add some colour to the place don't they?" Jess asked and paused for Sean's agreement, which never came.

"Don't they?" She reiterated the question and dug him in his side with her foot.

"I suppose they do my master! It's just a pity that they're so . . . insular! Isn't it?" He replied in a disinterested monotone.

"Yeah, I suppose you're right! But then again they've let me in to their insular world haven't they? Maybe if people didn't judge them and view them so suspiciously they'd be more open to outsiders!" Jess reasoned.

"Yes master!" Sean killed the increasingly annoying topic with an obviously sarcastic compliance.

After a light, late lunch they began to ready themselves for the party. Jess had her music on loud in their upstairs lounge and sitting at her dressing table applied her seldom-used make-up. For the first time Sean was dressed in black and white and sporting a black-backed, silvery fronted waistcoat. Jess chose to wear an off the shoulder sparkly scarlet, knee length dress with a new pair of red stiletto's. She looked awesomely sublime and Sean had to sit on the bed and stare at her as she clipped her hair loosely up so that several strands were left to hang down past her clavicle. Sean pressed his lips to her shoulder breathing in her perfume in a single long, deep intake. It was time for him to bring the car around and he didn't want to take his eyes from her. He needed to keep this image of her forever to go with the night she'd slept bathed in moonlight amongst many others but this was the surely the second time she'd ever looked so jaw-droppingly divine. This moment however, he could have help remembering and went to fetch the camera. Jess was, as ever, camera shy and he had to plead with her to take the shots he wanted. Finally under his direction she posed for him with her hands on the back of her head as if she was still doing her hair and looking into the mirror. Sean snapped photo after photo of her until whirred into automatic rewind. Content that the moment was forever captured on film he went to fetch the car.

Two beeps on the horn told Jess the car was out the front. Closing the door behind her she walked to the car where Sean was holding the passenger side door for her to embark. Amber's Audi was parked at the front of the manor along with Poy's Freelander and Tracy's Honda Civic. There was also a Jaguar X type he deduced would belong to Richard and a tatty Volks-wagon camper van that probably belonged to Becky and Dan. The front door was open and they could hear the Sting track, fields of gold playing loudly as they walked through to the sitting room. Amber dressed in a white, toga styled and figure-hugging dress a with silver clasp made a B-line for Jess and hugged her for longer than Jess felt comfortable with. Poy in a white Marylin Monroe pleated dress was next up to greet Jess, her

120

eyebrows raised she lavished almost worshipful praise on how fantastic she looked. Tracy in a very little black number escorted Poy over but stayed far enough back not to be drawn into the Jess worship and turned instead to talk with Becky in a flowing red dress that matched her flame red hair brilliantly. Finally as the huddle fanned out Tracy approached Sean and Richard. Standing between them and linking arms she led them to the quiet corner. Confident she had captured them she released them in front of her intended seat and sat down to ever so slowly cross her legs in a perfectly re-enacted Sharon Stone movement. She left them in no doubt at all that she was without undergarments and smiled at their noticing. She pulled at her dress in an even more shameful pretence of modesty and waved them down to sit either side of her. Richard immediately took his appointed position but Sean politely declined and pointed out that for now his place was with Jess and moved to stand with her and chat along with Amber and Andrew. For now there were three distinct camps. Poy and Robert were joined to Becky and Dan. Amber and Andrew were with Jess and Sean and Tracy had laid claim to Richard.

Jess whispered in Sean's ear that Raymond's name was actually Richard.

"It's not my fault his parents gave him the wrong name!" Sean joked.

Jess just rolled her eyes and holding his hand led him to the Poy camp. With the three ladies engaged in conversation Sean invited Dan over to the drinks table for a refill. They were soon joined by Andrew and began to ingest alcohol at an increased rate finishing the punch and starting on the wine. Richard peeled away from Tracy and Amber and joined them at the table refusing the wine in favour of the whiskey. Andrew took it upon himself to load a tray with seven glasses of wine and offer them around the room.

Amber had Richard turn the music down a fraction as she proposed three toasts, one to Rebecca who couldn't be with them, one to the fantastic work done so far and finally to Andrew who'd had his plans for the Health club accepted. Richard turned the music up beyond its previous setting and Tracy pulled him out to the middle of the room for a one to one dance. Soon everyone's inhibitions and barriers were broken down by alcohol and everyone, including the timid Robert were enjoying dancing and mingling freely. Richard rejoined Sean and Andrew bringing two extra glasses of whiskey with him.

"Cheers Roger!" Sean said draining his wine to take the offered tumbler.

"You'll run out of names beginning with R soon enough!" Richard told him.

"Roger that Rudolph!" Sean replied and winked at a perplexed looking Andrew.

Sean scanned the room for Jess but she was nowhere to be seen. He waited for ten minutes or so then interrupted Amber and Tracy.

"Have you seen Jess lately?" He asked.

"Yes Sean, She wasn't feeling too good so I took her home in the car half an hour ago! She insisted that you stayed as you've earned a good blow out and should stay and enjoy yourself, she really didn't want to worry you!" Amber told him.

The whiskey had done its work and Sean didn't want to get any drunker. Concerned for Jess he slipped away and drove down the track and back to the farm. Drunk or not he thought, there was no way that Jess would be alone in the house after dark. Checking every room and calling out to her she was nowhere to be found. He began to get seriously worried and decided that before raising the alarm he'd check out the only light that he'd seen on the farm . . . a light from one of the mobile homes. He approached the home and peered through a gap of white light in the orange curtains.

Jess was there, stood in the middle of the lounge. She was holding her red dress up to her waist and with her eyes closed tight she was biting her bottom lip in apparent ecstasy. T.C was down on her and Sara was licking her behind. Furious at her deceit he watched for information and ammunition why he would no longer be hers to command and betray. T.C pushed her fingers inside her and her put her mouth back to work on her clit. He couldn't watch anymore. His blood boiled then ran cold and he didn't know what to do, feel or think. Finally he grasped the loudest thought in his head. He'd dramatically disappear from her life and not allow her to keep him lingering on in her life as she gradually neglected him and acclimatised him to her prolonged absences. A clean and immediate break of the relationship was the only answer to her actions. He ran back to the farm and quickly gathered his things. He phoned a taxi to meet him at the village pub and clipped Molly's lead on. His holdall over his shoulder he walked the pitch-black road the lonely mile to the village.

He paid the eight-five pounds taxi fare and went indoors stepping over the pile of letters and junk mail. Lying on the sofa he stared across the room at nothing and Molly sensing his upset settled down beside him. The expected phone call came at one-thirty.

"Where the fuck are you?" Jess's voice rang out angrily.

He put the phone down without a word and held it out waiting for it to ring again. It did and he let the answering service take it. It rang again and he answered it.

"Don't fuck me about! Where are you?" She asked in a softer but still stern voice.

"I'm home now!" He said slowly and deliberately.

"Home? What home? This is your home and you're not here! Why aren't you here?" Her voice wavered.

"I wanted to make the world good enough for you to live in and I think I've done that now!" His face screwed up as if he'd just sucked on a lemon and he fought hard not to open the floodgates to his tears.

"What are you talking about? You're very drunk Sean and not thinking straight! You're my world!" She insisted.

"Not any longer!" He told her and turned his phone off.

Sean woke up on the sofa feeling very cold and went to bed fully dressed wrapping himself in the crumpled duvet.

Come the morning and he turned his phone back on. He played his full answering service messages of ten messages from an angry Jess, a very angry Jess and a crying Jess and finally a pleading Jess. Walking down to the corner shop to get some milk his phone rang again.

"Hello!" He answered.

"Sean! What's going on? Jess is beside herself! She's distraught and I want to know why you're doing this to her?" Amber insisted.

"Amber! It's clear to me now she doesn't need me! She wants . . . something else! I love her and this isn't easy but it's better than a long, lingering slow death!" He told her.

"A slow death is what you'll get if you persist in fucking with her head. If it's over at least have the balls to tell ME why Sean?" Amber told him.

" . . . I thought it was strange that she'd go back to the farm alone. She never stays in the house alone at night! She wasn't home! She was having . . . she was with your lesbian friends if you see what I mean!" He divulged expecting Amber to suddenly understand and soften.

"So what! She hasn't moved them in and you out has she? Get a fucking grip Sean. If they left here last night instead of you, would she be in the state she is in now . . . No! They . . . mean. . . . Fuck. . . . All to her! So get back here, forgive her . . . experimentation and get on with life! You're a couple, a perfect couple and she couldn't give a flying fuck for them girls! You however, she needs!" Amber told him making light of the betrayal he felt.

"No! Not after that, I can't! That's not what I'm about! I gave myself one hundred percent and expect one hundred percent loyalty and commitment back! What will happen next if I accept this betrayal?" He turned the phone off.

After two perfect coffees he returned his phone to active and listened to Ambers one and only message. . . . "Sean. Don't be ruled by jealousy! If you could see her now your heart would break and you know it! That's why you had to leave like you did! I've spoken to Jess and she regrets what she did last night. She's told me to tell you that nobody on this earth could take your place. And Sean she hasn't stopped crying. Please Sean get back here and make her crying stop! You shouldn't be putting her through this!" The message did melt his heart at the thought of her in pieces but he wouldn't be rushed into an immediate decision. He sat and pulled out the cigarettes he'd bought along with the milk and lit one. Happily puffing away with the thought of Jess regretting her actions he pondered what to do for the best outcome.

In the garden with another cigarette he knew that he would undoubtedly return to her in time. Jess had deceived and betrayed him and her tears didn't set things to rights. For now he would make her wish that she'd treated him better. He'd hold out for a few days or maybe as long as a week and get her to understand that she had a duty to him as great as his was to her. No more would she take him for granted and have him polish the boots of her intended lovers. His worship of her was still in tact hidden by a thin veneer of hurt. She was still his perfect Goddess but he would have her rule him with respect and take some responsibility towards his feelings. From here on in she would rule justly and with appreciation of his commitment to her.

His phone rang again. "Sean you hard bastard! You get back here . . . if only to give Jess the respect and closure she deserves! You can't fuck with her like this! And definitely not with me! If you aren't back here by eight tonight it'll be enough for me to take charge of the situation! It's up to you Sean, you do the right thing or I'll have to step in and sort it out, and I really don't want it to go that far. . . . Well . . . are you coming?" She asked.

"No! I'm not! I won't come crawling back at the drop of a hat and a few tears. Amber you don't know how I feel! I don't know how I feel so I will take my time to think without time limits, deadlines and threats! Thank you!" He told her as calmly as he could.

"Eight o'clock Sean!" Amber ended the call.

Unable to get the image of the crying Jess out of his head he turned his thoughts to the near future and how he'd again live his life to serve her needs and make her perpetually happy. He'd lived under the shadow of her power over him and gladly complied with everything she wanted of him. Now she could see that he too had power and though she would never live under its shadow, she would know of its existence and possibilities.

That night he again fell asleep on the sofa watching the television. It felt as if he'd only just closed his eyes when he felt an enormous pressure pushing him into the sofa.

At first he thought that he was having the same dream as before. Only the pain in his back and his having to turn his head to get a breath of air told him this was real. He was yanked up to stand as Molly barked and danced around two figures dressed entirely in black. His dream was real. Molly snapped at one of his assailant's legs and received a powerful kick, which sent her to threaten at them from the other side of the room. Sean was hooded and bundled into the kitchen where he was beaten, thumped and kneed in the stomach. A single blisteringly fast blow to the head sent him into unconsciousness.

He came to securely bound and rolling around in the confined space of a car boot. He knew where he was being taken and why but who they were he could only guess at. Poy, Rebecca's sergeant and probably the capable Richard had been sent to retrieve him. The car stopped and the engine was cut as he waited the short time to be unceremoniously pulled from the vehicle.

"Merci Robespierre!" Sean said as he was led away ending up in the last of the Hay barns illuminated in part by several figures with torches and then by Amber's Audi's headlights. His hands were untied from behind his back and retied at his front then he was hoisted from the ground and suspended against a wall of hay bails.

"You made this happen Sean! You not me remember that when we've decided to do with you whatever is nessaccary! The only thing I can think of is to beat you near to death! Maybe then you will take me seriously and your responsibilities to Jess to heart! We're breaking new ground here Sean so . . . I suppose you should be honoured to be helping us write the book!" Amber's voice announced.

Everything went quiet. Sean couldn't hear anything but the flick of the hay across his forehead as he turned his head and strained to hear . . . something. He thought of saying something himself but faced with a captor that admitted that they didn't know what to do with him, he stayed silent.

Suddenly he heard footsteps in the hay and a bail being dropped at his side. Maybe the beating and being brought forcefully back was an adequate punishment for Jess's tears and he was about to be released.

Sean had his shirt cut from his back and almost immediately a lash from something far larger than a riding crop cut into him. He called out the pain and gathered his strength and courage to bare the inevitable next lash. Three of these and I've proved my metal in another way he thought and stayed silent.

"We can't hide this from Jess so she too will have to learn from it!" Amber called to him and another lash caused him to cry out in shock and terrible, excruciating pain! Seconds passed then finally Amber spoke into his ear. "I'll kill you if you hurt her like this again! I'll shoot your selfish heart out then blow your brains out!"

Sean didn't doubt she meant her words and braced himself for the next shocking impact. It came to him mercifully quickly and after calling out the pain allowed himself to cry; no longer afraid to show his fear.

"I fucked up! It won't happen again! I knew I'd come back, I worship the fucking ground that girl walks on . . . and I was stupid!" He shouted out his words fast to deter her from hurting him again.

"You caused her to cry Sean and I had to watch her suffer unable to do anything about it . . . until now! I asked you to stop it but you didn't fucking want to did you? So maybe you want me to stop hurting you . . . but will I? Do I want to stop your hurt? Did you want to stop hers or did you revel in it?" Amber had taken over whip and applied it four more times with just two seconds between each strike. Ignoring his screams she paused for his pleading to die down then applied the lash twice more in quick succession then moved to whisper up to him . . . "Maybe . . . next time Jess has her cunt licked by the lezzies you will forgive her sooner . . . you see I too like to have my sessions with them! Do you think I have a problem? Do you think that Andrew's ever done to me what you've done to Jess?"

"No . . . Amber!" He spoke back. "I'm sorry for this! I was stupid . . . selfish!" He submitted trying to stay conscious in case she took his silence for defiance.

"Then you are going to put things right with her?" She asked.

"Yes! Yes! Please!" He said, his voice little more than a whisper as he neared blacking out with pain.

A minute or two went by then he was cut down and had a blanket placed over him as far as he could make out by Richard. Amber's car revved up and reversed out the barn leaving the area in darkness.

A short time later Jess led by Richard holding a torch entered the barn. She ran to kneel at his side and on pulling back the blanket gasped at his bloodied back and semi conscious state. Bursting into a flood of tears she bellowed venomously at Richard to get him back to the house. Richard handed her the torch and as carefully as he could he hoisted Sean up and over his shoulder in a fire-mans lift. Sean groaned at the stretching of his skin that tore at the ends of his open wounds. Jess held and stroked his dangling hand as they picked their way back towards the farmhouse.

Richard lowered Sean onto the bed and led him on his side.

"Amber stated that if requested Andrew will come and attend him but you have to ask her to send him! I can dress his wounds but . . . well Andrew's more proficient at this than I am!" Richard informed her sympathetically.

"Tell Amber that she's done enough!" Jess insisted through gritted teeth, tears still streaming from her eyes and herself nearing a state of panic.

"I wish I had stopped it. I should've prevented it. I'm sorry!" Richard said softly as he backed out of the room.

Jess went to get a bowl of warm water and a flannel to clean Sean's cuts. She'd just begun to clean him up when Andrew appeared and made Jess promise that it was to be their secret. He checked over Jess's cleaning of Sean's wounds and cleaned where Jess had feared would cause more pain.

"Ideally I'd like to take him to the hospital but lets strap him up and see how he is in the morning before I make that decision. I don't know how we could possibly explain this so lets try and keep it to ourselves!" Andrew offered Jess a smile but she could see straight through it and knew that Sean was in trouble.

He finished the job she'd started and told her that they should let him rest and led her away in his arms to the kitchen. Sitting opposite her at the table he began to explain Amber's motives and his own personal slant on the nights events.

"Amber has acted in the only way that was left to her! Sean forced her hand?" If Amber hadn't intervened in the way she did, this whole mess would've dragged on and on and she couldn't bear to see you in the state you were in. He provoked this to happen, not you and not Amber! Okay? Anyway you've got him back now and I don't think you'd ever be without him again would you? He asked.

"No! I'd never want to be without him, but neither would I ever beat him half to FUCKING DEATH!" Jess lost her self-control.

Andrew rushed to hold her and quieten her down but Jess wouldn't let him near her.

"Fuck you and your stiff upper lip! Fuck your fucked up sense of reasoning. I CAUSED THIS! HE COULD FUCKING DIE AND IT'S ALL DOWN TO ME!" Jess ceased her ranting and stood shaking uncontrollably.

"He's not going to die! He's as strong as an ox that one. Keep calm, stay by his bedside and watch over him. I'm going to get Molly, if you need me phone me but I'll come straight back here." Andrew told her

CHAPTER FOURTEEN

Jess looked after Sean consulting only Andrew on his healing wounds and getting him to set the big black television up in the bedroom for the first few days of his recovery. His right eye became so severely swollen that it closed up entirely, his bruised ribs and stomach turned a deep purple but it was the terrible scarring on his back that always made Jess look away when Andrew came to clean and dress them. The final dressing was applied thirteen days after the event and left them in no doubt that the scars would never disappear. Jess took it upon herself to walk Molly everyday even though there were plenty of people she could have designated the job to. She refused Tracy entry to see Sean telling her that he wasn't to be displayed like a zoological rarity. No one was to see Sean but herself and Andrew and she'd effectively cut all contact with Amber to zero. For the first time in her life she was at odds with her older sister and had absolute right on her side. They were the talk of the farm after the event, which came to be known as Sean's folly.

Enduring his lengthening recovery he needed to be busy and more importantly to him, to get back to ordinary life with Jess. He wanted to show her that he was still the man she'd first met and his little escapade was no more than a blip on the screen. Day by day he took on more responsibilities and duties from her. Through his lovemaking he made it plain that he was hers and that he wouldn't have it any other way. On one occasion he found the words to tell her that she was welcome to do what ever she wanted with who ever she wanted but that he drew the line at her taking a male lover. Male lovers were taboo and the only thing that would tare them asunder.

During his recovery they both found it easy to become the gentlest of lovers. There were no raised voices and no demands apart from those spoken in the softest of tones. They both still felt the pangs of guilt but this was still early days. Their time together in the confines of the house healed and bonded them to beyond the tactile and they were seldom not physically touching. Sean had returned to writing his book and in the last two weeks he'd completed his halted chapter and begun the next.

In his lengthening absence the work on the renovations had almost ground to a complete halt. Andrew gave his time more extensively to compensate but without Sean's zeal, he thought too much and did too little. The novelty of having their own quarters began to wane with the weekenders and there were few of them willing to take direction from the patronising and sometimes dictatorial Andrew.

The word spread around the farm and filtered down to the weekenders that Sean was set to return to work. On the appointed day almost all the part-time paying male members had arrived to help out. Andrew was baffled as to how they all held Sean in such high esteem.

The full story of what had happened to Sean was supposed to be a closely held secret and for the most part it was. Resident members were to neither confirm nor deny any of the rumours that bandied around farm.

Amber arrived at the farm before eight in the morning. She let herself in and busied herself arranging the flowers she'd bought for Jess en route at a petrol station. With no signs of life in the downstairs she bellowed up the stairs.

"Hello! Good morning! I've got the kettle on! Do I have to make tea for three?"

Sean heard the voice he'd not heard since the night of the flogging. For an instant he froze then as Jess swung her legs free of him he went to the door and shouted down that he'd make the tea in just a few moments. Jess had her Jeans on by the time he turned around and he hurried to dress and get his re-acquaintance to Amber begun and over with as soon as possible. He hurtled down the stairs and paused to compose himself before entering the kitchen where Amber waited at the table.

"Good morning Amber. . . . Did you want tea or . . . or coffee? He asked with a sudden tremble in his voice.

"Tea please Sean!" She said, as she turned side on in her chair to observe him closely.

Realising he was unexpectedly in the grip of fear his mouth dried up and a very visibly obvious tremble travelled throughout his body to his hands and legs. Suddenly he felt like a drug addict at the onset of cold turkey. He needed not to be in the room alone with her. His palms began to sweat and he ran them down his trousers in an attempt to halt their shaking. As he waited for the kettle to return to the boil his memories of that night flooded uninvited to his mind. Amber's voice and the words she used came all too clear to the forefront of his mind. The stretching of his skin when he was hoisted from the ground, the prick of the hay on his face and the awesome shock of the whip, its burn and terrifying sound came more clear to him than when it had taken place. She meant every word she uttered and would surely keep to her promise and the next time he was cause for concern, she would gun him down.

The kettle clicked off and he waited the thirty seconds for it to come off the boil in silence. Amber said nothing but he could feel her eyes burning into the back of his head. He strained to hear the longed for sound of Jess descending the stairs but there were no such welcome sounds. Amber must've been waiting for him to say something but what she would be wanting to hear he couldn't think. His tremble worsened and even the heavy kettle wavered in his hand.

"I'm sorry about that evening!" He spoke to her with his back to her and his head hung low watching the teabags darken the water in the cups.

"Sorry for what?" Amber snapped.

"For . . . for making it all nessaccary!" He told her gripping the work surface tight in both hands.

"Of course you are!" Amber submitted in a tone that may have suggested that she didn't believe him.

Sean began to squeeze the bags against the side of each cup. Amber watched him falling to pieces in front of her eyes and did and said nothing to calm him. Sean still had his back to her and the tea was nearly made. His eyes welled up and tears began to run down his face then the floodgates opened and from somewhere behind his face he cried aloud. His struggle to suppress his crying only made its sound dramatically more outlandish.

"I think you'd better sit down and I'll finish the tea!" Amber told him and pulled him by the arm to be seated in her chair.

Sean hid his face in his trembling hands and fought on to cease his uncontrollable, shameful performance. Amber finished off the tea and brought two cups to the table just as Jess entered the room.

"What's going on? Why is he upset? What have you said?" She asked and pressed her face to the side of his and put her arm around him.

"He's having a panic attack that's all! He'll be fine in a moment or two it's a natural reaction to trauma! The trauma of seeing me no doubt!" Amber informed her.

Jess squeezed onto his lap and put her arms around his neck as he held her around the waist.

"Come on now Sean! I'm not here to punish you or make you miserable! I just came to see how you both are and see how the work is coming along!" Amber told him looking into his eyes for the first time that morning.

"The work's isn't coming along is it? Hardly anything has happened out there since Sean was. . . . Hurt!" Jess snapped at her.

"I know! Andrew's told me how Sean has endeared himself to the entire workforce!" Amber said stroking her mug of tea.

"Workforce? He is the bloody workforce! Without him the plan was to hire a bloody construction company!" Jess was furious at Amber's unappreciative, suspicious tone.

"Yes and just about every member of the society are going to be out there today to see him. I'm just a bit worried about how all this . . . hero worship is going to affect him. I'm also concerned about what Sean's going to say to them!" Amber revealed.

"So you're not here to bring him flowers as a peace offering and see. . . ." Jess was suddenly interrupted.

"They're for you!" Amber told her.

"Well you're not here to bring ME flowers! You're here to find out what he's going to say!" Jess kept the pressure on Amber.

"Yes that's right! So . . . Sean, what are you going to say?" She asked.

"Keep it simple I think is best! I was playing a stupid game that went beyond the society's boundaries of acceptable behaviour and was brought back and confined to the house as a punishment!" He answered.

"Perfect! Simple, explanatory and myth-busting!" Amber declared with a smile. "However, they're going to know you took a beating by your eye! Its still a bit . . . well, puffy!

"That was all part of the punishment and unavoidable! I could've returned to work the next day but was confined to house!" He submitted.

"Thank you Sean! Let this be the start a new understanding between us! We're friends again . . . as we were before!" Amber told him and for the first time that morning had some genuine emotion in her voice.

"We'll always be friends! This is the end of that unfortunate chapter . . . a blip on the screen and no more than that!" He told her.

Together the three of them walked out into the courtyard to inspect the work so far. The weekenders were all in the canteen waiting to be collected and given their jobs. They all went to the windows as Sean, Amber and Jess walked to the unit that would be the ladies club. Tracy, Poy and Robert had their table nearest the window and Tracy bellowed at the workforce to sit the fuck back down! After a short conversation Amber left them and they walked to the canteen to organise the workers.

Tracy and Robert stood up to greet them only Poy remained seated to offer her cheery good morning solely to Jess. They sat at the table and discussed who would be working where and what needed to done that day. Jess rubbed Sean's arm as he told them what he wanted then as Tracy began to bark orders at the crew Jess made her way back home and left them to it.

Alone in the house Jess was un-nerved and couldn't settle at anything. Wherever she went in the house she felt as if she were being watched. After just twenty minutes she returned to Sean in the courtyard and asked if she could keep Molly with her in the house until Tracy was free to accompany her and do some admin. Sean smiled and told her to call Molly and she would follow.

To Sean it was a great day! He applied himself to every job in turn with his mind constantly processing what needed doing next. Inevitably the question of his mysterious disappearance arose within minutes of work commencing. Ray backed up by Keith stood before him and asked the question. Sean gave them his prepared answer with a determined air of nonchalance.

"So you weren't horsewhipped near to death?" Keith asked seemingly disappointed at his decidedly unexciting means of punishment.

"Horsewhipped?" Sean smiled and showed them his surprise and amusement at the notion. "No! Well no more than I like to be!" He told him with a convincing chuckle. "Horsewhipped indeed!" He added for effect and let out a very genuine sounding laugh.

Ray went to pat Sean on the back but Sean's sixth sense told him it was coming and he sidestepped the incoming hand with the skill of a martial arts expert. Thwarted for the time being Ray went back to scrubbing the walls with his wire brush. They worked through the rest of the morning singing along to the radio happy at their work until Tracy and Poy returned with the others for the dinner hour. Sean refused dinner in the canteen insisting on checking on Jess at the house. He found her in the office and called her in for tea and sandwiches. Jess told him that Amber had bought Andrew a car so that he could get around independently of her. Andrew was over the moon with his new Ford Focus and was on his way to the farm to show it off. Sean thought on the possibility of his impending news but couldn't divulge to Jess what had put such a big smile on his face. The estate agency that she believed was arranging the letting of his house had an interested couple. They'd viewed the property twice and were expected to make an offer any day. Sean explained that he was simply happy for Andrew and thought that he could drive him home so he could pick up his Daytona and keep it at the farm from now on.

The days were lengthening and the sun still shone brightly when the working day was over. Sean could've easily worked on but for his hunger and want of seeing Jess. As the workers marched off to the canteen he went home. The smell of dinner hung heavy in the air and Jess had been busy making the kitchen a complete mess. The dinner itself however was one less chore than he expected and thoroughly enjoyable.

CHAPTER FIFTEEN

Jess and Tracy planned the grand opening as they travelled far and wide purchasing all the required furnishings. The return to normality and long working days also spelled a gradual warming in the relationship between Amber and Jess. On the evening of their total reconciliation Amber had arranged a family meal and turned up at the farm with a vast array of curry dishes bought from their old, usual supplier. She couldn't afford the risk of heightening emotions with alcohol so brought with her a selection of flavoured waters and fruit juices. Their evening went well and ended with Jess accepting a goodnight kiss from Amber before they all retired to their respective ends of the farmhouse.

Rebecca was back at the manor and Richard had moved into one of the mobile homes; having most of the living space being taken up by his surveillance equipment and computers. Sean helped him move in and sensed his sadness at Rebecca's not insisting that he moved into the manor.

Amber and Andrew stayed more frequently at the farmhouse and the return to an extended family life suited Jess perfectly. She felt far more at ease when the house was populated and enjoyed the return of the family evenings immensely.

The morning of the grand opening came and Sean didn't need reminding to be dressed in black and white. It was a fortuitous sunny day and the courtyard had been swept so clean that it resembled more of a film set than an actual working farm. Everything had been newly painted, windows cleaned even the moss on the rooftops had been swept, much to the consternation of Ray and Keith who'd been allocated that particular duty for being the biggest pair of gossip mongers on the farm.

Under Tracy's direction all the women were in their black and whites and the men in their reverse black and whites lined up on opposite sides. Richard drove Rebecca in the Range Rover to the entrance of the courtyard as Andrew ran around taking photographs from every angle then positioned himself for the cutting of the ribbon. Rebecca was the only person not dressed wholly in black and white. Instead she wore her red riding tunic with black trim and walked smiling contagiously at everyone to the red ribbon.

"I'd like to thank everyone for their extremely hard work and devoted support in getting this venture up and running ahead of time and would like to take this opportunity to ask for the same efforts to be made on the next project I believe is already underway! Thank you everyone! WE WILL CHANGE THE WORLD!" Rebecca cut the ribbon to a rapturous applause. Next Rebecca flanked by Richard and Poy walked to the table set up outside the canteen and waited for Amber to open the first bottle of champagne. With everybody crowded behind Rebecca, Amber offered her thanks to Rebecca on behalf of everyone for making it all possible and popped the first cork. As the cheers died down the sound of Rebecca's favourite Vaughan Williams composition of The lark ascending sounded from the speakers mounted outside the canteen. Amber took her around for her first viewing of the vastly transformed units. She was delighted with what she saw and on entering the ladies club became visibly emotional.

"This is just what I imagined, more so in fact! I will be using this as my showpiece and my blueprint for what I will do everywhere else!" She announced to Amber taking it all in wide-eyed and smiling. Amber gave her the news that Jess had booked all four apartments to be taken by the first of the new members due to arrive that afternoon.

"I think it would be a good idea for Jess and Tracy to come travelling with me to America and imitate exactly what they have done so very well here!" Rebecca told her.

"We'll need them here surely!" Amber replied concerned for her own free time.

"Quite right! But only until we can get someone else to run the farm in their absence!" Rebecca replied defiantly.

Richard drove Rebecca home where they were joined by Amber and Andrew to discuss matters other than the farm. Even Becky and Dan had slipped away and were last seen heading for the manor. Poy left Robert with Sean and also drove down to the manor for the hush, hush meeting. Tracy and Jess were left guessing as to why they weren't included then reasoned that it probably had something to do with them and their efforts on the project.

Jess had Sean and Robert mill around the car park on look out duty to meet and greet the newcomers and show them to the canteen. Two rings on her mobile would tell her they'd arrived and either she or Tracy would officially greet them. A cold easterly wind blew across the open fields and through the car park making Sean's job an even more miserable non-event. He made a mental note to suggest constructing something that would serve as a gatehouse or kiosk that would also add security. From where he stood he spotted the windows in the hayloft of the stables. With Robert in full agreement they scaled the ladder to the loft and threw down a thick blanket of hay so they could lie down and look out from the floor level window. Out of the biting wind they could stare down the track and chat in comfort. Forty minutes of yes and no answers from Robert was sending Sean into an internal rage. No wonder Poy would so often beat him he was the dullest person he'd ever met. Emotionless, monotone and perpetually miserable Sean could have raped him and not received a response of more than one syllable. The thought of masturbating his way through the boredom and it seemed an ever more likely pastime than trying to get a conversation going with Robert. Sean laughed and at his wayward thoughts and prompted a sideways glance from Robert. Finally a car appeared on the horizon and Sean rang Jess. Making sure that Robert knew to stay and lookout for further vehicles he made his way joyfully down the ladder and out to the car park. The silver Alpha Romeo pulled up at the nearest edge and a very preened, professional lady in her mid fifty's stepped out wearing black trousers and tweed jacket. Her short light brown, styled hair suited her well and she had a pleasant smile. Clutching her handbag she waited for him to approach. She introduced herself a Stella and led him to the boot to retrieve her bags. Taking her laptop from the back seat she walked beside him carrying her medium sized red suitcase and Luton bag. Jess joined them in the canteen and gave Sean the key to take Stella's bags through to her apartment. Raymond and Keith spoke with Sean then took their positions in the hayloft with Robert freeing Sean to return home and prepare dinner.

Jess arrived home happy that the day had gone swimmingly well. The new arrivals seemed very pleased with the apartments. They were made aware that they were the vanguard of new members and any suggestions and expectations they had would be gratefully received. Jess explained that Keith and Raymond were working the bar together both hoping to be noticed and desired. The thought of Tweedle Dee and Tweedle Dum vying for attention forced another smile to Sean's face.

Amber and Andrew popped home on their way to the clubhouse and invited Sean and Jess along. Together they entered the club with Amber and Jess immediately mingling with the newcomers. Sean ordered a drink from Ray and Andrew immediately cancelled it.

"It's a Ladies club! We're here in a completely different capacity!" He informed him.

Sean accepted the disappointing news and wondered why on earth he'd agreed to attend. Soon Rebecca, Richard and Poy arrived and introduced themselves around. Richard joined Sean and Andrew, leant over the bar and ordered a whiskey.

"It's a Ladies club Roland! We're here in a completely different capacity!" Sean had pleasure in informing him adding some tutting for good measure.

"Oh Cock!" Richard replied with a pained look on his face. "Why are we here then? Let's leave the women in the perfectly capable hands of Keith and Ray and get some drinks down our necks back at mine shall we?"

It was down to Richard to inform Rebecca and the others of the plan to slip away. Amber insisted that Andrew stayed and Jess believing that Amber only intended to stay a short while longer also refused to let Sean go.

With three cola's the men stood away from the bar and chatted around the podium and laid plans for having a den of their own somewhere. Andrew was adamant that they didn't need such a thing. As he saw it, it would cut them off from their main reason for being there in the first place and would become a bone of contention.

"Your problem Andrew is that you revere all women; whereas Sean and myself are here solely for our . . . better half's!" Richard pointed out.

Andrew wasn't impressed by his comment but had no prepared argument to put against it. He hoped it would quickly pass into history but then Sean openly agreed with Richard and expressed his gratitude for articulating the fact that he himself hadn't realised until then.

"So really we are here solely for our partners and on an equal basis to everyone else?" Sean told them his thoughts as they came to him.

"No! That's how the outside world works. Here we show greater respect for women in accordance to our beliefs that they are all to be revered." Andrew argued. "You wouldn't tell Jess and Rebecca . . . I don't respect women as a whole I only respect you! Well . . . would you?" Andrew made his point.

"No!" Sean agreed and thought on.

"Yes! Yes I would and I have!" Richard informed them.

"Then that's probably the main reason for you living in a mobile home and not at the manor with her!" Andrew pointed out glad to have the upper hand at last.

"I agree with how the farm functions whole-heartedly but this is simply the fantasy island, money spinner for the serious work we do. Don't take this as the reality of the society. It's a means to an end. It's a money making venture for a crusade!" Richard pointed out his heartfelt opinion on the farm.

"Um excuse me. What serious work? What crusade?" Sean asked looking at each of them in turn.

Richard looked to Andrew who shook his head to say it wasn't time to tell him any more. Richard shook his head back at Andrew and Andrew responded by waving a warning finger and increasing the seriousness of his stare.

"If anyone has earned the right to know what we really do its Sean for Fuck sake!" Richard leant over the podium to face Andrew down.

Andrew said nothing and put his arms up in surrender and non-involvement before taking his drink to rejoin Amber. Richard spoke quickly to divulge as much as he could before Andrew could return with reinforcements.

"We rescue trafficked sex slaves, prostitutes, abused spouses and when we can we dispense some . . . retribution and justice of our own to their abusers. That's what we're about, not what you see here but . . . what you don't see here!" Richard revealed and looked over his shoulder expecting to see his fellow conspirators bearing across the room at him but they were still happily chatting. Andrew had not betrayed him but neither would he take the steps that Richard found nessaccary and bring Sean further into their confidence.

"Very noble! Something worthwhile." Sean said. "Who's involved in this secret army?" He asked wondering if Jess had kept this secret from him.

"There are five, sorry seven of us now. Becky and Dan have just come aboard. There's Rebecca and myself, Amber and Andrew and Poy and now Becky and Dan too." Richard told him.

"So . . . Jess doesn't even know about this and neither does Robert?" Sean asked.

"No! We are very particular and very careful. We have to be." Richard explained and pulled a displeased face at his cola drink.

"How did all this come about? How did you all discover each other?" Sean was eager to learn more.

"Rebecca employed me to tail her philandering and abusive husband then as he gambled and put all her savings up his nose she paid me to follow him to America. He never returned from there. As for Rebecca and Amber they met through me. Amber was the investigating officer in a case that I was . . . involved with. Amber met Andrew here at the farm and Amber met Poy also through the course of her role in the C.I.D. We've all been touched . . . in no small way by the injustice we are now fighting." Richard told him.

"But Andrew met Amber through his work as an architect?" Sean queried him.

"Yes but he was already known to her as the man she arrested for the attempted murder of a pub landlord. There was a little Thai girl working at the pub and Andrew found out that she was being offered around. He frequented the pub and one day could no longer bear to see her treatment and went behind the bar to end her employer's reign of abuse. It took four men to pull him off and he hospitalised two of them too." Richard recited the tale with a growing smile. "That young girl now works at the manor very happily and at the moment she's visiting her parents in Thailand. You met Wendy at the manor. She too was one of our rescues. She was one of six women from Ghana that were put to work in a brothel of such . . . depravity that they were just there waiting to die. The gang that ran the brothel were annihilated, probably by another, rival gang." Richard said with a smile to hint at the truth.

"What about Poy?" Sean next asked.

"Ah hers is story about sisterly love. She found out that her sister's husband had been constantly abusive. We can only guess at what he put her through. Poy only found out when she went to stay with them and received some of his special treatment. Unfortunately for him Poy was made of sterner stuff than her sister and the ensuing fracas ended in his rather gory death." Richard revealed.

"What about Dan and Becky?" Sean asked.

"Abusive boyfriend that she thought she'd never escape but she didn't count on the intervention of Dan. He lived next door and one night he'd decided he'd heard enough. He went next door and kicked the door down. Becky's brave boyfriend tried to run out the back but Dan brought him down and hospitalised him."

"What about you?" Sean asked to complete the set.

Richard took a deep breath and his eyes glazed over in an instant.

"Another time maybe. I can tell you their stories but as for my own . . . maybe another time." Richard drained his cola and told Sean that he'd return but needed a proper drink.

Sean looked around and viewed everybody he'd been told about in a whole new light. His thoughts went back to Richard and his untold story. Jess called Sean over to her table and told him that Stephanie would like to meet and talk with Keith and would he arrange it. Sean in turn told Keith that he'd caught Stephanie's eye and should leave the bar to Raymond to go and attend her. Keiths face lit up and Ray scowled a short while until he realised that alcohol was loosening their inhibitions and there were three other new guests. Jess withdrew from them and talked a while with Andrew and Sean at the podium then decided to return home with Sean.

"She was rather interested in you until I told her you were mine! Jess told him as they left the club.

Sean liked the bit when she'd said he was hers and kissed her hand. They were both very much in the mood for love and as soon as the bedroom door closed Jess became his master and had him on his knees. A dominant slap across the side of his face as he knelt let him know that the priestess survived in her. With his blood pumping he knew he'd missed her and had a very exciting next few hours ahead.

In the morning Jess went riding with Rebecca and two of the guests. Sean dressed for a day of digging the foundations for the Health club. Tracy caught him walking through the courtyard with a spade over his shoulder and asked if Ray could join him. Sean agreed happy for the company.

"He's missing his Tweedle Dee!" She told him and went to fetch him from his car washing duty.

Though the day still had a chilly breeze it was sunny and with the sun at its zenith and no wind reaching them in the trench Sean had to remove his sweatshirt. As he pulled it over his head it drew with it his T-shirt and Ray saw the scars on his back.

"Bloody Hell!" He exclaimed.

Sean knew what he'd seen and quickly pulled his T-shirt down.

"I told you I was a sick monkey!" Sean joked.

"That's from the time you disappeared isn't it?" Ray stopped work to question him.

"Around that time yes! But Ray . . . please say nothing not even to Keith . . . promise?" Sean asked of him.

"Okay! But why?" He asked.

"Because I don't want everyone knowing my business!"

"No I mean why did you get those, they look awful!" Ray continued.

"I don't know why! I was drunk and stupid and prompt action had to be taken!" He explained. "Now lets get on shall we?"

"Who gave you them? I can't see it being mistress Jess?" He went on.

"Ray! Leave it now!" Sean told him and dug his spade into the clay.

"I bet it was mistress Poy! She's got a mean temper on her that one!" Ray continued.

"ENOUGH ALREADY!" Sean raised his voice.

"I bet it was Poy who whipped you on Jess's behalf, that'd make sense!"

"Ray please mate, talk about something else!"

"So what was the argument about?" Ray persisted.

"FOR FUCK SAKE DROP IT!" Sean shouted raising his hands to the sky for the strength not to hit him with the spade.

"I wish someone cared enough to whip me!" He ventured on but with a tone that suggested it was his final remark.

"Some blokes would pay extra for that!" He found the will and the words to continue his bating of Sean. "Not that bad maybe, and they'd probably use a safe word like . . . Bananas, to call out when they'd reached their pain threshold!"

Sean threw the next spade full of mud over him and returned to the dig.

"I wouldn't have a safe word!" Ray said shaking some dirt from inside his shirt.

"Ray, please! If you don't shut up I'm going to get Poy to give you exactly what I got and you won't have to pay extra okay?" Sean reasoned with him.

"So it was Poy then! What's it feel like?" He continued.

"Ray . . . Mate . . . do you want to be whipped like a cunt for being a cunt because I can arrange it?" Sean informed him giving him a serious look and waiting for his considered answer.

"Well. . . . No! But if I was ever lucky enough to get someone like Jess I would expect to be whipped if I was stupid enough to disobey her!" He told him.

Sean knew then that Ray was more like him than he'd ever realised. The only difference was that Ray didn't yet have anyone to call his own. Ray knew what he wanted and had been with Tracy to experience it. He'd joined the farm to live it and find his great love. Sean had done things differently because he'd found Jess and only through her came to the farm.

"You'll find someone soon Ray! That's what this place is all about! Bringing people of the same ilk together for life, love and happiness!" He told him more considerately.

They had dinner together in the canteen and worked the remainder of the day actually getting to know each other instead of their usual joking around. Sean began to believe that Ray would keep his secret and that there was more to him than his light-hearted approach to life displayed. Ray was due to be working the bar again that evening as Keith had been claimed by Steph. They stopped work early to get cleaned up and Sean let Ray use their bathroom instead of just the sink in the slave quarters.

Andrew was milling around the house and showed Sean his photographs of the opening and his format for the newsletter he was developing. Sean saw through the kitchen window Amber going into the clubhouse rather than coming home. Dinner was on the table and with Jess home too and Amber not answering her phone the three of them went ahead with dinner without her. Finally Amber came in and was clearly drunk. Andrew attended her and led her to the small lounge and brought her dinner in to have on her lap. She picked at her dinner then cutting short her foot massage, handed Andrew her plate and told him she wanted to be left alone a while. Holding her plate in one hand Andrew tried to put her slipper back on one handed but only received an impatient kick to his leg for his efforts.

"She's had some upsetting news!" He announced on his return to the kitchen. "Somebody she knew and liked very much had just taken their own life jumping from a sixth storey hotel window!" He said quietly.

Hearing her sobbing Jess walked by Andrew and went to her. Andrew got his paperwork and photo's together ready to work on them with Tracy.

"She's upset and drunk! She'll be very volatile until morning so give her a very wide berth!" He explained before leaving.

Jess called for Andrew after a few minutes and Sean explained where he'd gone.

"You come in then Sean!" Amber told him. "You can rub my feet if Andrew's fucked off somewhere!"

Sean glanced at Jess who motioned to him with wide eyes and a nod to get started. Everything fell silent as Amber put her head back and tried to relax.

"She went through such a lot! From the age of eleven she was abused daily. She was twenty six years old and timid as a deer!" Amber broke the silence. "Seven years she was in that house then one day she found the strength to get out. Free of her abusers she trained to become a nurse then when she saw that they'd got another little girl she came to me!" Amber sat up and with tears streaming down her face she continued. "She didn't do it for herself but for the other little girl! We got him and we had him convicted! His pathetic wife was glad to be free of him too! Six years he got! Six years to relive his stories with his like in prison talking about his years of rape! How I hate and detest that word . . . RAPE!" Amber held her hands to her face. "I should've kept her close! I should've got her involved here and shown her that the human race does have a soul and that she was more worthy of a life than he was. . . . When she was told of his early release she ended it . . . her life! She needed to go somewhere he couldn't find her!" Amber broke down entirely taking Jess and Sean along with her.

Amber responded to Sean's lengthy exhalation and sat up.

"What would you do if you if you knew him? What would you do if you came face to face with the man who has done that to children?" Amber asked.

"I'd throw him out the very same window! Maybe let him dangle a while but let him know that he was on his way to meet his maker and reap Gods own justice. . . . Of course it should go without saying that his bollocks and prick should be kicked out of existence before he dies!" Sean told her with his blood pumping fast at the thought dispensing such blissful justice on a sick and evil man.

"Is that how you honestly feel?" Amber asked him her tears for now reserved.

"Yes! Scum like that . . . prison isn't enough! They prey on innocents and stalk society why the fuck do we let them ever walk the streets again?" Sean rattled off his heartfelt opinion.

"Well said and true!" Amber paused wiping her wet cheeks. "I want you to kill him for me, for Kate and for the sake of your own convictions! I want him dead! Are you up for it? Will you do this for me?" Amber looked into his wide, open eyes.

"Yes!" He replied with certainty.

"Wait a minute! Sean isn't going anywhere and doing any such thing! He'll end up in prison for more years than that scum has done!" Jess interceded.

"No he won't! We'll work together on this! Nobody is going to prison!" Amber insisted. "If the worst comes to the worst we will have the best lawyer in the country! We will pay the fucking judge! We will look after our own!" Amber insisted.

"No! Sean's not a killer! He'll fuck up!" Jess said rising from her chair.

"Sit down and listen!" Amber demanded. "We as a society have dispensed justice to the sick the warped and the downright evil because it makes us sleep better at night! We've all . . . taken people off this Earth. People we knew to have commited unspeakable horrors. They serve their time then when society tells them that they can have another chance . . . we step in and deny them that right. We have not fucked up and I'm not prepared to let this particular serial rapist to continue living is that quite clear?" Amber glared at Jess.

"How many people have you killed?" Jess asked with a look of horror.

"To date its two rapists, three paedophiles and one murderer! Two pimps have died at our hands and we've dished out heaven knows how many beatings! And that's only since we started acting as a unit." Amber recounted casually.

"You've killed seven people?" Jess asked her with an expression that revealed her horror.

"PEOPLE? No! Scum! Filth! Yes! We've wiped out some serious evil from this world!" Amber announced proudly.

"How many of them did you kill?" Jess asked fearing the answer.

"One! Mine was a particularly nasty paedophile. He served his sentence and I shot him in the back of the head shortly after his release! We've all killed! Now I'm asking Sean to commit to us!" She told her.

"And me?" Jess inquired.

"Killing's not for you!" Amber looked on her with sad eyes.

"So who is . . . all?" Jess inquired.

"Richard, Poy, Andrew and Myself! Becky and Dan are with us now but haven't performed the deed yet." She answered.

Jess done the maths. "So who of you has killed more than once?" She asked

"That would be Richard. He has the deepest rage in him. His daughter was abducted, raped and murdered. He . . . will never get over losing her. He sleeps well enough for a night after every execution; the rest of the time he drinks. He has to!" Amber informed them looking directly into Jess's eyes.

"So you want to turn my Sean into a killer for what?" Jess asked.

"Think on this girl and where she is now! Then think on him and where he is now! Who should be in the ground? Him or her I ask you?" Amber pulled her feet from Sean's lap and stood up. "We will pick our time! Richard will plan it out and Sean will do the deed. If Sean doesn't do it I will! Either way he's a dead man!" Amber stood before Jess and lifted her chin to see into her eyes.

Jess knocked her hand away and stormed out the room.

"If Jess doesn't want it then you can't go any further! Thank you for understanding Sean but I won't let it come between you!" She told him.

"If I can't talk her round, I'll do it without her knowledge. I want to be on board. I want to take this scum off the Earth! I'll do it for you, for me and for the group okay?" Sean said softly as he stood and walked slowly to the door.

Amber told him to stop and went to him. Holding him at the elbows she focussed on his eyes staring straight into him.

"I knew you were . . . special the first time I saw you that night! There's something about you that's trying to speak to me, I'm sure. Sean . . . when I beat you I was trying to exorcise my own demons!" Amber told him and pulled him in to kiss him on the mouth.

Amber suspected that he might try to pull away and placed a hand on the back of his head to prevent it. Sean didn't pull away or show any reluctance to let her give the kiss but neither did he reciprocate it. He trusted her never to do anything to hurt Jess! She'd brought him back for Jess . . . hadn't she? What did she mean when she said that she was trying to exorcise her demons. It was then that the penny dropped with Sean. He realised that Amber had had a thing for him since the night of their first meeting in the pub. If Jess walked back in he WAS in serious trouble. If he broke away from Amber he COULD be in trouble, especially in her Hate filled, remorse full and alcohol fuelled state. If he kissed her back he was sending the wrong message and giving her false hope. Suddenly he felt as if he wasn't alone in his head. Amber was in there with him and knew his most recent thoughts.

Suddenly Amber broke away from the kiss and rested her forehead against his. Cupping his face in her hands she breathed in deep.

"You mean to defy her? Knowing she doesn't want you to, you will go ahead and do it anyway?" Amber pulled away from him, her eyes squinting as she thought how to respond to his lack of response. "I should beat you again just for that! I've got to show you the error, the serious misjudgement in your thinking! I only want the best for my little sister and at the moment that's not you!" Amber pulled him forcibly by the collar and led him to the big lounge. Targeting his face and head she slapped him down with a series of forceful blows. With every blow she vented her rage until he fell on his knees and lowered his head to the floor and ultimately beyond her reach.

"If you've finished with me can I go now?" His muffled voice came up from the carpet.

"What? Go and live a lie with my little sister you mean?" Amber put a foot on his head to keep him down and with her.

"Can I go now please?" He reiterated his request.

She slid her foot from his head to his neck and pushed it into his shirt to rest between his shoulder blades.

"Not yet no! You can show me how far your lies and deceit go!"

"Only as far as ending the life of someone evil for you and keeping it from her!" Sean admitted to a silent Amber. "Amber you were crying and I thought I could help. I want to help that's all I swear it!" Sean added and again the room fell into silence. "Amber . . . I'm frightened! Right now I'm frightened of you . . . but I want to hold my head up high when I'm with Richard and Andrew . . . that's all!"

"Yes of course!" She said softly. "I'm . . . sorry! You're a good man I can see that! I've always seen it in you but I do . . . have to test you . . . from time to time! Tell Jess you won't be required on the evening! Its enough for me to know you're willing!" Amber walked deeper into the room and turned to watch him tuck his shirt back in and leave the room.

CHAPTER SIXTEEN

Jess had her breakfast in bed and sat out the morning hiding away in her lounge so as not to be confronted by the likes of Amber or Andrew. She stared blankly at the television her thoughts unable to move from Amber's revelation. Her attention was drawn into the television during the brief news headlines. They announced that a girl had gone missing from her home just outside Nottingham. She was fourteen years old and hadn't returned home after school on the previous day. There had been no family argument and her parents were distraught and hoping for the best. The photograph displayed showed her smiling dressed in her school uniform. Jess stared at the screen and didn't hear the remainder of the news. Suddenly she called for Sean.

"This man Amber wants dead . . . he should be made to feel the same horror as his victims did?" Jess asked as soon as Sean knelt before her.

"How do you make a grown man feel the same way as a terrified little girl?" Sean asked her. "Where do we keep him for years of . . . of what? That girl had to walk home from school every day knowing what was going to happen to her and hoping it wouldn't! How do we reconstruct that?" Sean spoke with conviction and with the presence of an underlying anger. "They should lock them up for life but they don't! What Amber and that are doing . . . especially Richard is wholly justifiable, wholly understandable and it's something I would gladly join them in!"

"Fuck sake Sean! You're not a killer! You can't even watch a medical program on television! You pick worms out of puddles and put them on the grass! How are you going to kill someone? And if you do you'll suffer from it! Amber is faced with that stuff every day and has become . . . de-sensitised to its gore and finality! Andrew and Richard have been in the army and done and seen God knows what! Poy did hers in the heat of the moment and in self-defence! You . . . what's influencing you? What gives you the edge, the determination to see it through?" Jess raged her argument at him.

143

"Didn't that story of Kate get your blood up? Do you want him walking around, sorry prowling around? The law hopes . . . HOPES he has learnt his lesson but one of his victims is dead because of what he put her through and at least one other mentally scarred for life. He . . . should . . . die for what he's done! If he smiles one solitary smile it's a smile to many! If he enjoys a song on the radio it's a song too many! Every breath he takes is a breath he's given up the right to!" Sean paced the floor in front of her. "And to be fair that worm was flailing around and struggling for its life and wasn't guilty of anything!"

"I'm not saying he doesn't deserve to die, far from it! It's you Sean! You can't do it, and if you did you'd suffer from it emotionally and have coping problems like Andrew has with his black dog depressions and Richard with his drinking and Amber and Poy with their anger issues! There's another possibility that scares me . . . you'll get caught and convicted and no longer be free to be mine! You'll get twelve years to his six!" Jess argued.

"Jess is right Sean. . . . On everything but Richard I agree with her! Richard drinks less now than he did . . . before! He resolves his problems and finds his peace of mind doing what he does now! You haven't got it in you to do what . . . we do and should stay that way! I shouldn't have asked it of you! Not you!" Amber walked slowly into the room. "This one's mine! I want you two to stay pure and not muddy your minds with dealing out death! Let's forget I ever mentioned it and put it behind us!"

"That'll do for me! Just leave me and Sean out of that side of things or we'll be gone from here for good!" Jess spat her words out at Amber.

"Good! That's settled then! We'll waste no more time on the subject!" Amber was relieved to announce and left the room.

"You see things so clearly! You look deeper into things and come up with . . . the right answers straight away! You know me better than I know myself and you've just proved it! Jess . . . I'm more in love with you today than I ever have been! I'll do anything for you including . . . not kill!" Sean smiled then sank to his knees kissing her hands to arouse her passion to his level and hopefully beyond.

Unseen and carrying her shoes Amber silently descended the final steps and went into the small lounge quietly closing the door behind her. Leaning back against the door she put her hands over her face then ran her fingers through her hair. She walked alone to the cold bedroom and fully clothed she wrapped herself in the duvet to summon sleep.

Jess's phone rang, finding Tracy on the other end of the line.

"Are you coming out to play today? I could really do with your help, our new members would like to go riding and if you're sending Sean out and about; can you get him to sort something out for Raymond? He's in the café and desperately bored!" Tracy said without so much as a hello.

"Yes! Sorry Trace! I'll meet you in the club; just give me half an hour!" Jess replied her voice tainted with guilt. "I have to do the rounds with Tracy! You can pick Ray up from the café and sort him something out a.s.a.p!" She told him forcing a smile.

144

Jess found conversation difficult from the start; it was all that she could do to be polite as her thoughts were transfixed on the mayhem of murder. She tried to recall any particular evening that Amber or Andrew may have shown in their behaviour that they had performed or were about to perform a killing. Nothing came to the fore. Amber all too often returned home late and in a foul mood because of the stress of her job and Andrew always had his true emotions well guarded by his typically British calm and stiff upper lip attitude. Tracy soon picked up on the fact that Jess's conversational skills were not up to standard. Taking her aside from the three new members she asked what was troubling her. Jess explained that she was having severe period pains and there was no way that she was able to go riding. She suggested that she phoned Amber and arranged her to go riding with them, as she was free all day and just hanging around the house at a loose end. Tracy agreed and returned to the group to make Jess's apologies and phone Amber to see if she could take the reins and the women for a canter on the hilltops. Amber didn't answer the call so Tracy left a desperate sounding message.

As they reached the stables her phone rang and Amber announced that she was coming to the rescue. By the time Becky and Dan had saddled up the four horses to be taken out Amber was in attention and happy to take a ride out.

Jess tried to recall Sean to the house but his mobile rang out on the kitchen windowsill next to her. Wherever he'd gone he'd taken Molly with him so she phoned Tracy and arranged for her to come round and keep her company promising to return the favour as soon as she felt better.

"Gimme an hour free range with Sean and we'll call it quits!" Tracy told her and ended the call before she could refuse.

Sean had taken Raymond to help him repair the wall along the roadside. They worked well together and in relative silence from the previous occasion with Ray's grating sense of humour noticeably absent. Sean picked his spirits up and let him know that two more ladies were due to arrive the next day. His news was well received by Ray and instantly raised his spirits giving him the hope of being snapped up just as Keith had been. Sean left Ray to hack through the undergrowth and retrieve more fallen boulders as he drove off to get a take-away lunch from the café. T.C and Sara were the only two in the café. They were playing backgammon and to Sean's surprise he was summoned over to their table. T.C enquired how Jess was and extended an invitation for both of them to pay a visit to their home that evening. Sean replied that though Jess was fine he couldn't be certain that they had the time in the evenings but would relay the invitation. With the silence that followed his answer he made his excuse to get his lunch and return to work. Neither of them acknowledged his goodbye keeping instead their eyes cast down at the game in hand so Sean walked back to the counter and collect his and Ray's food and drink.

After lunch it took just two more hours to get the wall finished and looking as if it had never been damaged. Sean drove Ray back to the Café and seeing T.C and Sara were still there turned instead to go home.

Tracy was still working with Jess on the kitchen table and looked pleased to see him. Jess however was glaring wildly at him.

"Where's your mobile?" She asked instead of returning his hello.

"Oh! I must've left it here somewhere!" Sean replied innocently.

Jess stood from the table and walked to the small lounge beckoning him with her finger to follow. Once inside the lounge Jess closed the door behind him and led him through to the big lounge where she closed that door too. She hadn't shown him genuine anger for weeks and suddenly here it was again. As the door clicked shut Jess slapped his face then as he faced her to ask she slapped him again. He was stood on the very spot where Amber had slapped him down and now Jess had chosen the same spot to punish him for leaving his phone at home.

"I wanted to be here with you today and told Tracy a lie so I could do just that!" Jess slapped him again.

Sean kept his eyes from her and simply stood within striking distance to take her anger. Jess struck out at him again and again until he turned his head away and waited for her to change her target. Jess ceased her slapping and stormed back out to the kitchen. Sean gathered his thoughts and followed her through a minute later. Jess threw his phone at him and angrily commanded him to go upstairs and wait for her.

Tracy understood that she was surplus to requirements and gathered her things.

"I think I'll leave you two to it!" She said rising from her chair.

Sean went up the stairs followed by Jess leaving Tracy to see herself out.

"Where do you want me?" He asked on the landing.

"Front room!" She said and pushed him towards it.

"Should I get excalibre?" He asked softly.

"No I'll beat you here with my slipper!" She told him commandingly.

Sean knelt in front of her, removed her slipper and handed it up to her. Squeezing the toe of her slipper into the palm of her hand she swung it at the back of his head. His hands made half the journey to cover his head then fell to his sides.

Re-settling the slipper in her hand Jess stepped back and swung it again to the side of his face. The sting burned into his cheek and persisted after the contact was broken. She swung it again and the burn made his eyes water. Not wanting to be hit in the same spot again he lowered his head and kissed her foot. Jess threw the slipper down and let him kiss on. "Bed!" She commanded and waited for him to lead the way.

CHAPTER SEVENTEEN

It took Jess three days before she returned to joining Amber and Andrew of an evening in the small lounge. Quiet at first she soon settled into the evening and put them further at ease when she relayed a joke Sean's friend had text him moments earlier. . . . A man staggers into casualty with concussion, bruises, two black eyes and a golf club wrapped around his neck. "What happened to you?" the doctor asked "Well I was playing golf with my wife and we both sliced our balls into a field of cows. I found one stuck in a cow's fanny. I yelled to my wife that this one looked like hers then everything went black and I don't remember what happened after that!" The ice was truly broken and they laughed hard and long sharing more jokes when they could stop laughing long enough to tell them.

Amber was drying her cheeks when Andrew caught her eye and tapped his watch.

"We have to go but we'll be home all night tomorrow and well crack open some wine and get Andrew to do us a nice fondu shall we?" Amber told Jess rising from her chair.

"There's nothing special on tonight is there?" Jess asked disappointed at their untimely breaking up of the party.

"I'm afraid so!" Amber said as she went through the door led by Andrew rattling his keys.

Jess caught up with her and asked who the meeting was with.

"It's just Richard, Poy, Andrew and myself!" Amber replied and stared at Jess waiting for her to understand by the party list that this wasn't a run of the mill meeting.

"Its that Paedophile's night tonight?" Jess asked staring at her.

"Yes!" Amber broke eye contact and resumed lacing her all black trainers.

"How?" Jess asked.

"White van, dark woods, deep hole, shotgun!" Amber replied not raising her head.

"Well take care . . . both of you! I can't offer you advice so just take care and don't take any risks!" Jess went to Amber and hugged her.

She walked with her to the door and put her hand on Andrew's shoulder as he exited behind Amber and left her to close the door behind them.

"The paedophile is getting their full attention tonight!" Jess told Sean on re-entering the lounge.

"Oh I see!"

"Do you still wish you were going with them?" She asked seeing the solemn look on his face.

"Well yes I do! Even if it was just in a supporting role, I'd like to be there and see him meet his end!" He told her honestly.

"Amber just mentioned white van, dark woods, deep grave and a shotgun." She told him and sat on the arm of his chair.

"You don't think they'd use the foundations trench you've been digging for the Health club do you! That's just too near home for my liking!" Jess said fearing an evil restless spirit.

"No not the foundations but the woods at the far end of the manor! I think they'll take him there!" Sean said almost certain of his guess.

"Let's go and see shall we? I'd rather now know where he is than fear where he might be!" Jess said her eyes lighting up at the thought of the midnight foray.

They busied themselves dressing in more appropriate clothes for a cold and damp nights adventuring. Jess wore her black, stonewashed jeans, black polo neck and black bomber jacket. Sean finished her off by pulling his woolly black scull cap over her head and couldn't resist kissing her with more passion than he anticipated. Jess pushed him away giving him a serious scowl and told him that they had to get going. Molly was ready to escort them and enjoy a foxhunt of her own. Sean stopped at reaching for her lead and turned to Jess.

"If we do find the grave shall we stick around and watch the goings on?" He asked.

Jess thought on it and Sean wondered if he'd ever actually get an answer.

"Yes!" Jess eventually replied.

"Sorry Moll' you can't come now! Hunter you might be but stealthy you are not!" Sean told her rubbing her under the chin.

Sean took both the big and little torches from the cupboard and stuffed Molly's blanket into his nap-sack. Reserving the batteries and not wanting to be observed by Tracy or anyone around the courtyard or mobile homes they walked down the track to the manor cloaked in darkness. Once past the manor Sean let Jess use her small torch to illuminate the way through the fields. The long dewy grass soaked their trousers to the knee and slowed their approach to the far woods. A fox's spring cry made Jess jump and a chill run up her spine. She put her arm in his and walked along leaning into him. Holding him tight to her they came to the intensi-fied dark of the hedgerow and had to find the overgrown stile that led to the final field and into the woods.

Finally at the edge of the woods Sean suggested that they split up and went in separate directions to save on time.

"No way! I . . . have to be here to protect you!" Jess told him.

"Well if Amber said the grave was deep then it won't be in amongst the trees because of the roots. They've probably dug it at the edge or in the clearing at the center!" Sean reasoned to her and began to shine his torch around them.

"ARGH! OH MY GOD!" He suddenly exclaimed, flicked his torch off and ran at full pelt from the woods towards home.

"AH! WHAT IS IT? WHAT IS IT? SEAN STOP! STOP RUNNING!" Jess yelled out and took off in his general direction. Shining her torch to locate and run to him Jess let out a terrified high- pitched scream. "Arrrgghhhhh!"

Sean stopped his run as Jess passed him determined to have him between her and whatever had frightened him so much. He bent double and let out his laughter as she too ceased her run and shone her torch at him in his fit of hysterics.

"YOU BASTARD SEAN! I'll get excalibre out to you just for that! You see if I don't!" Jess shouted at him holding back the sudden urge to join in his laughter.

"So much . . . for you . . . protecting me! You were . . . outpacing me! Tell you there's a ghost behind you . . . and you could . . . you could run for England! Your feet were . . . hardly touching the ground! You give new meaning to . . . having it away . . . on your toes!" Sean told her between deep breaths and laughter.

Jess approached him and thumped him in the stomach.

"No more joking around! Okay. . . . Promise?" She asked ready to thump him again.

"No more! I promise!" He told her.

They walked to the nearest edge of the woods to begin the search. Sweeping their torches in wide arcs they moved parallel with the tree line. A barn owl flew low over their heads its sudden appearance, silent flight and brilliant whiteness against the navy blue sky made them both see it as a ghostly apparition, even Sean jumped and had to re-settle his nerves. At the farthest edge of the woods they stopped and Sean suggested they searched the grassy glade in the middle of the woods. Jess agreed and they entered the woods inching their way forward and stepping sometimes on and sometimes over rotten branches. A quick sweep of the glade revealed nothing and they retraced their steps back out.

"What now?" Jess asked.

"We should try the younger, little copse at the rivers edge!" Sean told her and set off in the new direction before she could answer him.

At the nearest edge to the river they began their search and walked towards the stone wall. Sean's beam of light hit a brown mound then another mound of lighter coloured clay and a third larger mound of chalky spoil.

"This is it!" They approached the mounds and found the excavation between the two largest piles of earth. Sean shone his torch down into it.

"Strewth! That's deep! They only stopped digging when they hit the water table!" He exclaimed.

"Where do we watch from?" Jess asked swallowing hard as the gravity of the situation began to dawn on her.

Sean shone his torch the opposite side of the wall and climbed over.

"From here!" He told her trampling down the tall, skeletal thistles making a flattened area for two then spread the blanket out to give their knees a degree of protection.

"They'll drive up to here so we should watch and listen out for them! When they come we'll take our position behind the wall. Are you still okay with this?" He asked holding her hands.

"Yes I'm fine! It's just sad to think that it's up to us to do this! When they get them, they should never let them out!" She told him in a hushed tone as if they might be overheard.

With their torches switched off they stood looking in the direction of the farm and at the base of the hill. They waited and waited then began to mill around both wondering if the operation had been thwarted or called off. Suddenly Sean called for total silence and held his breath to hear the faintest sound of an engine. The glow of headlights came into view and they cautiously made their way to the hiding place. The sound of the angry engine grew louder as Sean checked his mobile. It was twenty minutes to two and the van drew up to within twenty feet of the mounds and cut its engine. Sean and Jess knelt and watched over the wall. Doors opened and two figures emerged. From the rear of the van came three more figures the middle figure being obviously supported on either side. Escorted to the graveside he was left to drop heavily to the ground.

The tall figure from the front of the van carried a baseball bat over to the condemned man and stood ready with the bat resting on his shoulder. They strained to hear what the voices were saying but couldn't make anything out. Suddenly in a burst of action the ground-hugging figure had a white pillowcase put over his head and pulled tight around his neck. Trying to lower his head the figure that had hooded him straddled him and hoisted him up by the neck. The bat was swung into the exposed white ball that was his head. The crack of bone and teeth made Sean lower his head and momentarily shut his eyes tight. A muffled and panicked series of cries came from the hooded man as the white hood began to turn red. The bat was swung into his face again then the swinger changed position and swung once more. The hooded man continued to emit a series of pitiful whimpers trying to achieve greater volume but failing fast.

"Why don't they kill him quickly? Why are they dragging it out?" Jess asked hoping to see it end.

"They're knocking his teeth out!" He whispered back to her.

The bloodied hood was carefully pulled off and the gag tied at the back of his head was removed. Looking around at each of his attackers in turn for a sign of pity he kept up a scream of a terrified, cornered and cowering monkey. No words came from him just the same repeated scream over and over again until he lowered his head and sobbed. It was too distorted for Jess and Sean to make out what he was trying to say apart from the repeated word. . . . Please. Amber's voice clearly rang out in response to his pleading.

"Did Kate ever say Please don't? Did you listen to her cries? Or was she too fucking scared to even ask to be left alone? Left alone to be just a little girl? You sick, evil CUNT of a man!" She kicked him in the stomach and two other figures joined in and kicked repeatedly as he rolled nearer the pit.

Closer now to Jess and Sean's hiding place they could more clearly make out the words he was attempting to call out whilst also expelling the torrent of blood.

"He's trying to say he loved her!" Sean whispered.

The two figures, that of Richard and Poy unceremoniously stripped him of his clothes as he more desperately continued to plead with them whilst frantically expelling the blood from his mouth to plead more clearly. On his hands and knees Poy and Richard kicked him back towards the pit and finally with a scream and a splatter of muddy water, into it. Only his struggling around in the watery grave could be heard until he again called out that he loved her. Amber approached the edge of the pit.

"Your kind of love she'd have been better off not knowing! Your kind of love comes straight from Hell so you can take it back there with you!" She said and let off both barrels into the pit.

Poy led Amber away and walked with her slowly homewards. Richard and Andrew began to shovel the chalky spoil back into the pit. Jess and Sean settled back down on the blanket and Jess moved slowly to hold him tightly in her arms. Soon her lips travelled over his face and down to his neck as her hands wandered onto his groin. Sean responded positively and held her head to kiss her deep in her mouth. Breathing heavily and moving slowly he undone her jeans and pulled them down to her knees. Doing the same for him she took him into her and held his head to her face to kiss him and to share his breath. Slow grinding movements gave way quickly to sudden deliberate thrusts as they dared each other to make the first audible sound. Jess came in a series of quickened, short thrusts and jolts. Sean smiled and stayed deep inside her until he too came, not daring to make the sounds he felt attempting to escape from deep within him.

They redressed slower and with more care than when they'd undressed then sat with their backs against the wall listening to the shovelling of earth.

"They're going to take ages to fill that in!" He told her eager to get her home and again make her moan in ecstasy and warmth.

"Shall we help them?" Jess asked with a devilish stifled laugh.

"We could scare the shit out of them couldn't we? I could take my clothes off and pretend to be the ghost of the man they're burying." He said and held his hand over his mouth.

"Okay do it!" Jess said quickly reaching to undo his belt.

Sean piled his clothes on the blanket and was completely naked in the cold night air. He knew instantly what he wanted to do and told Jess that he would keep his eyes closed for as long as he could so as not to laugh at their fright. It was for her switch the torch on and then view the scene to relay it to him anything he'd miss. Sean stuffed the torch into his empty boot and positioned it to shine where he would be standing.

Quickly and silently he balanced himself standing on the wall with his arms outstretched. Then as Jess turned switched the light on he forced the smile from his face, closed his eyes and in his deepest voice began to chant.

"Gow Day Tay, Gow Day Tay Criss Super Star Kiss. Ex Maria Virgin Man Ganaine Tain." He opened his eyes to see Richard on his knees at the top of the mound clutching his spade as if he were a crusader knight at prayer. He sought to find Andrew and located his silhouette some fifteen feet beyond Richard. His laughter burst from him even louder than his chant. The cold was no longer a factor, he jumped off the wall and approached Richard stopping after just a few steps to double himself up and fall to his knees in a fit of uncontrollable hysterics. Richard went towards him holding his spade in a very threatening manner then held it out as if he were about to take a swing at him with it. In the distance a deep chesty and sporadic laugh could be heard coming from Andrew. Jess clambered over the wall and jumped around the kneeling Sean and the pale Richard pointing and mocking him with her laughter.

"FUCKING HELL! You are a right pair!" Richard exclaimed and again sank to the ground to complete his recovery.

Andrew approached and Jess's laughter intensified at the memory of his throwing his spade towards Sean before hurtling off in the opposite direction.

"Is that what they taught you in the army? Throw your spade at the enemy and fuck off sharpish?" She asked.

Andrew held her in his arms as Sean went to get his clothes and dress.

"I don't know what was going through my head except that you weren't of this world. You skinny bastard!" Richard exclaimed as Sean hopped about putting one leg in his trousers.

Andrew went to find his spade as the funning around died down. Richard rescaled the mound and resumed shovelling the spoil back into the pit. Joined by Andrew Sean and Jess flicked their torches on and headed off to the farm. Jess increased her walking speed to try and catch up with Amber. She called out to them and waved her torch in the air as they neared the lake. Amber was shocked to hear Jess's voice call out to her. When they finally met she was at a loss to see Jess laughing and joking around. Jess explained what they'd done and both Amber and Poy joined in her laughter.

"And . . . how do you feel?" Amber asked.

"Feel? I feel fine! The next one's mine! Mine and Sean's okay?" Jess answered.